D0367461

SBYA
42
.99
p1

the reckoning of noah shaw

WITHDRAWN

ALSO BY MICHELLE HODKIN

THE MARA DYER TRILOGY

The Unbecoming of Mara Dyer

The Evolution of Mara Dyer

The Retribution of Mara Dyer

THE SHAW CONFESSIONS TRILOGY

The Becoming of Noah Shaw

An imprint of Simon & Schuster Children's Publishing Division
1230 Avenue of the Americas, New York, New York 10020
This book is a work of fiction. Any references to historical events,
real people, or real places are used fictitiously. Other names, characters, places,
and events are products of the author's imagination, and any resemblance to actual
events or places or persons, living or dead, is entirely coincidental.
Text copyright © 2018 by Michelle Hodkin
Cover photograph copyright © 2018 by Chris Crisman
All rights reserved, including the right of reproduction in whole or in part in any form.
SIMON & SCHUSTER BFYR is a trademark of Simon & Schuster, Inc.
For information about special discounts for bulk purchases, please contact Simon &
Schuster Special Sales at 1-866-506-1949 or business@simonandschuster.com.
The Simon & Schuster Speakers Bureau can bring authors to your live event. For
more information or to book an event, contact the Simon & Schuster Speakers
Bureau at 1-866-248-3049 or visit our website at www.simonspeakers.com.
Also available in a SIMON & SCHUSTER BFYR hardcover edition
Book design by Lucy Ruth Cummins
The text for this book was set in Caslon.
Manufactured in the United States of America
First SIMON & SCHUSTER BFYR paperback edition November 2019
2 4 6 8 10 9 7 5 3 1
The Library of Congress has cataloged the hardcover edition as follows:
Names: Hodkin, Michelle, author.
Title: The reckoning of Noah Shaw / Michelle Hodkin.
Description: First edition. | New York : Simon & Schuster BFYR, [2018] |
Series: The Shaw confessions ; volume 2 | Summary: Legacies are
revealed, lies unraveled, and new alliances forged as Noah tries to escape the
consequences of his choices and move forward without first confronting his past.
Identifiers: LCCN 2018022691| ISBN 9781481456463 (hardback) |
ISBN 9781481456470 (pbk) | ISBN 9781481456487 (eBook)
Subjects: | CYAC: Supernatural—Fiction. | Genetics—Fiction. |
Ability—Fiction. | Suicide—Fiction. |
Classification: LCC PZ7.H66vloc.gov/2018022691

the Shaw Confessions VOLUME 2

the reckoning of noah shaw

MICHELLE HODKIN

SIMON & SCHUSTER BFYR

NEW YORK LONDON TORONTO SYDNEY NEW DELHI

Caldwell County
Public Library
63 N Main St
Granite Falls, NC 28630

For Janie, may her memory be blessed.

And for my grandfather,
Robert Kramer, the strongest person I know.

the
reckoning
of
noah
shaw

Mara,

If your story was a memoir, then mine is a confession. My confession is that I regret it. I never thought it was possible. I didn't think there would ever be a day, a moment, a second, when I would look back and wish I'd never met you, but that is my every moment, now.

You are an ocean away at a café on Fulton Street. We've been there together, I know the address and the name. But you aren't with me. And I miss you. You are missing from me.

I want you here, now, more than I've ever wanted you anywhere. I want to breathe you, drink you, devour you—I want you inside me so that I never have to miss you again.

I want to own you, is what I want, and yes, I do know how fucked up that is, thanks. But we've always been fucked up, really, and we said we would never lie to each other, didn't we? (Though, we have lied to each other, haven't we?) So I'm telling you the truth now. I want you to belong to me. I want to ask you if you're mine, and I want you to say yes.

It's funny, or not funny, but ironic, but not really ironic—the point is, once, not very long ago in fact, I claimed you before I'd even kissed you. I did it so easily, thoughtlessly, because we both knew it wasn't real, though I knew, even if you didn't, that I wanted it to be real. And then, after I did kiss you, there was a time when you wanted me to claim you. I could ask "Are you mine?" and you would say yes.

But I can't ask you now. Or I could, but I don't know what you'll say anymore, and I'm too much of a pussy to risk it. So I'm writing this to you, even though you're never going to read it, in the hope that I can exorcise these thoughts, these words from my mind. Are you mine? Were you ever mine? Or were we always what we said we'd never be, idiots who made promises to each other that we would choose not to keep?

Because it is a choice, after all. You can choose to be claimed, or refuse. You can choose to claim someone, or choose not to. You can leave them unclaimed, alone. And no matter what we say to each other—no matter what we've said to each other not even two weeks ago, breathless and sweaty with love in our eyes and lies on our tongues, both of us knew, and know, the truth. You are not mine. You never were mine. But right now, I feel like I would do anything to have you—leash you, cage you, trap you, so that you'll have to be mine, whether you want it or not.

You once told me that you were poison, and I was the drug that made you forget it. You were right and wrong; I'm not a drug, I'm a wound. And your poison is in me.

It feels like lightning and tastes like sugar, a fevered sweetness that I would give anything, anything to forget. I would tie stones to the memories of you and drown them before tying myself to you again. I would beg for nothingness, pray for blankness, but there's no one to beg. I know no God but you.

I have nowhere to send this, and no reason to believe you wish to receive it. I can feel the night behind me as I write these words to feed to the flames. You wrote because you had something to prove. I write because I have to speak, and there's no one left to listen.

Yours, still,

Noah

Part I

the truth is a snare: you cannot have it,
without being caught.

—Søren Kierkegaard

1

MY TRAGIC HEROINE

HE DAY STELLA JUMPED, THE DAY MARA left, her grandmother turned up in a white dress and a black car and told me to get in if I wanted to save her.

She looks so much like Mara.

Or rather, she looks like someone Mara'll look like someday, a living, breathing perversion of her. The shadow of laughter behind her eyes when something amuses her but she won't share. When Mara closes her eyes to search for just the right word, she closes hers as well. The shape of Mara's mouth when she's hiding a secret behind her lips is the shape her grandmother's takes, too.

The first thing I asked her wasn't how she was alive or why, but—

"What shall I call you?"

She sits beside me, looking straight ahead, but I see her smile in profile. "I told you my name."

"I can't call you . . ."

"Mara?" She finishes for me. "Why not?"

Because her name sticks in my throat. Because the sound of it might kill me.

"It was my name first," she says.

Her voice snaps me back to attention, to this moment, facing this not-Mara beside me.

"Fine," I say. "Your family name, then."

"Which one?"

Her eyes are quick, laughing.

"If you don't give me a name, I'll choose one for you myself," I say.

She arches an eyebrow. "Go on, then."

My thoughts are furred, though, and even as I try and think the name *Mara*, I'm hardly able to get past the first letter.

"M," I say.

One of her hands reaches for the collar of her white silk dress. She rubs the fabric with her thumb and studies me. "Good choice," she says eventually.

Her stare is bold, unflinching, and as the silence stretches between us, I feel more exposed, more raw. "Why are you here?"

She blinks, once. "I told you. I need your help."

A matter of life and death, she said. Someone we both love.

"Right. That got me in the car," I concede. "But I'll need more if you want me to stay."

She watches me, unnaturally still and calm. "You have questions."

"You have no idea."

That cryptic, smug smile again. "I have some idea."

It helps, her smiling like that. It's harder to be awed by someone so irritating. "Your family thinks you're dead," I say.

"Yes."

"Mara saw it." Not strictly true, but it catches M's attention.

"What did she say?"

I reach back through the door in my mind, the one I closed on Mara minutes or hours ago, God knows which, wincing in anticipation of the memory of her voice, and hear—

Nothing. Silence.

M waits.

This is what I remember instead: my father's ghastly Florida mansion. An unused sitting room with furniture draped in drop cloths. Mara's tentative, shaking hands lifting a soft, crude little doll between two pinched fingers, then tossing it forcefully into a fire. The smell of burning hair. The curl of singed paper.

That was what we thought was left of Mara's

grandmother—that doll, the pendant sewn inside of it, and the ashes of her suicide note. The note Mara saw—*remembered*—M writing.

I look at her grandmother now and consider, not for the first time, that I might be well and truly mad. Maybe something broke in me the moment Mara left. Maybe it broke before.

It's a strange and unfamiliar sensation, not knowing whether to trust your own mind. Not knowing if your own senses are betraying you. I never quite got what it was like for Mara, when we met. Never quite understood why she'd wanted me to keep that journal, writing about her, for her, when she thought she was losing her mind. Losing herself.

I'm beginning to get it now.

M watches me expectantly, head tilted, a fall of black hair curling on her left shoulder.

"Mara said you killed yourself when she was three days old," I manage to say.

"That is what her mother believes, and so that is what she was told."

Told? "No. Mara *saw* you. She remembered—"

Everything. Mara remembered everything, and she recounted it in extraordinary detail. The scents of the village her grandmother had lived in as a girl. The hushed voice of an older girl sitting beside her, sewing her a friend. My own memory of that day plays like a silent film in my mind; Mara desperate for answers, Mara desperate for my help. Mara's face open and earnest and trusting—

The memory stings, and I shy away from it. "Did you come back?" I ask stupidly, filling the silence to drown out my thoughts.

"From . . . ?"

"Did you die?"

"Not yet."

A start. "How old are you, then?"

"How old do I look?" she asks, amused.

Mara and I did the maths once, back when I'd found a photograph of my mother at Cambridge, with M standing beside her. My mother couldn't have been more than twenty-one, twenty-two perhaps. The woman sitting beside me looks exactly the same.

"I don't know," I say casually. "Thirties, I suppose?"

She tips her head, acknowledging. "Thirty-six."

"How long have you been thirty-six?"

"A while." She grins, light and teasing.

"Cute," I say. The car hits a pothole, reminding me that we're being driven somewhere. Which begs the question—

"Where are we going?" I glance out the window, but all I see is city, still, and traffic.

M doesn't answer right away. When I turn around, her expression's shifted again, into something blank and unreadable. And then she says, "Home."

2

FOR WHICH I AM WILLING

MY FIRST INSTINCT IS TO THINK: I'M homeless. Mara was my home and I left her, scorching the earth behind me. I burned down our house thinking it would set me free, but instead I'm like a dog, circling the ashes, hoping the only family I've ever known will one day come back.

I say none of this, obviously. Instead, I ask, "Which home?"

"The flight will take you back to England."

"*England?* Why?"

"I told you—"

"You haven't told me anything," I say, feeling frustrated and bitter and sorry for myself.

M, meanwhile, is maddeningly calm. "I told you it's a matter of life and death, which is true. I told you I need your help, which is also true."

"Why me? I'm sure Mara would be quite interested to meet you," I say, gauging her reaction.

"She can't know about me, not yet."

"And what if I tell her?"

"You won't," she says plainly. She looks out the window at the passing streets. "Mara's chosen a different path, and a different person to lead her through it," she says to the glass. Then, to me, "If she reaches out to you again, it won't be *her* reaching. It'll be him."

Him.

She could be referencing almost anyone, technically, but the pendant around my neck feels heavy, oppressive, and my anger knows its target. "The professor."

She nods once.

"How do you know who she's with right now? What she's doing?"

"Just because I can't see the people I care about doesn't mean I've stopped caring. Surely you understand that."

An artful dodge. "You haven't answered the question."

Her expression shifts. "It would be hard to explain if I had a lifetime to do it, let alone a single conversation," she says, sounding older for a moment. Her left hand drifts to the collar of her dress again, but this time, her thumb rubs the hollow of her throat. "We're connected to those who share our Afflictions," she says. "Particularly those who share our genetics."

My mind darts back to Mara, to Florida, to her memories of M. To the book I'd thought I found at random, *New Theories in Genetics*, authored by the professor, though I didn't know it then. "Genetic memory," I say aloud, remembering the passage I read to Mara. An explanation for what was happening to her, impossible as it seemed.

M smiles approvingly. "Some of us find ourselves remembering things that didn't happen to us, but rather someone who shared our Afflictions, or our genes. A relative, usually, but not always."

I think of what she said about Mara, and what M seems to know about her now. Has she lived any of Mara's memories? "Does it go both ways?" I ask.

"It can."

"But I've never experienced . . ." What are they? Fits? Hallucinations? "Memories. Not like that."

"Because you've closed yourself off from them," she says.

I bristle at her tone. "You seem quite sure about that."

She ignores my stare, looking out the window instead. "If your mind was as open as Mara's, she would be here and safe."

She doesn't finish the rest of that sentence, so I do. "Here and safe, instead of with the professor and not, you mean."

A pause. "Something like that."

Anger rises, coiling at the back of my throat. I gave Mara a choice; she *chose* not to be here. "Hate to be the bearer of bad news," I say, "But if Mara's with the professor right now, it's likely *his* safety you ought to be worrying about." She doesn't respond. "Right, I think we're done here—"

"The professor was my professor, once," she says, cutting me off. Then turns to stare at me directly. "Did you know?"

Words written in elegant longhand appear in my mind.

Mr. Grimsby calls him the professor, and everyone seems to accept that.

"He was my tutor," M continues. "When I was first brought to London." She swallows. "I know him. He'll use her as he used me."

The words hang in the air, sticky and rotting. "I'm sorry," I say carefully. "For whatever . . . happened. But I don't know what you expect me to do about it."

She exhales through her nose. "Mara's memories of me helped her understand what was happening to her. She found answers in them, sometimes to questions she couldn't voice." She leans forward slightly, encouraging. "I think you'll find the same is true for you, and that once you let them in, you'll unearth answers that can help her."

"How would *my* memories help her?"

"You're her balance," she says.

Her words provoke a bitter smile.

"Your fates are tied together."

You will love him to ruins.

I *feel* ruined. Ruined and wretched. Maybe fate was right.

"I don't believe in fate," I say indifferently.

"You don't have to. You're connected to each other, in ways you can't begin to appreciate. She needs you."

My voice goes flat. "She doesn't need anyone. She can take care of herself."

"You're wrong about that."

"Am I?" She seems genuinely hopeful, which only proves that whatever she thinks she knows about Mara, whatever she's seen, fails to account for one fundamental truth:

"Mara doesn't want help," I say. She doesn't want to be fixed. She doesn't need to be saved.

"She does." The way M says it, I half-wonder whether she's heard the thoughts I haven't voiced.

"She does want your help. She just doesn't know it yet. But she will, and it will bring her back to you."

It is shameful how badly I want that to be true. To realise that *that's* why I'm still sitting here, allowing myself to be led by the collar in the hope that I'll be taken in a direction that'll bring her back to me. I might've thrown Mara away, but I haven't let her go. Not really. Not yet.

"If you believe that, then you don't know her any more than you know me," I say, rather snottily.

She looks at me, her dark eyes narrowing slightly. "Your mother's chin would lift and her lip would curl in exactly the same way yours is doing right now, when she got defensive. And you could always tell David Shaw was lying if he met your gaze without blinking."

The mention of my parents brings me up short. I swallow hard, collecting myself. "You knew *them*. You don't know me."

"Perhaps I know more than you think."

Whatever cards she thought she was playing, she's played them wrong. "I guess we'll never know," I snap. Then, leaning forward, "Stop the car," I say to the driver.

The driver meets M's eyes in the rearview mirror. "Ma'am?"

"Keep going," she says to him. Then, before I can protest, "I didn't just know your parents," she says. "I knew everyone in your family—or at least, everyone after the first Simon. You were supposed to have his name, actually."

"My father wanted me named Elliot, for his father," I argue despite myself. I try to remember when he said that, because I'm certain of it.

"That was the compromise he reached with Naomi. She hated Simon." She half smiles. "So you ended up with two middle names instead of merely the one."

"Cool story," I say tonelessly. The anger is still there, white and cold and familiar. Anger at her for tempting me, and at myself for being tempted. "I'm not interested, all right? I've already watched my mother die the once. I don't need to pry open her memories and relive it."

M looks incredulous. "Noah, your mother had an ability,

but she wasn't the only one. You did know that, right?"

Wrong. "Who else, then?"

She runs both hands through her hair, and in that moment she looks like Daniel, surprised and frustrated at once. "Your grandfather's grandfather. The one who took me."

"*Took* you?"

She inclines her head a bit. "Found me. Claimed me. Took me."

"From whom? Where?"

"I don't remember," she says, her voice flattening out. Then she looks out the window, at the city. "I remember jungle. Trees that grew so thick and wild you'd think they were sentient. Stars that jewelled a sky a richer shade of indigo than the ink we used to write with." She inhales deeply. "The words I have now can't do it justice. And the languages I knew then were . . . not common." She pauses a beat too long, and her tone shifts again. "Plus there was no one to talk to when I was that young, anyway."

"Surely you had parents . . ."

She turns her gaze back to me. "Surely I did, but I don't remember them."

"Maybe it's not the worst thing," I say, thinking of my own father. "What you don't know can't hurt you."

She fixes me with a stare that raises the hair on the back of my neck. "You've never been more wrong about anything in your life."

The silence stretches out, spiky and oppressive. Then she says, "Mara needs—"

"You don't know *what* she needs," I snap. "You might be her family, technically, but really you're just a stranger. You don't know her, what she's done or why, and you know even less about me." I glance out the window; we're on the FDR, but if the car pulls over I could get a taxi, if I manage not to get hit. Hitchhike, if it comes to it.

"I know she's seventeen years old, and that people make stupid decisions when they're seventeen."

"I'm seventeen as well."

"Precisely."

"You're not helping your case," I say. "Mara's not stupid, or naïve. She made her choice, eyes wide open."

M tilts her head to one side. "If you spend your life in a house with no windows and no doors, if you've never seen a tree reaching for the sky, or felt grass under your feet, or heard a bird's wings beat the air, your eyes might be open, but how much can you see?" She pauses. "I was told, once, that killing myself could save her. Prevent her death. But when she was born and I looked in her eyes, I knew that it would change nothing. That I'd been lied to, by someone who built a house with no doors or windows around me, someone who told me the sky was red and grass is poisonous. I almost died believing it," she says. "I almost killed myself because he told me to."

"Mara wouldn't." The words come immediately. "She wouldn't kill herself."

"Would you bet her life on it?" she asks, just as quickly.

My stomach clenches with nausea. I turn away to hide it, but my limbs grow heavy with the memory of Mara's weight in my arms, the ghost of her lips at my neck as she thanked me for stopping her heart.

She made that choice with her eyes open, too. Her life for Daniel's, when my father forced her to choose. And I agreed to it. I'll never not loathe myself for agreeing to it.

But at least I respected her freedom to make a choice that I hated, loathed, rebelled against with every cell in my body. Mara swore, before she left me, that she'd never grant *me* that freedom. She'd end a thousand lives to save my useless one, no matter what *I* want.

The car stops in traffic and I reach for the door handle. "It's Mara's choice," I say, my voice low and cold. "Her life. She can live it as she chooses. *With* whomever she chooses," I add, unlocking the door. If that's the professor, so be it.

"Your abilities are gone," M says quickly. "I can help you get them back."

"Not interested." I step out onto the pavement, not caring about the cars. Not caring how she knows, about my ability and the lack of it.

M's tone shifts into something sharper. "The life I have now began when I was taken. Your family owes me a debt."

"Let me know where to send the cheque."

"All right," M says, her voice clipped but louder, now, to rise above the noise of New York at night. "I'll keep your friend Alastair in my thoughts."

The words catch me just as I'm about to close the car door on her. My fingers tighten on the steel frame, and I lean down to meet her eyes. "What?"

"He's in the hospital, isn't he?"

A car honks insistently behind us, which sets the other cars off. I don't give a single fuck. "How do you know?"

"Your other friend attempted suicide. It was all over the news."

"That's not an answer."

"That's true," she says.

I don't like the way she says it.

"There's been a rash of them lately, hasn't there been?" She holds my gaze. "Teen suicides?"

I'm supposed to ask what she knows about it. To ask her for answers. Let her drive me in the direction of *her* choice. She's waiting for me to say the words.

I could. I could get back in the car, follow her to England, turn out the pockets of my memories or my mother's memories or whoever's memories and offer her whatever shakes out. Or I could slam the door behind me and walk away.

I shut the door. I don't look back.

3

UNDERSTOOD BACKWARDS

IT'S ONLY ONCE THE TAXI ARRIVES AT MOUNT SINAI that I realise my wallet and phone are missing, and only after the driver grudgingly lets me go without paying that I remember Goose isn't even at the hospital anymore. Jamie had said he checked out—yesterday, was it? Time feels elastic. Warped.

Which is why I'm brought up short by the sight of Goose in the hospital lobby, chatting with a blonde in a tan pantsuit.

"Goose!" I shout, turning a few heads.

A broad grin appears on his lips when he spots me, and he takes his leave of the blonde.

"Mate," he says, pulling me in for a one-armed hug. "What are you doing here?" we both say at once.

"I thought you checked out?" I ask first.

"Tried to. A doctor came in at the last minute, though, said I'd be leaving 'against medical advice.' Wanted me overnight for more tests." He shrugs.

"You all right?" I ask, leaning in a bit to look at his eyes. His pupils are blown.

"Smashing," he says brightly. I can't help but think of what M said, though. Keeping Goose in her thoughts. Did she know something? Was it a threat, maybe?

"What did they see, on the tests?" I ask him.

Goose sighs, adding an eye roll. "A teensy little skull fracture. I fainted after your friend . . ."

After Stella dove off the Manhattan Bridge, neither of us says. An image of her shoe floating in the East River surfaces in my mind.

"Apparently I've got an extraordinarily hard head—didn't even need staples. It's hardly even sore." He reaches around to feel the back of his head. "They gave me splendid drugs, though." He sticks his other hand in his pocket, rattling a bottle of pills. "Not that I'll need them, now that you're here, right? Or is that not how it works?"

About that. "About that . . ." I start. The words drift in the air as I realise I've no idea how to finish that sentence. "Did

Jamie mention anything before he left?" Better off changing the subject.

Goose shakes his head. "Just that he was heading to his aunt's, that your flat would be mad what with . . . what happened . . ." He shifts uncomfortably. "He mentioned that Daniel and Leo and Sophie were being questioned, I think? Said I ought to check into a hotel before heading home."

"Home?" The word feels loaded, now.

Goose shrugs one shoulder. "Guess he assumed I'd head back to London? Oh! He said something about Mara's dad— or mum, maybe?—being a solicitor?"

"Dad," I say. Marcus Dyer's a criminal defence lawyer.

"Right. He gave me his number in case the police wanted a chat." Goose looks over his shoulder, toward the lift. "Have you heard anything?" he asks in a low voice. "About what happened?"

I follow his gaze. Two police officers are talking whilst waiting for the doors to open.

There are a thousand reasons for them to be there, of course, reasons that have nothing to do with me or Stella or any of us. "No," I say. "It's been . . . an odd day." My eyes drift from the police to the lobby's other occupants. The woman Goose had been talking to is standing in my line of sight, texting.

"Who is that?" I ask, tipping my head toward her.

"Mmm . . . Mandy, maybe?" He presses his forefinger to his lip. "Mattie? Something like that. Works for the hospital, I think. The nurse who brought me down here was called away, so she came to let me know the car was here to pick me up."

Thank fuck. "Brilliant. Where are you staying?"

Goose looks puzzled.

"Where's the car dropping you off?"

He cocks his head to one side. "I thought you'd sent for it?"

I shake my head once, then look at the large windows facing the street. Three cars are waiting by the curb in the dark. Two are black.

"Maybe Jamie called it," he suggests. "Or Mara?"

"Doubtful." I look back over at the woman Goose had been talking to. Her phone is at her ear, now, and she's approaching the lift.

"We ought to go," I say, feeling slightly paranoid and greatly annoyed about it.

"Right," Goose says. Then, "Where?"

Fair question. "I've lost my mobile and wallet, I think," I say. "You've got yours?"

"Wallet, no mobile," he says. "Might've dropped it on the bridge."

Bloody hell. "You all right to walk?"

"Of course, but we could just take the car, no?"

"Rather not," I say, after a moment. We've barely made it out of doors, though, before Goose trips. I catch his arm. "Careful, mate."

"I'm fine," he insists. "Look." He points to his left shoe—his laces are undone.

"Mr. Greaves?" a voice asks in an Eastern European accent. We both look up. An older man is holding open the door of one of the black cars.

"Well spotted," Goose says to the driver, who doesn't smile.

"What car service are you with?" I ask.

"Eastern," he says. He points to a small placard in the front window.

At least it's a real car service, one I've heard of. "Where are you headed?"

"Teterboro."

I exhale through my nose. "Well done, M," I mumble under my breath.

"Pardon?" Goose asks.

"We're being herded, I think."

"Herded . . . where?"

"England," I say.

"Could do." Goose nods amiably, until he notices my expression. "Unless you've got something else in mind?"

"Not quite."

"Are we waiting on Jamie or Mara to join us?" he asks slowly.

I shake my head once.

"Right, then," he says. "Is there some other reason we should look this gift horse in the mouth?"

I'm not used to being cautious, but I feel responsible for

Goose. "Chalk it up to past experience," is all I say.

"Fair, I suppose." Goose bites his lower lip. "What are you worried about, though, exactly? Think there'll be a gingerbread cottage at the other end of the flight?"

"It's not entirely out of the realm of possibility," I say.

"It's only England, mate. Not the edge of the world. Why not go until things die down, here?"

"Unfortunate choice of words," I say.

"Perhaps. But look." He points to the car. "It's a Honda Civic. People don't get kidnapped in Hondas." The driver looks on, unsmiling.

I can't help my grin. "All right, you've made your point."

"Marvellous," he says, climbing in. He pats the seat beside him. "See? No bloodstains or anything." Once I'm in, he leans his head back, closing his eyes as the car starts.

"Are you allowed to sleep with a concussion?" I ask.

"They encourage it, actually. Says it helps the brain heal." He lets out a contented sigh. "Wake me up when we get there." Within minutes, he's unconscious.

I can't remember when I last slept. The night before last, maybe? I let my eyes close on the blink.

An afterimage of Mara's face appears in darkness, after kissing me awake in the middle of the night. My hands ache with the memory of her heat, her softness.

Fuck. We've barely started the trip, but I can't stand the stillness.

"How much longer?" I ask the driver, after a few more minutes.

"Twenty minutes," he says. "No traffic."

I run my hands through my hair, crackling and restless as I watch the clock. I nearly leap out of the car once it comes to a stop.

I give Goose a shake. "We're here."

He yawns. "Pip pip," he says groggily, before letting himself out.

"Mr. Shaw?" the driver asks through his open window. I haven't mentioned my name once. He hasn't asked.

"Yes?"

He nods once, gruffly, and offers me a plain white envelope with no name on it, no address.

"What's this?"

"This for you," he says, extending his arm farther out of the car.

I take it. He drives off that same second, leaving Goose and me to stare at the planes lined up.

"Which plane's ours?" Goose asks beside me.

"Don't know," I say.

"Maybe it's in there?" He tips his head at the envelope. I open it.

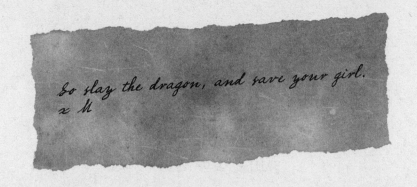

So slay the dragon, and save your girl.
x M

SMILING VANITY

"**A**NY HINTS IN THERE?" GOOSE ASKS.

"Not as such, no." I fold the note back up and pocket it. The sound of heeled footsteps approaches, and a cheerful crew member introduces herself as Madison, before leading us to a plane Goose is damn near giddy about. She offers him a tour before we take off, and I settle into one of the white leather seats.

A second flight attendant appears, offers me a drink.

"What've you got?"

She tips her close-cropped head at a glossy bar at the far end of the cabin. "Everything."

"Whiskey, then. Neat."

"I'll have what he's having." Goose reappears, sinks into the seat opposite me. "Quite something, I must say."

I arch an eyebrow. "Doesn't your family have a plane?"

"We're only Embraer rich, not Gulfstream rich." He takes a sip from my glass. "Mmm."

"My theory is that the size of one's private jet is inversely proportional to the size of one's cock," I say, unimpressed.

"Interesting," Goose says, setting his glass down on the side table. He presses a button by his seat, and a head pops out from the galley.

"Is there something I can get for you?" the attendant asks Goose.

"There is, in fact, Jessa. Do you happen to know whose plane this is?"

She flashes a smile. "This is the newest member of EIC's fleet."

"Thanks ever so."

"Anytime."

Goose raises his glass, pretending to examine the amber liquid in the glow of the reading light. "EIC," he says slowly. "That would make this *your* plane, wouldn't it?" He lifts the glass to his grinning mouth.

I nod slowly. "Walked right into that," I say.

"Without so much as a setup. A thing of beauty." He clinks his glass with mine. "To your plane, and your cock."

I wake up just as the wheels touch the ground. My head throbs and my mouth is dry and bitter.

"Goose," I say, and he startles awake.

"Shite, was I out the whole flight?"

"Think so."

"You?"

I nod, a bit wary. I never sleep on flights.

"Good morning," one of the flight attendants says. Jessa, was it?

"What time is it?" I ask.

"About noon. Are you hungry?"

"Famished," Goose says, just as I say, "Not really."

"I can have something prepared for you if you like, before you deplane?"

I look out the window, expecting to see London City Airport, but this isn't it. "Where are we?"

"Darlington."

"Darlington?" Goose repeats.

Jessa nods. "Your driver is already here and waiting to take you to the house."

Goose looks at me quizzically. "What house?"

"Noah." The crew member who gave Goose the tour last night appears from the rear of the plane. "I have Victoria Gao on the line for you."

"Who?" Goose asks me.

The last time I heard from my father's solicitor was at his

funeral, I think, when she handed me my inheritance. Her assistant has helped sort out a few things since then, but that's all. "Back in a sec," I say to Goose.

Madison hands me the phone, then excuses herself wordlessly. "Hello?"

"Next time you decide to take one of the planes, I'd appreciate at least a day's notice," Ms. Gao says. My memory of her is one of elegance, composure. She sounds surprisingly put out.

"Sorry 'bout that," I say, glancing at the exit door. "Trip came together at the last minute."

"Well. At least you're all right," she says.

Odd thing for her to say, isn't it? "Why wouldn't I be?"

"No one's heard from you in days. I've left several messages, texts, and emails," she says.

"I left my mobile in New York," I say slowly. "Wallet, too."

"I'll send someone over to check the flat," she replies, matter-of-fact.

"You have keys?"

"It would've been rather difficult to move your furniture in without them," she says. She has a point, but the thought is mildly unsettling anyway. "As I said, I'll send someone to check the loft, and have your things sent to you if they're found."

"Sent where?" I ask.

"The manor," she says, as if it's obvious. "Your grandparents will be relieved to have you there, I'm sure."

"It hasn't been *that* long since I've called," I say.

"Things are a bit sticky in New York, at the moment. Better you're in England just now, and out of the press."

"*Sticky?*" Her tone gets my back up. "A girl died, another's on life support in hospital."

"Felicity Melrose is on camera having set fire to company property. You're a minor still, in America. There's no evidence that you even knew her."

Knew Stella, though. From Horizons. But Ms. Gao doesn't mention her, or acknowledge that I have.

"Doesn't it look rather dodgy, me leaving the country?"

"If you'd asked my advice before you left . . ." Her voice trails off. "I might've suggested adjusting the timing of your trip. But we can work with it. Your family's in the UK, after all, and the archives incident is a civil matter, at best."

The archives incident. Still no mention of what happened on the bridge.

"What about Stella?" I ask. The line is silent. "Hello?"

"Sorry, you cut out for a moment."

"I asked, what about Stella," I repeat.

"Stella . . . Benicia?"

"Yes," I say, growing annoyed. "The girl who live-streamed her suicide attempt to the world." Victoria Gao must know of her. What's she playing at?

"What about her?" she asks perfunctorily.

"I knew her," I persist. "I was there, when she jumped."

Silence on the line again. Then, after a beat, "We'll get it sorted."

Sorted. A practical word. Efficient. Fitting, for Ms. Gao. She seems like a practical, efficient person.

If she has keys to my flat, it's likely she has keys to other things. The archives, no doubt.

What else has she sorted?

A burst of laughter erupts from the front of the plane. A woman and a man I can't remember meeting are doubled over at something Goose has said.

I shift away, leaning down a bit to look out the window. "How did you know I was here?" I ask Ms. Gao.

"We keep track of our investments," she says, not at all ominously. "The Gulfstream's brand-new. The shareholders would have my head if it was lost on my watch."

"I see," I say. "For a second I thought you were referring to me," I add drily.

"I'm afraid the board is less compelled by nonmonetary value. Though of course it's good to know where you are. I am here to help you, whatever you need."

"Thanks," I say, with sarcasm.

"You're welcome," she says without it. "I'll have your things shipped from New York within the week, along with Mr. Greaves's belongings. Madison will show you where to meet the car. Safe travels," she says, and hangs up.

5

I SHALL FETCH HER UP

"SO MUCH FOR THE GINGERBREAD HOUSE," Goose says, when he hears where we're going.

"Early days, yet," I reply, as we're driven through the Yorkshire Dales.

"Disappointed to have had our conspiracy theories dashed, are we?"

Not disappointed, but not relieved, either.

The problem with Goose is that he's not wrong; in his position, I'd be equally sceptical. It's just that I've spent the past year falling in love with a serial murderer, finding out that my father helped arrange it, discovering that a centuries-old man engineered my parents' own marriage and my existence, and learning that everything I spent the first sixteen years of my life believing is wrong.

I *could* try explaining all that to Goose—he'd probably take it in stride, like he has everything else. But his perspective is limited. I can't rely on it.

Daniel's perspective would be useful, though. I wonder what he'd make of M's reemergence? Or of the mission she tasked me with, which I seem to be unwillingly complying with despite my best efforts?

He'd never answer, if I messaged him. He'd be likelier to hit me for hurting his sister. And it's hard to imagine him hitting anyone.

"Never thought I'd be spending my gap year at home," Goose says, looking out the window. A mist of rain clings to the glass, fogs the air outside.

"We won't be here long," I say. "Our things'll be shipped in the next week, the lawyer said. We can leave after that." I don't love the idea of strangers rummaging through my things, or of Ms. Gao having my mobile, but the thought of missing a text or a call from Mara is unbearable.

If she reaches out to you again, it won't be her *reaching. It'll be* him.

"Or we could leave before," I add, remembering M's words. "I don't much care," I lie.

"A week in the country," Goose says, with a definitive nod. "Could be refreshing."

"Could be," I say. M could be wrong about Mara and the professor. She could be lying.

"Just what the doctor ordered."

"Quite," I agree. What did the professor write, in Mara's letter? *If you put it on, I will know.* Something like that?

"Will Mara be joining us?"

She might not be wearing it. My hand rises to my neck, finding my pendant beneath the collar of my shirt.

Even if she is wearing it, though—who bloody cares? I'm wearing mine. It's not the One Ring. She's not a slave to him any more than I am. I press the point of the pendant into the underside of my thumb.

You kind of are, though.

The thought echoes in my skull, in Mara's voice. I grit my teeth.

I mean, you're here, just like they wanted.

"They?"

"Mate?"

The sound of Goose's voice surprises me, and I look over at him. He seems puzzled, and a tad worried, which makes sense because I've just talked to myself. Out loud.

"Stop," I say to the driver.

"Sir?"

I lean forward in the seat. "Pull over whenever you can."

"Of course, sir."

"You all right?" Goose asks.

"I'm fine." Just mental. "Just need a bit of air."

"Very well, sir." He pulls onto a side road and I get out. Goose follows.

I take a few long strides away from the car. There's a white sign marking the crossroads to a small village just outside the borders of the estate. "I'm fine," I repeat, convincing absolutely no one. "Really."

"Of course you are. You haven't mentioned Mara once in the past twenty-four hours, but coincidence, surely."

"I'd rather not deal with family shite right now," is all I say, staring fixedly at the sign.

Goose comes to stand beside me. "All right, fuck the country, then. London's calling."

Not far enough.

I shake my head. "We'll run into people we know."

"Madrid? Paris?"

"Maybe," I say, trying to imagine it. Disappearing into another city. An anonymous tourist like anyone else.

"Fine, I'll choose. But first I've got to eat, mate. Let's find a pub, shall we?"

"If you're buying," I say, when another thought occurs to me. "You've got cash?"

Goose reaches into his pockets. "A bit."

"Enough for a taxi?"

"For a short ride, yeah."

I nod. "Let's do it."

"Do . . . what, exactly?"

"Walk to town, get a ride someplace else."

He places a hand on the sign. "A stupid question, probably, but . . . why?"

Because I don't like being used. Because I like being tracked even less.

And because I can't even think here without Mara invading my mind. Going back to the place where my father's corpse is rotting won't help me be rid of her, knowing she's the one who put it there.

Goose is looking at me with concern. "Is there something wrong with the car we've got?"

"No," I say, searching for a reason that won't sound mad. "Except that the family solicitor hired it, and I just want a day or two to myself. Where no one knows where I am or what I'm doing and I'm not responsible for anything."

Goose hovers for a moment, between believing me and not. When he sighs, I know I've got him. "Fine. But if I pass out, you're carrying me."

6

THE TRAGIC CLOWN

WE DISMISS THE DRIVER WITHOUT incident, but after that, our options thin. We end up walking into a car park outside a closed pub in Darlington, and stumble upon a couple of Dutch tourists on their way to Whitby who offer to bring us along.

Working out the lodging situation is a bit of a challenge, as I have to convince Goose not to use his credit cards without sounding mental. He ends up borrowing the Dutchman's mobile, hacking into his brother's Airbnb account, and stealing some of his credits. ("He invested early. He can afford it.")

The scenery changes from moor to seaside, and it's late

afternoon by the time the car pulls up to a row of small houses that hug the edge of the cliffs, in full view of Whitby Harbour.

"Lovely people, the Dutch," Goose says, waving goodbye as their car pulls away. I lean back against a low stone wall for a moment, closing my eyes. I've been running on anger and annoyance—mostly anger—but now I'm just fucking tired.

"I haven't been here in ages," he says. "Not since I was little and my brothers thought to scare me by making me walk the graveyard at night. Ever done that?"

I shake my head, letting the unfamiliar scents of the harbour and the sounds of the village work on my restless senses.

"Let's go, then," Goose says. "After we get pissed."

If I could, it'd be brilliant. I wonder how much alcohol it'd take to get me there in my newly nonhealing state.

"Got enough money for it?" I ask.

"Not to get totally rinsed. We'll have to get by on our considerable charm." He loops his arm around my shoulders. "Or, my charm, rather. I've got enough for both of us. Oh my God, this place!" He's stopped us in front of a quaint little white shop with black windows. "I love this place!"

"Humble Pie and Mash," I read the sign.

"Perfect for you," he says, dropping his arm and opening the door.

It's not a pub, but it smells good enough to make me not care, for the moment. A white pit bull is lounging beside a table with its chin on its paws.

"Welcome," the hostess says in a northern accent. "Sit any where you like." She hands us two menus.

"They don't serve alcohol," I say dejectedly.

"No, but they do serve haggis and neep pies." Goose turns over the menu, then sniffs the air. "Is it my concussion, or do I smell beer?"

A group sitting a few tables away is passing bottles around.

"The Endeavour just down the road'll bring a couple o' pints over," the waitress says, coming round. "Pop on over the road to pay and they'll bring 'em by for a quid."

Goose stands immediately, nearly knocking over his chair. "I'll be right back."

The waitress raises her considerable eyebrows as he leaves.

"Apologies for my friend," I say. "For both of us, actually, in advance."

"No worries, what can I get you?"

"I'll have the steak and stout," I say, reading the cheerfully illustrated menu. "He'll have the Yorkshire sausage and black pudding."

"Right then, anything to drink?"

"A glass of milk for him, and mushy peas with his pie as well?"

"Lovely. Do let me know if there's anything else."

I thank her again, then look around. There's a fire going, and the place is done up to look like a quaint little cottage that a kindly grandmother might live in; flowered tablecloths, stucco walls, and painted cabinets with little oddments arranged on top. A framed note on the wall says everything displayed has been found in the attics and old rooms by previous and current owners of the building, which started as a bakery in 1843. The more you know.

Goose arrives before the pies do, carrying two full pint glasses of beer and a bottle-shaped paper bag under his arm.

"Impressive," I say.

"Isn't it? We're too skint for delivery, but look!" He sets the bag on the table, scrunching the edges down dramatically.

"A half-consumed bottle of Jack Daniel's," I say. "Wow."

"They're not supposed to sell bottles."

"And yet."

"*And yet.*" He holds his pint aloft. "Cheers."

"Cheers."

"Gods, that's good," he says. After a few swallows, his glass is already a quarter empty. "We can ask for shot glasses for the whiskey, drop them in."

"Here you go, lads," the waitress says, setting down two plates loaded with peas and mash and pie and gravy. She sets a tall glass of milk in front of Goose.

"*What* did you do?" he drawls.

"Yorkshire sausage and blood pudding and a glass of milk," she says to Goose, "and steak and stout for you. Will there be anything else?"

"Two shot glasses?"

"Sorry, don't have 'em."

"Two extra glasses, then," Goose says.

"Thanks," I add.

"No worries," she says brightly. "Enjoy!"

Once she leaves, Goose shakes his head slowly at his thoroughly English meal.

"The milk makes it art, don't you think?" I ask.

"Was the mushy peas that did me in." He picks up his fork and cracks the surface of the pie. "I rather like blood pudding, actually." He loads up his fork and shoves it into his grinning mouth. "Mmm," he groans. "Delicious," he says with his mouth full, spraying crumbs onto the table.

This is good, this moment. I feel less haunted already. "Last time you had it?"

"Last summer, could be? *You're* the one who forgot your roots, mate."

"I imagine that's why I'm back here. To dig them up," I mumble.

Goose tilts his head quizzically. Then says, "So," drawing out the word. "Where's Mara right now, do you think?"

"Which one," I say tonelessly, pushing one of my glasses around with my knuckles.

"Pardon?"

I blink at Goose, enviably clueless. I'm not quite sure how to tell him that there are two Maras, the first of whom has been alive for at least a hundred and fifty years.

Easier just to drink. "I ended it. With Mara."

"Got that feeling. Really sorry, mate," he says. "You can cry in front of me, if you like. Better out than in."

"Thanks," I say drily.

He leans his elbows on the table. "Know what I think?"

I raise my eyebrows.

"Forget Madrid. Let's go to Ibiza, or Crete. Someplace where everyone'll be wearing less clothing, yeah?"

If this had happened last year, before everything, before *her*? It's exactly what I'd do.

"We can pop off to the manor once our things've arrived or get money wired here, even. Then set out."

Something itches at the back of my mind, but I can't quite find it beneath the haze of alcohol. "You don't have to stay."

"I like Whitby," Goose says. "It's adorable."

"No, I mean, after."

"I like Ibiza, too."

"You could walk away, still," I say hopefully. "From all this." He seems appropriately confused, given how little he knows, how little I've told him. I ought to fix that. "Everything that's happened—" I start.

But Goose stops me. "Whatever happened, happened. It's in the past. You can't change it, but you can leave it there, mate."

Tempting. But true?

I brought Mara to New York and had Jamie come to live

with us and tried to act like the shite that had brought us together didn't matter. One could ask Stella how well that turned out. Or not, seeing as how she'll never speak again.

Unless . . . M said she could help get my ability back.

I'll keep your friend Alastair in my thoughts, she said too.

If he's next, I won't know it without my ability.

But if he's next, how much help would I be, with it? How much did I help Felicity or Beth or Sam?

Or Mara, for that matter? If I'd been with her at Horizons, at the end—she couldn't have gotten to this place. She can't have wanted this for herself. For us.

My thoughts spin and stutter. I can't think through the noise of them.

Better not think at all. I pour another glass of whiskey, only just realising I've finished my first, and a pint besides. For the first time in years, I feel the sharp click of the alcohol, filling me with warmth. The illusion of fullness is preferable to the reality of emptiness.

Maybe Goose *is* right. Whatever happened, happened. I can't fix what's broken, but I can leave it behind. Stop dragging it with me.

I raise my glass in the air. Goose follows suit. "What are we toasting?" he asks.

"A clean break."

7

HEREIN LIES THE JUSTIFICATION

WE PAY THE BILL, THEN HEAD OUT IN search of somewhere we can buy or borrow more whiskey, because fuck it, why not.

We're thoroughly, delightfully wasted by the time we start toward Whitby Abbey, which doesn't prevent either of us from enjoying some of Goose's Percocet and chasing it with the bottles of Guinness we begged off a bartender at the last pub of the night. The abbey ruins are surrounded by a considerable stone wall. The graveyard, however, is not.

Goose picks an unsteady path through the headstones. "Stoker used some of the names from the graveyard in *Dracula*," he says, leaning over one of the headstones. "Can't read most of them." Then he raises his arm, pointing over a cliff. "That's where the *Demeter* ran aground."

"What?"

"The ship? In the book?"

"Don't remember," I say, settling down on the grass. Goose slouches down against a headstone. I'm up against one shaped like a cross, for the symbolism.

"Liar," he says. "Even Neirin had to study at least *once*. You'd never taken so much as a note. If we hadn't liked you so much, we'd've loathed you. You remembered *everything*."

I take the bottle of Guinness from him. "Maybe that's gone now too."

"Hmm?"

I take a long sip. Then, "Our abilities are gone," I find myself saying.

"What, you mean . . ." He stares at my hand, lying palm up on the grass. With significance.

"Mmm," is all I manage to get out.

"I need a bit more than that, mate."

I glance at it, my scarred palm. I drew it with a knife myself, for Goose's benefit ostensibly, but also for mine. "I don't heal anymore, is what I'm saying. Poorly."

"How do you know?"

"Well," I say, holding the bottle up. "I can get properly fucked up, for one thing."

"Cheers to that," Goose says, taking the bottle from me.

"Also, Jamie said something about it before we left the city."

"Do tell."

"Said the power's out, for all of us."

"Us . . ."

"Gifted. Carriers. Afflicted, whatever."

"So you, Jamie, Mara, Leo, Sophie—all of you?"

"All of *us*," I say. Except Mara. I remember her expression, or her lack of one, rather, when she said, "*Mine isn't.*" Wish I could forget it.

I leave that bit out. I hold my hand out for the bottle.

He passes it to me. "As of when?" he asks, mercifully.

"The bridge, I think? Something happened there, I think. Not sure what. Jamie tried to use his ability . . . it didn't work."

"He told you, or you saw it not work?"

"It's all rather vague." My mind skips through still frames of that moment, but they're out of order. "It's all jumbled up with . . . I tried to heal Stella. I think." Seems like something I would do.

"Maybe it's not you. Maybe she was too far gone?"

"Maybe," I say. "Doubt it, though. Mara's father, Marcus— he was shot, once. Nearly died. I saved him." An angry mother had aimed a gun at his client, but let's be honest—Mara pulled the trigger. First time I saw her choose to be judge and jury and executioner. Memories.

"Maybe it's only temporary?" Goose suggests. "Like a bruise or something."

"Maybe," I echo.

"Think mine's gone as well?" Goose asks.

"Probably. Do you feel any different?"

"No. Never have, though. Honestly, I wouldn't have believed you if I hadn't seen you do"—he picks up my hand, lets it fall to the ground limply—"what you did." He sighs. "Shame, really."

"Mara's grandmother said something about helping us get them back."

"Mara's—what?"

Shit.

"How drunk are you, exactly?"

"Sublimely," I say. "Is that a word? It doesn't sound like a word. I don't care, if it isn't. It ought to be."

He crouches up, takes the bottle from me as I converse with myself.

"So what did she say?" he prods.

Goose thinks I'm talking about *my* Mara. I'm not sure I have the energy to correct him.

"She wasn't . . . specific. But coming here was a part of it, I think."

"So, you left her, but she told you to come here? To England?"

Fuck it. I give up. "I left *Mara*. Her grandmother is also named Mara."

Goose's expression betrays that he's currently evaluating how drunk *he* is.

"Thing is," I say, staring straight ahead. "Everyone in her family thinks her grandmother's dead."

"Sounds complicated."

"Indeed it is. Turns out, she's been alive for over a century . . . ?" I say, as Goose's head continues to tilt on its axis. "About a hundred and fifty years?"

"Of course."

Neither of us says anything.

"Does she have a necklace?" Goose asks.

How does he know? "As it happens, yes," I say, thinking of the pendant I now wear, the mirror image of the one that belonged to M. The one she left for Mara. "Why do you ask?"

"*Game of Thrones*. The Red Woman. She'll probably crumble to dust if she takes it off."

"No," I say. "She gave her necklace to Mara," I add, then amend, "She left it for her." Inside a doll stuffed with human hair that we burned. I leave that bit out.

"What's it look like?"

"The doll?"

"What doll?" Goose asks.

"Oh, the necklace, you meant. Like this." I pull mine from beneath my collar.

He looks it over, confused. "You've always had that."

"Sort of. My mother left hers for me when she died."

"Wait, it's the same one that Mara has?"

"Spitting image," I say, glancing down at the oxidised silver. "Mirror image, I mean."

"And I'm guessing you're going to tell me it's not a coincidence."

I don't know if it's the alcohol or the drugs or my angst, but that's the moment I break. I tell Goose everything. About how I heard Mara before I met her. About realising we were the same, mirror images of each other. I tell him about the professor, my father, filling in the gaps around the experiments and Horizons as much as I can, given that there are gaps in my own memory as well.

I get as far as the bit just before Mara leaves before realising I can't say the actual words. The vowels and consonants crystallise in my throat, sharp and piercing. Like I've swallowed a mouthful of razor blades and now they're just lodged there, slicing me to ribbons.

"I've never seen you this fucked up over a girl. Over anything."

"I'm not."

"You *are*, though."

"Fuck right off."

"*She's* what this is all about, for you," he says, stabbing the air with his Guinness hand. "Not the suicides, or that old professor chap, or any of it."

"All just subplot?"

"Precisely."

"So where does that leave me?" I ask. My voice sounds less flat than I'd hoped.

"Well, do you want her back?"

"No," I say, but not quite fast enough. My head feels thick, hazy. I exhale on the word "Yes." My eyes close against the memories. What I said. What she did. "I don't know."

"I think you do know. But you can't say it because the answer's loathsome."

"What's that?" I murmur, leaning my head back against the cross.

"You care less about the fate of the world than you do about pussy."

"God help me."

"I don't think he will, mate. I think you're on your own."

BEFORE

No Name Island, Florida

I OPEN MY EYES AND SEE NOTHING BUT WHITE.

It is blinding after the dimness of my dreams. The dark halls of Horizons absent all sound—except for the occasional sob and scream. Mara's silhouette, the way she looks in Jude's arms as he edges her toward the shadows, a blade at her neck, his animal hands on her body. The memories have merged, meshed with others—my mother's blood soaking into my skin, Mara's voice in my ears as she begged Jude for her life. They've formed an endless nightmare from which I've no hope of waking.

Until now.

I blink and blink again. The whiteness dulls; it's only

fluorescent lighting, hidden in the recesses of the smooth, white ceiling.

A hospital ceiling?

I flip off the sheet covering my body and sit up. Pain spikes through my head and I close my eyes and grit my teeth.

"Careful," a tinny, bodiless voice says.

It's the voice of the person who betrayed us—who betrayed Mara most of all. The voice of the person who abused her trust. Who violated her home. Who watched on her monitor as Jude, that animal, crept into her room to watch her sleep, to scrawl messages in blood on her mirror, to torment and torture her until she broke.

It is Dr. Kells's voice.

I open my eyes again, wincing as my vision clears. I'm not in a hospital room; I'm in some sort of cell. There's a sink, and a toilet, and the white bed I was lying in just seconds ago. Three walls are concrete, and painted white. The fourth is glass.

"Where is she?" I say to the empty room, gripping the mattress. I feel the urge to tear it apart.

Dr. Kells can hear me, but she doesn't answer my question. Instead she asks, "How are you feeling?"

"Where is she?" I ask again.

"When you stand up, you may want to do it carefully. The drugs may not have worn off completely yet."

As if I care about being careful. As if I care about the drugs. I stare at the glass, at the white concrete walls beyond it, at nothing. I wonder, fleetingly, if I could use the bed frame to shatter it. And then I remember trying something similar with a chair in the dining hall at Horizons, before we found Jude. Before he found us.

Before Dr. Kells led him to us.

The glass there didn't shatter. It didn't even crack. I would need to come up with something else. But first—"Where is she?" I repeat.

"Where is who, Noah?"

"Don't fuck with me."

"I'm not fucking with you, as you put it. I'm merely trying to ascertain to whom you are referring. Are you referring to Mara Dyer?"

"Yes," I sneer.

"In that case, she's safe."

"Safe *where?*"

"We can talk about that further, but I would like to discuss some other things with you first."

"You cannot fathom the immensity of the fucks I do not give about what you would *like*," I say, crossing the cell until I stand just inches from the glass. I see my reflection in it; my eyes are red rimmed and my face is pale. My jaw is rough, but only mildly—a day unshaven, perhaps two. I'm dressed in white scrubs.

"I want to see her," I say. "I want to see her now. Perhaps afterward, if I'm feeling generous—which is, I'll admit, a tremendous if—we can talk further about how you've been torturing us and why. But if you think I'm going to say another word to you before I've seen that Mara is safe, you are not only sick, but stupid as well."

"Actually, Noah, *here's* how this is going to work. You will be *allowed* to see Mara if, and only if, you cooperate with me."

"Fuck you."

"Good night, Noah."

The lights in the cell go out and I'm plunged into darkness. I slam my fist into the glass.

The pain is beautiful.

9

MERIT OF HEROES

Whitby, England

W E'RE WOKEN IN THE GRAVEYARD BY A cloud of bats screeching overhead, returning to the abbey before dawn.

Or rather, that's how Goose claims to have been woken, before he shakes me awake. Which happens to be right when a short, balding caretaker sort appears in the graveyard, staring at us with an expression that reads *They don't pay me enough for this shit.*

"Jesus fuck," Goose mumbles as I rise. "What happened to your hand?"

I look down at my right fist. My knuckles are split, bleeding. I try extending my fingers and the pain is extraordinary. I place my other hand on the cross, steadying myself, and notice my blood on the stone.

"You punched a bloody grave," he says finally. "Literally."

"Seems so."

"May I ask why?"

"Do I need a reason?"

Goose bends to try and read the headstone. "Apologies on my friend's behalf, Miss Milnes."

A finger of ice straightens my spine. "What?"

"The name on the grave. Allegra Milnes."

I bend to read the inscription, but most of it's eroded away by wind and rain and time. There's a thought trying to pierce the surface of my blinding hangover, but Goose takes my elbow before it can coalesce.

"Come on, mate," he says. The caretaker's hangdog eyes follow us with reproach, so Goose apologises to him, now, and collects the remains of our binge from the graves we slept on.

"We're vile," I say, trying not to further desecrate or stumble over any headstones and failing.

"The worst," Goose agrees amiably. "Though at the moment, you're vastly more pathetic."

Undeniable. The sun's beginning to rise in direct proportion to the arrowing pain in my temples. Or the other way around. Or something. It's shit, is the point.

"Least we're not far from the cottage," Goose says in an

attempt at cheeriness. "We can ask the host for a doctor nearby or something—"

I try shaking my head—a grievous error. "No," I say instead.

"I'm relatively certain your wrist isn't supposed to bend at that angle."

"Nevertheless."

"Fine. Then we'll order some takeaway or something, get some protein in you."

The thought of food roils my stomach. "Mention food again, and I'll vomit on those stupidly expensive shoes of yours."

"They've seen worse."

"I have a headache in my eye."

"Buck up, mate. And walk in a straight line, if you can. Preferably not dead centre of the street."

"If I get run over by a car, I'll die," I muse. "Fascinating."

Goose has an arm around my shoulder, which only works because he's just slightly taller than I. "Be fascinated later. We're almost there."

I'm overwhelmed by an urge to laugh and throw up simultaneously; mercifully it passes once we arrive at the house. The keys are hidden beneath a little red-hatted garden gnome, and Goose unlocks the back door. We're immediately confronted by a massive staircase.

"I won't make it, mate. Go on without me," I say solemnly.

"You've been resurrected before. You can climb a flight of stairs."

"Good morning!" a round, happy voice exclaims from somewhere behind me. I try to locate the source of it, but can't seem to move my head without seeing spots.

"Morning," Goose replies. I catch a flash of his toothy grin in my peripheral vision.

"Welcome to East Cottage!" the woman says. "I'm Jane Corbin! You boys have fun last night?"

"Celebrating my mate's homecoming," Goose says. "A bit overenthusiastically."

Jane is no stranger to enthusiasm, clearly. Every sentence is punctuated with a verbal exclamation point. "Of course, of course! Well, welcome, as I said! There's plenty of food in the fridge, my husband Roger will be down in a bit before he heads to work, and then you'll have the place to yourselves for the rest of your stay!"

"Thanks," I say, trying to smile like Goose. I think it frightens her.

"You're most welcome," she says. No exclamation point, that time. "Oh, love! What happened to your hand?"

"Slammed a door on it," I lie. "Jet lag and alcohol don't mix."

She offers a sympathetic look. "They certainly don't. You ought to get that looked at—my husband's a medic, he can—"

"I'll be fine, just need a sleep."

"Of course, of course," she says, fluttering her hands. "Off to Bedfordshire with you."

I haul myself up the stairs, my jaw clenching with each step. I've no idea how many bedrooms are in the cottage or which ones are ours, I realise, at about the same time I realise I don't care. The first one with a made bed is the one I end up in. I kick the door shut, and fall onto it stomach first, a massive mistake.

I lie there, unwilling to moan even a bit, because I'm going to suffer *silently*, with *dignity*. People who moan are intolerable. *Just be sick already. Get it over with.*

"Fuck off," I say to no one, staring at the white beadboard on the lower half of the white walls. There's a fireplace in the room. *Charmant.*

Just being able to rise up onto my elbows is a monumental achievement, on par with space exploration and stem cell research. The prospect of death is always tempting, but never more so when compared to the prospect of standing.

"Get up, twat," I growl at myself. Gendered insults work on my ignorant psyche, apparently, because I *am* standing. Unfortunately I can't remember why.

Also unfortunately, I'm facing a mirror, which seems spectacularly unfair. I look the way I deserve to look, which is to say, ill and wretched.

I allow myself to wallow in it instead of focusing on any of the more global concerns, like whether Daniel or Jamie has been co-opted into one of the respective shadow organisations that have taken an interest in us over the year, or Mara's current whereabouts and welfare, or whether I'll wake up to find Goose missing and then dead.

Or that dream from this morning, or last night, or whenever it was. That Horizons dream.

Too much. The best course of action is oblivion, obviously, which leads me to do the perfunctory knock-then-open on the doors of the other rooms until I find Goose sprawled on a large canopy bed in one of them, snoring lightly.

He had the pills in his jeans pocket, which he's still wearing, which is why my hand is on his ass as a man dressed in white scrubs—Roger, presumably?—walks by, as I've left the bedroom door open.

"What!" I shout slowly.

He backs away with raised eyebrows, which is ideal, as it allows me to (1) avoid conversation and (2) withdraw the bottle from the still-sleeping Goose, shake out a few pills, and summon enough saliva to swallow them without water (an important life skill) before stomping back across the hall, my teeth rattling in my skull.

Without alcohol to help the pills along this morning, I remain upright and conscious, jittery and chattery. My fist throbs, but I don't want to think about it because that means thinking about the nightmare and the grave and the name of the woman buried in it when I don't want to think about anything at all, so instead I'm opening the various doors in the bedroom I've landed in—a cupboard and a loo, should I decide to force my body to empty my stomach of its poisonous contents, though I already know I won't. "It would be disrespectful to waste Goose's beneficence so thoughtlessly," I say aloud, to no one, as I wait for the pills to kick in.

The effects are disappointing, to be honest. I'd hoped for instant sleep—the exhaustion plus sedatives plus leftover alcohol ought to be enough to down a bull elephant, one would think, but all I get instead is a mild reprieve from my vengeful headache and the twisting in my stomach, along with a general creeping tiredness. I lie down, but can't close my eyes. The curtains in the room are drawn, and daylight sneaks in from the edges, slicing bars and shadows on the wall. The room feels raw, eerie, wrong in the daylight. Coffinlike and close.

I'm gripped by a wave of paranoia, suddenly—like I've got an audience in my head. Fucking drugs. I'd thought that at least they'd quiet my mind.

Because my mind is most definitely the problem. How do you escape when the enemy is you?

Part II

Before

No Name Island, Florida

The most painful state of being is
remembering the future, particularly
the one you'll never have.

—Søren Kierkegaard

FREE TO IMAGINE

IT'S DARK FOR HOURS OR DAYS, BUT AT HORIZONS, I
don't sleep. I sit against the wall, my back hunched, staring
at the concrete floor. I imagine Mara, sitting next to me, her
head on my shoulder. Her hair tickling my neck. I imagine—

"Good morning, Noah," Dr. Kells says as the lights come on.

I wince, blinking against them. This room is slightly
different from the last, I think. Or perhaps they've simply
replaced the glass panel I shattered with my fist, which is
already healing. Wasn't reinforced glass after all. An important lesson, and a reminder; trust nothing here. No one.

"How do you feel?" Kells asks.

I look up at the ceiling. "I want to see her."

"Are you ready to cooperate with me?"

I close my eyes. If I say no, the lights will go out. I'll be locked in here, away from her, still. But if I say yes—there's a chance.

I need to see her.

"Yes," I say between clenched teeth.

"That's good news. Now, tell me how you're feeling."

"Fine," I say, my voice clipped.

"Describe it," Dr. Kells says.

I inhale slowly and look up at the ceiling, trying to identify the source of the voice. There are no identifiable speakers in the room, nor are there cameras—but I'm most definitely being watched. Recorded, likely. I choose my words carefully. "I have a headache. The lights—it's too bright in here. I feel"—I run my hand over my jaw—"I feel hungover."

"That's probably the ketamine," Dr. Kells says.

Not likely.

"You look surprised, Noah."

So she can see me, then. I flick a glance at the darkened glass wall, but all I can see is my reflection.

"Why is that?" she asks.

I shrug.

"Have you been on ketamine before, Noah?"

Indeed. Once upon a time, I would crush and inhale and inject anything anyone gave me, just to see if I could feel it. To see if I could feel anything.

I didn't.

"Noah? Have you been on ketamine before?"

"Yes."

"What did it feel like?"

I shrug casually. "I don't remember," I lie.

Dr. Kells seems satisfied nevertheless, because she continues. "You were given a combination of ketamine and Telazol. Your body metabolises them so efficiently that we had to give you a rather large dose."

Kells knows about me, then. About what I can do. "How much?" I ask her, because despite everything, I can't help my curiosity.

"How much what?"

"How much did you give me?"

"Enough to down a bull elephant."

I almost smile at that.

"And that was only enough to put you down for twelve hours or so."

Twelve hours. Is that how long it has been since the torture garden? Since I saw Mara in Jude's arms—since she slammed him against the wall at Horizons. Since he fell with a sickening crack to the tiled floor and she lifted him—with just one hand around his throat. Until—

A hissing sound—coming from the vents. That blank scent drifting in the air.

They gassed her. I didn't realise it, not until it was too late.

Mara fell, and Jude fell with her. Jamie and Stella and that girl, Megan, the screamer—they were gone by then. Slunk off into the shadows or the patient rooms to hide from Jude or to try and escape and run.

But I didn't run. And I didn't fall. I was conscious, and ran to Mara, held her face in my hands. Swept the hair from her pale skin, checked to make sure she was breathing. In the second before I felt her breath against my cheek, I thought I might die. And then, a sting—

I raise my hand to my neck, exposed in the white scrubs.

"It was a tranquilliser dart," Dr. Kells says, as if she knows what I must be thinking.

There's no puncture wound. Of course not.

"We needed to be able to move you safely."

At this, I laugh.

"That amuses you?"

I raise my eyes to the glass. "It does, in fact. Yes."

"Why is that?"

Her words are nearly drowned out by the images in my head. I see the body of a girl lying in the sand, her white shirt soaked red with her blood. I see Phoebe, her wrists slit in her Horizons bed. "Because you don't give a shit about our safety. You told Mara she was delusional. Insane. You made her *feel* insane. You made her feel sick, but you were the one *making* her sick."

"I'm afraid you have no idea what you're talking about. I'm trying to help her get better."

"Bullshit."

"I'll show you."

I hold my breath. "When?"

"I'll send someone down to your room now."

"My cell, you mean."

"When he arrives, you're going to put your hands on the glass and allow him to restrain you."

Is that so?

"Otherwise I'll have to give you another dose of ketamine and Telazol, and I'll make sure the lights stay off for a full week. Do you understand?"

I run my hands through my hair. "Yes."

"And it could be a very long time before you see Mara again."

"I understand," I say.

"Good. Then I'll see you in a few minutes."

Can't fucking wait.

I spend the next four minutes planning my attack on the unfortunate person sent to restrain me. But the person who comes to a stop in front of the glass is not the two-hundred-and-thirty-pound guard of my imagination; she is female. And small—about Mara's height, and she only looks a few years older. She wears glasses, and has a light splash of freckles across her nose. Her white lab coat grazes the knees of her trousers, and she carries a pair of leather and metal restraints in her hands.

"Hello, Noah," she says in a delicate voice. "I need you to put your hands on the glass for me now. Can you do that?"

I don't answer, but I do as she says.

"Thank you. I'm going to come around and put these on you." She holds up the restraints. "That's not going to be a problem, is it?"

I study the woman through the glass. I could overpower her in a fraction of a second—I could break her neck before Kells could have me tranquillised. There's no chance the good doctor doesn't know this, which means two things: First, that Kells thinks I'm less likely to fight her because she's female. Second, that whoever this woman is, she's expendable. Kells had to account for the fact that I might hurt her—and sending her to me means that Kells is fine with it. Which ultimately means that she's useless, as a hostage. I exhale through my nostrils and nod.

"Good. Thank you. I'm going to come in, now, but I need you to keep your hands on the glass. Will you do that for me?"

"Yes," I say.

She nods slightly, just once, and then walks off to the left. Seconds later, I hear a hiss, and half turn my head. I notice a seam in the white wall—the door opens and the woman stands in the back of the cell.

"Place your forehead against the glass, please."

I do.

I hear her approach. "Now lower your hands slowly, and angle them toward your back."

I do. She fits my wrists into the restraints and buckles them tightly. I am motionless.

"All right, then," she says. "Thank you for your cooperation."

"You're welcome," I say smoothly, still facing the glass.

She smiles. "You're going to follow me out of your room, and then we're going to walk down the hallway side by side. Do you understand?"

"Yes."

"Good. I would hate for there to be any problems. You can turn around now."

I do, then incline my head at the door. "After you," I say.

The woman nods, and then walks through the narrow frame. I slide past her, nearly touching, and I make eye contact as I do. I can hear her heart rate increase.

An idea begins to form. I take two steps, and on the third, I stumble. The woman reaches out, grabbing me by the arm to steady me.

I offer her a sheepish smile. "Sorry," I say. "I'm a bit—I'm not usually so clumsy."

"I'm not surprised," she says, smiling back. "To be honest, I'm shocked you're on your feet at all."

"Would you mind?" I ask, looking from her hand to my arm. "Just until I'm—a bit steadier."

The woman looks up at me—I'm over a head taller than she is. I don't meet her gaze, but look at the floor instead. She takes my arm and her heart is still racing, and *then* I meet her eyes, my expression unguarded. "Thank you," I say sincerely.

"Sure," she says, her cheeks flushing.

We walk down a long, featureless white corridor, flanked by mirrored walls. I note each turn so that I can remember. "What's your name?" I ask, to distract her.

"Dr. Walsh."

"I asked for your name, not your title."

She hesitates for a moment, still staring ahead, then says, "Hannah Walsh."

"And what is it you're a doctor of, Hannah Walsh?"

"I'm an anaesthesiologist."

"So you could render me helpless in seconds," I say.

She smiles a little. "Only if you don't behave."

I give a slight shake of my head. "That won't be a problem."

"I'm glad to hear that," she says as we come to a stop in front of a door. "Because we're here."

11

THE ABYSS OF DESPAIR

D R. WALSH DIPS HER HAND INTO HER POCKET and withdraws a key card. She raises it to the wall, and something blinks green through the white paint. There's another hiss, and the door swings open. Dr. Walsh lets go of my arm and gestures to the room. I look at her.

"You're not coming in?"

"No. But I'll be back to get you when you're finished."

"Thank you," I say as I walk past her.

She nods, smiles, and then closes the door behind me. I hear it lock.

The room is white and nondescript, with two

hotel-appropriate pastel paintings on the walls. A plastic chair sits in the centre of the room, facing a mirror. An unseen clock ticks away each second. The lights dim, and the mirrored glass turns transparent.

Beyond it is another room. Mara lies in a twin bed, an IV connected to her arm, her hair fanned out over the white pillow. My heart turns over at the sight of her and I rush to the glass.

"It's reinforced glass." Dr. Kells's voice slides into the room through an intercom. Another lie, or the truth, this time? "You're not going to be able to get through. In any case, she's unconscious."

"What did you do to her?"

"She's sedated. That's all."

"How do I know she isn't—she isn't dead?" I ask, forcing the word.

"Would you like me to wake her up?"

Yes. "Yes," I say.

"All right, Noah. I'll wake her up. And then you and I are going to talk. Do we understand each other?"

I nod.

"Out loud, please."

"Yes."

"Good."

The sound clicks off. Minutes later, Dr. Kells walks into Mara's room. My heart begins to pound and I move until I'm mere inches away from the glass. Kells injects something into the IV line, and then sits in a chair beside the bed. I count the seconds until Mara's eyelids flutter open.

I nearly collapse with relief when they do. "Thank you," I whisper to no one, my forehead against the glass. "Thank you."

"Good morning, Mara," Dr. Kells says to her. "Do you know where you are?"

I don't breathe as I wait for her answer. She blinks and turns her head to one side, then the other. Her eyes roam the room, but her expression is blank. Unfamiliar.

"Do you know who I am?" Kells asks Mara.

I need to hear her. I'm desperate for her to answer.

After a few seconds, she does. "Yes," is all she says. But in a voice that isn't hers.

I would recognise Mara's voice in a sea of thousands of others. That familiar alto with a slight growl, giving every word a faintly sarcastic edge. And when Mara speaks, her tone is the same, but the edge is gone. My hands curl into fists.

Dr. Kells smooths her skirt. "I have some things I'd like to talk with you about, but first, I want to let you know that you've been given an infusion of a variant of sodium amytal. Have you heard of sodium amytal?"

Mara says no. She hasn't.

I have, though.

"Colloquially, they call it truth serum," Kells explains. "That's not entirely accurate—but it can be used to help relieve certain types of suffering. We sometimes use it in experimental psychiatry to give patients a respite from a manic or catatonic episode." She leans in closer to Mara—my heart thrashes against my ribs. "You've been suffering, Mara, haven't you?"

Mara says yes in that dead voice.

I can't listen to this.

Kells nods her head, then says to Mara, "We think the variant we've developed will help with your . . . unique issues. We're on your side. We want to help you." Her expression is benevolent, her voice smooth and calm. "Will you let us help you?"

She's speaking to Mara, but she glances over her shoulder at me.

I have never wanted to murder someone more than in that second.

Mara doesn't look at me, though. She has no idea I'm here, even. If she did, I don't know if she would recognise me with whatever poison is galloping through her veins.

Mara answers yes, but even behind glass, even through speakers, I can tell that her words are slow. Her tongue is thick.

"I'm glad," Kells says, smiling, and I feel a gush of rage. She reaches down to the floor and picks something up. A remote.

"Let me show you something," she says to Mara. Then, to no one, she says, "Screen."

Mara's eyes are drawn to the ceiling to her right, where a thin screen lowers before her. Her eyes flick toward the glass, then, and my heart pounds for a second, irrationally hoping that she'll know I'm here. But she passes right over me, glancing instead at something I can't see.

"Monitors," Dr. Kells calls out. An insistent, steady beeping begins. Kells is monitoring Mara's heartbeat.

"Lights," she says, and Mara's room goes dark. The screen lights up. I see shaky images of a dark-skinned, dark-haired girl in winter clothes, her breath turning to steam in the beam of light from the camera. She smiles and the camera pans and swings over rotting wood floors, over peeling walls—over a blackboard with names on it, and then, finally, I know what I'm watching.

It's footage from that night. From the asylum. The girl I'm seeing is Rachel, Mara's best friend. The camera must be Claire's. I watch, rapt, as scenes change, and the girls' words turn to screams. The screen goes dark and after the ringing slam of dozens of iron doors, after the collapse, I hear laughter.

It is Mara's, without question.

But then. The shadows on the screen move. The camera is being lifted by someone offscreen. And then I see Kells's face before the video ends.

"You've been a participant in a blind study, Mara," Dr. Kells says to her. "That means that most of your treating doctors and counsellors have been unaware of your participation. Your parents are unaware as well. The reason you've been selected for this study is because you have a condition, a gene that is harming you."

My eyes narrow.

"It makes you act in a way that is causing you to be a danger to yourself and others. Do you understand?"

"Yes," Mara says.

"Some of your friends are also carriers of this gene, which has been disrupting your normal lives."

I watch Mara's face for some indication, any hint that she's even aware of what she's saying, but there is none, and it terrifies me.

"Your condition has caused pain to the people you love, Mara. Do you want to cause pain to the people you love?"

"No," she says, and this time, for the first time, I think I hear an echo of her sound. Of her voice. Of *her*.

"I know you don't," Kells says. "And I am truly sorry we weren't able to help you before now. We had hoped to be able to sedate you before you collapsed the building. We tried very hard to save all of your friends."

The monitor goes silent for a moment that lasts an eternity. I scream Mara's name.

The monitor beeps again.

"We didn't anticipate that things would happen quite the way they did—as it was, we were lucky to be able to extract Jamie Roth, Stella Benicia, and Megan Cannon before they were seriously harmed. We just couldn't get to Noah Shaw."

12

IN HER MOUTH

I WATCH WITH REVULSION AND DREAD AS DR. KELLS calmly, clinically lies to Mara, describing how and where and when I died. I watch Dr. Kells tell Mara that I was too close when Mara brought Horizons down. I scream Mara's name, begging a God I don't believe in to let her hear me, just let her hear me. But she doesn't. She lies there with a kind of radical passivity, her face a mask. One tear rolls down her cheek, though. Just one.

A shadow grows inside me as I watch it fall.

Dr. Kells asks Mara if she wants to get better, to *be* better, and I watch as Mara says yes in that alien voice, absent the fire I love, absent feeling. I am drowning in darkness and I need to shatter the glass that separates us to breathe. I need to lift her out of that bed and carry her out of this place and into a different world, where nothing is broken and everything is as beautiful as she is.

And I can't. I am as powerless now as I was when Jude took her. I fail Mara again and again and the rush of remembering comes in a wave and hollows me out.

The glass darkens, rendering Mara invisible again, throwing my own reflection back at me instead. I look like the ghost of a stranger. I stand there for minutes or hours, I don't know.

"Noah?" Dr. Kells's poisonous voice interrupts the extreme silence. I don't answer.

"Would you like to be taken back to your room?"

I am quiet.

"The silent treatment?" she asks, dripping sarcasm. "That's a bit juvenile, no?"

I stay calm, and manage to speak instead of scream. "What point is there in talking to you? Every word that comes out of your mouth is a lie."

A slight pause. Then, "You can tell when someone's lying, can't you?" Kells asks.

I ignore the question.

"You can hear the spike in a person's heartbeat. A faster pulse. You can hear physical stress, can't you, Noah?"

"Is that why you refuse to be in the same room as me?" I

ask her disembodied voice whilst staring at my own empty eyes.

"On the contrary. I would very much like to be in the same room with you."

"And yet."

"All right," she says. "Let's change that. I want nothing more than to have an honest conversation with you—"

"I doubt that very much."

"And I want you to be able to hear that what I'm telling you is the truth," she continues. "I'll have someone arrive to escort you to someplace we can talk."

"Why bother?" I ask, not moving. "I'm right here."

"That room isn't suitable."

"Oh?"

"There's only one chair," she explains.

My eyes narrow. "Which I'm not sitting in."

"I'd like for both of us to be comfortable."

"Then you can bring another. The mathematical possibilities are endless."

Kells ignores this.

"It wouldn't be because the glass isn't reinforced, there, would it? You wouldn't have lied about that, right?"

"I'll send someone right away to pick you up." The sound clicks off.

Dr. Hannah Walsh, anaesthesiologist, arrives a few moments later. The door unlocks, swings in. Dr. Walsh doesn't move, but she does smile when she sees me.

It takes an extreme act of will to force a smile in return, but I do it. If I can't charm her then I can't use her, and if I can't use her then I can't get us out.

But I *will* get us out. Even if I have to *make* my own key.

She leads me to a different room, this time—an open space, echoing the shape and expanse of the Zen garden at Horizons. But instead of manicured trees and sand and bamboo in the centre, *this* room features a barred cell. A cage.

The walls are striped, pea green and off-white, giving it the feel of an old hospital, or a gymnasium. Dr. Walsh glances up at me once we arrive. "I'm going to change your restraints, now." I hear a tremor of uncertainty in her voice. She is nervous.

"Why?" I ask plainly.

Her tone shifts. She's *professional* now. "Is it going to be a problem?"

I raise my eyebrows. "No," I say. "Just curious."

She takes my arm and leads me to a chair beside the cage, where a set of metal wrist and ankle shackles rests. "These should allow you a bit more freedom," she says, showing them to me, and it's all I can do not to glare. "They're forward facing, so your shoulders will get a break," she explains.

And they will make it impossible to run. "More freedom?" I ask, casting them a lingering look.

Dr. Walsh doesn't answer my question. She just leans in,

tilting her head up toward my ear, and says, "As long as you're calm, everything's going to be fine."

I can't remember the last time anything was fine.

She indicates for me to sit. I obey. I allow Dr. Walsh to remove the buckles from my wrists, and once they're gone, my shoulders roll forward, aching with the movement. It doesn't quite hurt, but I wince anyway.

"Painful?" she asks.

I nearly laugh. Instead, I cast my eyes down to the tile floor. "I've had worse," I say, injecting a hint of vulnerability into my voice. A quick glance at her, meeting her eyes. Then away, feigning embarrassment.

"I'll see what I can do about getting you some pain meds," she says, and holds out her hands.

In the few seconds before my hands are shackled together once more, I could hit her. For these few seconds, I am free and she is vulnerable. I remember it, watching her hands as they buckle and tighten and snap leather and metal into place on my wrists, my ankles. I memorise it.

After Dr. Walsh finishes, I ask her, shyly, to help me stand. She bites her bottom lip; her fingers graze my biceps tentatively at first. I allow the corner of my mouth to lift in a smile. "Thank you," I say, my voice low.

Her grip tightens, solid on my arm as I allow her to guide me into the cage. She withdraws something from her pocket— another mistake. She ought to have already had it out; in the four seconds before she locks the barred door, I could slam it back and knock her over.

I remember that, too.

Just as Dr. Walsh locks it behind me with a manual key, I hear the click of an approaching pair of heels on the tile. Dr. Kells emerges from the hallway just as Dr. Walsh turns to leave.

I am fighting for calm.

"Hello, Noah," she says with freshly lacquered lips. She's dressed as if she's the head of Human Resources—which, in a way, actually, she is. The sleeves of her lab coat are rolled up over a silk blouse and pencil skirt; her Horizons uniform. She walks to a table rather far from the cage, and sits behind it. "Have a seat," she says smoothly.

I do as she says, maintaining eye contact the entire time.

"On the floor in front of you is a piece of paper," she says, tipping her head at it. "You should still be able to pick it up in that position."

I am, and I do. I crouch down, lift it, and read what it says:

Double-Blind

S. Benicia, manifested (G1821 carrier, origin unknown); side effects(?): anorexia, bulimia, self-harm. Responsive to administered pharmaceuticals. Contraindications suspected but unknown.

T. Burrows, non-carrier, deceased.

M. Cannon, non-carrier, sedated.

M. Dyer, manifesting (G1821 carrier, original); side effects: co-occurring PTSD, hallucinations, self-harm, poss. schizophrenia/

paranoid subtype. Responsive to midazolam. Contraindications: suspected n.e.s.s.?

J. Roth, manifesting (G1821 carrier, suspected original), induced; side effects: poss. borderline personality disorder, poss. mood disorder. Contraindications suspected but unknown.

A. Kendall: non-carrier, deceased.

J. L.: artificially manifested, Lenaurd protocol, early induction. Side effects: multiple personality disorder (unresponsive), antisocial personality disorder (unresponsive); migraines, extreme aggression (unresponsive). No known contraindications.

C. L.: artificially manifested, Lenaurd protocol, early induction, deceased.

P. Reynard: non-carrier, deceased.

N. Shaw: manifested (G1821 original carrier); side effects(?): self-harm, poss. oppositional defiant disorder (unresponsive), conduct disorder? (unresponsive); tested: class a barbiturates (unresponsive), class b (unresponsive), class c (unresponsive); unresponsive to all classes; (test m.a.d.), deceased.

Generalised side effects: nausea, elevated temp., insomnia, night terrors.

My eyes linger on certain words:

Carrier. Manifesting. Side effects. Lenaurd.

Deceased.

"I'd like to explain what you're looking at," Dr. Kells says, "if you'll allow me."

Everything I see, hear, read, experience in this place, at

Horizons, leads to question after question. I can't keep them straight, but it hardly matters. Dr. Kells is a manipulator. A liar. Better, possibly, than even me.

"I'll take your silence as assent," she says, seeming excited. "The gene indicated on that list you just read, G1821, operates in many ways like cancer. There are environmental and genetic factors that can trigger it, and when triggered, the gene turns on, like a switch, activating an ability in its host. But as you've witnessed," she says, offering me a narrow look, "the gene also appears to turn off certain switches." She pauses. "Like the instinct for self-preservation."

Her pulse is even and steady. I listen so I can remember the sound, the rhythm, should it change.

"Certain thoughts and behaviours can become compulsive, such as the urge to self-harm. That seems to be true in your case, yes? You're able to heal, but you experience suicidal ideation, don't you?"

My face is blank.

"That was a question, if you couldn't tell."

"I could tell."

Dr. Kells leans forward on her hands just slightly. "How about this," she says, considering me. "I'll answer one of your questions, and then you answer one of mine."

"Fine," I say flatly. "I'll go first." There's quite a lot I'm desperate to know, but I ask the only thing that matters. "What did you do to Mara?"

"I gave her an infusion of a variant of sodium amytal we've developed—it's called Anemosyne."

"What does it do?"

"It ameliorates her agency."

"Meaning?"

"Technically, that would be three questions," she says. "What I gave her, and what it does, and the impact it will have on her."

My eyes narrow to slits as I expect her to shut me down, to deflect and redirect back to me. She answers, though, surprisingly. "The drug separates the borders between the unconscious and the conscious. We think what's happening to Mara— and, quite possibly, all of you—is that when G1821 is activated, when that switch turns on, your conscious thoughts and unconscious desires and instincts merge. It acts somewhat like a reflex. In Mara's case—you've heard the term 'id,' I gather?"

I listen to the steady beat of her heart. "Yes," I say.

"Good. That will make this easier to explain." She takes out a notebook and writes three words, holding them up for me to read: "id," "ego," "superego."

It's a good thing I'm in shackles, because Freud bores the shit out of me.

"If the ego is the organised part of her mind, and the superego plays the moralising role, allowing her to distinguish between good and evil, then the id is just a bundle of instincts. It strives only to satisfy its own basic needs, like hunger and the drive for sex. It knows no judgements and does not distinguish between moral or amoral.

"In normal people, non-carriers, the ego mediates between the id—what a person wants—and reality. It satisfies a person's instincts using reason. The superego acts as the conscience; it punishes through feelings of remorse and guilt. These feelings are powerful, and in normal people, the ego and the superego dominate the id." She puts the notebook down. "Mara is not a normal person."

"Shocking," I say.

Kells goes on, as if she hasn't heard me. It's less of a conversation than a performance. "As you've seen," she says, "Mara appears to have the ability to manifest thought into action, but it's dependent on the presence of fear or stress, as I believe it is for the other carriers, though Roth's manifestation is in its infancy so there can be no confirmation yet. In any case, G1821 makes Mara's id reflexive; if she is afraid, or stressed, her ego and superego don't function. And the consequences, as you've seen, can be disastrous. Her ugliest, most destructive thoughts become reality."

"The solution seems simple," I say.

"Does it?"

"Stop fucking with her."

Kells leans forward, eyebrows raised. "Was that what her Spanish teacher did? Gave her a failing grade, signed her own death warrant?"

"Mara didn't know what she could do then," I say defensively. "I've wished several people dead over the course of my teenage life." I lean back, raise an eyebrow. "I'm wishing one of them dead right now."

"But *your* desires don't come true," Kells says. "The only person you're able to hurt is yourself." She cocks her head, and a curious little smile overtakes her mouth for a split second before her personality evaporates again. "Mara doesn't even always have to be *aware* of these thoughts, of her intent behind them. If the right mixture of fear or stress is present, her instinctual drives take over. And there's a Freudian theory that along with the creative instinct—the libido—a death instinct also exists. A destructive urge directed against the world and other organisms." She clears her throat. "My working theory is that carriers of G1821 have an exaggerated death instinct, which manifests for each of you in different ways, making some of you vulnerable and some of you dangerous. And Mara's more dangerous than any of you."

"You can't punish her for something she can't control."

"As I said, I'm not attempting to punish her, I'm attempting to help her. The drug we've developed will, we hope, reactivate the barrier between her id and her ego and superego; it's designed to prevent any negative intent from becoming action. The dose needs to be adjusted, however, and I can't study Mara on drugs. And she's too unstable to be studied without them. So," Kells says, drawing herself up, "I need to study you."

13

THINGS CANNOT BE OTHERWISE

S o Mara was bait," I say slowly. "To get me here." My voice sounds distant, faraway, to my own ears.

"Partly true," Kells concedes. "I did need Mara here at Horizons because, at the absolute least, she needs to be receiving a constant, consistent dose of Anemosyne in order to separate her conscious thought from her unconscious thought. To prevent her thoughts—which are often negative, if you noticed—from becoming reality."

And to make her sound like that *thing* in there, that not-Mara I heard, speaking with that deadened voice I'd do anything to forget.

"So what, exactly, do you plan to do with the rest of us? You have Jamie and Stella here as well, yes?"

"Yes."

"Three drugged dolls at your disposal, which you've just acknowledged renders them useless to you. So why bother keeping them at all?"

"To help—"

"Like you helped Phoebe?"

"Phoebe's death was unfortunate—"

"Interesting choice of words."

"If you'd let me finish a sentence, I'd explain." She shoots me a pointed look. "They could also be a danger to themselves or others, just like Mara. Stella perhaps less so than Jamie—her status is less clear. But the point is, G1821 expresses itself differently in different people, and like many other genes linked to diseases, the symptoms vary. Jamie, for example, is earlier on in his manifestation than Mara—in his case, G1821 was only recently triggered."

"How?" I ask.

"We think it might be linked to the physical development you undergo as teenagers. The teenage brain is physically different from an adult brain. Right now, it looks like the process is slightly different for all of you, accounting for all sorts of environmental and genetic factors, somewhat like puberty. Everyone develops at a different rate. The same is true for G1821." She gestures, palms up. "Sometimes, in order to bring the greatest good to the greatest number of people, a few are hurt in the process."

"Not hurt," I say, leaning forward. "Murdered." My face is stone, impassive, and my voice is sharp. "You allowed—no," I say, shaking my head. "You *invited* a psychopath into Horizons and allowed him to murder two girls—or was it more?"

"I assume you're referring to Jude Lowe?" Kells asks.

"You *assume* correctly," I snap. "I fail to see how any part of what you've done to Mara—to anyone—can at all qualify as *good.*"

"Jude was needed to trigger Mara," she says. "We know that at least two of the triggers for G1821 are fear and stress."

Fight or flight.

"And in order to see what Mara was capable of, she needed to be pushed."

"Provoked," I say evenly, though inside, I am seething.

"In a sense," Kells says, "yes. But I prefer the term 'exposed.'"

"I bet you do."

A muscle twitches in her jaw. "Jude was needed in order to expose Mara to what she was most afraid of, in order to know whether her ability would manifest, and in order to study it—its consequences and its limitations for her eventual benefit and for the benefit of everyone around her. Exposure therapy is used in order to accommodate patients to their triggers and their fears—"

I bite back the anger because I need to stay calm. Focused.

"That's not what you were doing," I say. "You weren't confronting Mara with her worst fears and showing her that they were meaningless, harmless, so she could overcome them, so she could get better. You were provoking her, terrifying her to get her to react—you wanted to make her worse."

Kells shakes her head. "No. Look what happened at the final stage—she overcame her fear of Jude and fought back. She unlocked reserves she didn't even know she had."

For a moment, I can't speak. Kells isn't lying—she actually believes in what she's saying. "You sent that animal into her house to torment just so you could *watch*," I say. Unconsciously, my hands have curled into fists. Kells notices. I struggle to relax. "Like some attack dog, like a pet—"

"He's not a pet, Noah. He's a participant in the program."

"Why would *anyone* be a part of this?" I ask, but even as I do, I remember Jude's words, what he said to Mara, what Stella heard in his mind—

"You told him Mara could bring Claire back," I say. "You promised him the thing he wanted most. Something Mara couldn't deliver, to trigger *him* into triggering her."

"To *expose* her—"

"You're using him the way you're using all of us."

"I'm trying to help Jude, too, Noah. The applications—the benefits—of what we're doing here outweigh the risks. I've tried to study Mara as noninvasively as I could, which is why I had her behaviour recorded before I took any specific action."

I swallow even though I want to scream. "How did you get into her house?"

"I didn't. Jude did."

"I never saw any cameras."

"That's because there weren't any." She clears her throat again. "We used fibre optics, installed in her home while she and her family were not present to observe and record her behaviour before it escalated."

"You are sick," I say.

"*Mara* is sick, Noah."

"If that's true, it's because you made her that way."

"No," Kells says through clenched teeth. "She was *born* that way. I can't learn how to help Mara until I fully understand what's *wrong* with her, and I can't do that without you."

"How about this," I say. "Get fucked."

"I'm disappointed to hear that."

"You'll get used to it."

"I would have thought you'd want to see Mara again," she says, rising from her chair.

"Not like that," I say. Never like that.

She pauses for a moment, watching me. "What if you could be together? You and Mara? On your own."

Everything in me wants her offer to be genuine, even knowing that it can't be. I watch Kells, I listen—her heartbeat is steady, her breathing calm. She isn't lying.

"Wouldn't that be complicated somewhat by the fact that

I just witnessed you telling Mara I was dead?"

"I wasn't truthful with Mara because I needed to attempt to trigger her—to be sure that she was responding to the medications. To give her the worst possible news—to say the worst possible thing, and make sure she wouldn't react." She inclines her head a bit. "And it worked. I can just as easily bring you to her, prove to her that you're alive and well, and let you have some time alone with each other."

I don't believe her. I'm desperate to believe her.

"I regret the way I treated you when you first woke up," she says. "Mara's heart stopped when she was told that you were dead. I have no desire to torture her, or you, which is why I've answered all of your questions in good faith. I've explained everything to you, and have asked for nothing from you in return except your cooperation."

I extend my forearm, my hand curled into a fist. "Take my blood and be done with it, then."

"The answer isn't in your blood. It's in your brain. Your telomeres do replicate and show no sign of stopping, which we think allows for your own rapid cellular regeneration. But you're able to heal not only yourself—you can heal other people, other things, too, right?"

I stay silent.

"Genes alter and degrade over time, and this one changes your brain chemistry, or triggers nerve processing that unlocks your ability to influence cells or action, possibly. The truth is that I don't understand enough about how yours works. I do know that I need to study patients while they're awake, and conscious."

"Well, you've got the rest of the weekend. What do you want me to do?"

Her eyebrows rise. "The weekend?"

"For the retreat? The bullshit pretext under which you had parents who thought their kids had depression or anxiety or an eating disorder or whatever and sent them to you for help, not knowing they were handing them over for human experimentation? Those parents are going to wonder where their children are, eventually. Mine included. You do know who my father is, I'm sure."

"Of course I do," she says plainly. "He hired me."

"To fix me, no doubt."

Kells allows herself a smile. Says nothing.

"He's hired you and a dozen other psychologists over the course of my childhood. You're a member of quite an unillustrious club, I'm afraid."

She observes me calmly. "I started working at a subsidiary of the EIC when I was twenty, just out of college," she says. "David Shaw recruited me. Sponsored my doctoral research. Your father knows what you are. He knows what *Mara* is. His company's been conducting research that probably spawned a clutch of Carriers all over the world. You're here anyway."

It's my pulse that hammers, now. My heart that stutters.

"Do you understand what I'm saying to you, Noah? Your father *left* you here *anyway*."

"You're lying," I say through clenched teeth.

"Listen to my pulse."

"You're regulating it," I snap. "You're just trying to provoke me, trigger me, like you've done to Mara."

"Why? What good would that do me?" She rises from her chair. Walks up to the cage. Unlocks it. Meets my eyes.

"I know you want to believe that I'm lying. But you know your father," she says, indicating my shackled wrists. "You know the truth, even if you're too ashamed or afraid to admit it to yourself."

"Why would I be either of those things?" My words come out in a whisper.

She doesn't answer, and it tortures me. "He wants her put to sleep. I think she can be saved. Will you prove me right, or wrong?" She holds up the keys in her hand.

I don't have enough time. To think. To decide. Which is why I make the wrong choice. "Take me to her."

14

MY CREATION

THE SIGHT OF HER BREAKS MY HEART.

It's been less than a day. Minutes, really, since I watched her through the glass. It feels like an era, like I've seen civilisations rise and fall in the time we've been apart, and now I'm left, staring at the ashes.

That's what she looks like since Kells told her I died. Like the ashes.

I breathe her name from the doorway of the same room I last saw her in, newly unshackled but testing my steps. She doesn't respond. I can't even tell if she knows I'm here.

I turn to Kells. "Is she awake?"

Dr. Kells looks at a tablet. "Seems to be."

"What did you do to her?"

"Only what you saw."

I look back at Mara, lying in a metal bed in the centre of the room, dwarfed by negative space. Her eyes are open, looking at nothing. She doesn't respond to my voice. It's as if by telling Mara I no longer exist, I've stopped existing for her, and I am close to breaking.

"Is she paralysed?" I ask Kells, who pauses before answering.

"No. The medication helps her be . . . present, as I explained. She's likely experiencing strong emotions, which have triggered stress responses. They'll come and go like waves, and she'll be able to ride them out. She *could* move. She chooses not to."

I take a step toward her, and when Kells doesn't stop me, I take more until I'm by her side. Her features don't look relaxed, just . . . slack. She looks uninhabited. Like an abandoned house.

There's nothing I wouldn't do to bring her back. Nothing.

There's an IV running into her arm, and a few monitors, but nothing else I can see, nothing I can use, to get us out.

All of Kells's words reverberate in my skull—about my father. About Mara. "What will it take," I begin to say, "for you to let us go?"

"Your honest answers to my questions, for a start, beginning with how you first discovered your ability. Then we'll reevaluate from there. But if you prove to me that I can trust you, I will prove that you can trust me. Your mind is the key, Noah. I need you to let me in."

I've sworn at her. I've threatened her. I haven't begged yet—I could try that, I suppose. But invoking my father has done something nothing else has managed to, yet. His power has opened doors for me my entire life, but for the first time, I'm now on the other side of it, that power. Nothing I've ever done has been any match for it. Nothing *I* could do could match it.

"You promised me a moment alone with her," I say to Kells. "Give me that, and I'll give you what you want."

She inclines her head, with the good grace not to smile, at least, and leaves the room.

A wave of sadness threatens to choke me.

Sadness tightens your chest and throat and lungs—you can't breathe for it. You can only turn your grief over and over.

Anger, though—anger can be used. If you can swallow the ache in your chest and let bitterness rise in your throat, you can burn it like fuel.

I choose anger over sadness.

I reach out to Mara's face. She doesn't react when I sweep the hair back from her pale forehead. Her eyes are fixed and staring, even as I lean in, until my lips are at her ear.

"Get out," I purr. "Then kill them. Kill them all."

Part III

After

Whitby, England

Blessed are the forgetful, for they get
the better even of their blunders.

—Friedrich Nietzsche

15

THE LEAST ENLIGHTENED

I'VE ALWAYS BEEN SHITE AT ADVICE.

The room is dark when I awaken. Vague outlines begin to take shape in the dimness—a fireplace, and a bed I seem to be looming *over*, instead of lying *in*. Beyond it, the postcard-perfect view of the unmistakable Whitby Abbey, lit up in the night.

It *is* interesting that I've begun to hallucinate, but only mildly. Obviously the drugs and the previous night's binge drinking were a monumental mistake; this is not a normal reaction. And I don't want to fucking imagine Horizons, of all places. Or Mara, of all people.

But now that I have, it's that dead voice of hers that echoes in my mind. Those vacant eyes that didn't register my face. I want to scrub them from my skull.

I peel off my clothes as if I can shed the images with them, and run the shower at scalding. I vaguely hear a phone ring, somewhere. I press my palms against the white tile and bow my head, trying to ignore it as the water scorches my skin. Finally the ringing stops.

I shut off the water and catch a glimpse of myself in the mirrored medicine cabinet. My fist is a bruised, possibly broken mess, and I take obscene pleasure in it.

I was fifteen when I first learned that I could heal. I'd been coolly informed by my father's secretary that we were moving the next day, to the United States. To Miami. No warning. No notice. I spent the evening at the pub with friends, getting piss drunk not because I cared but because I didn't. I should have, but I felt nothing, and that, more than anything else, terrified me.

I stumbled into my father's study—he was gone, as usual. I didn't know what I was looking for. Liquor possibly. Probably. Every part of me was numb. I skirted the desk my father never sat at and walked slowly toward the bar. The walls were gauzy and insubstantial, not shimmering, not moving, just . . . barely there. My hands roamed the surface of the bar. They found a knife.

Everything was out of focus, and then, when my fingers touched the handle, not. The grooved bone handle—or was it ivory?—felt so real in my palm, like the only real thing in the room. Including myself. The edge of the blade was sharp and gorgeous, and suddenly—strangely, I remember thinking—the hand that held it looked sharp as well. My hand. The rest of me didn't seem to be there. Not real. And then I thought that if I wasn't real, I couldn't bleed. I was made of nothing and so if I cut myself, nothing would happen. There was a pinprick of wrongness about it, but it faded quickly. I took the blade to my forearm, feeling a—a pressure, unlike anything I'd ever felt. I *needed* to do it.

Everything shivered into focus at the touch of the metal on my skin. I inhaled and the air was cold and gleaming and I laughed, because it felt real and magical at once. I didn't hesitate the way you should when you anticipate pain. I was ready. I wanted it. I dragged the knife across my arm.

I closed my eyes and pressed harder. A rushing sound filled me and my heart beat again, almost against the blade, it felt like. I watched, surprised—astonished, really—as blood welled in the line of the cut and spilled over onto the floor. It was slow-seeming and yet happened faster than I'd imagined it would, because I hadn't imagined I would bleed at all.

My arm throbbed, and I slid down against the bar until I found myself sitting on the floor, legs askew, propped against the furniture. *Everything* was real, then. The pull of the cabinet bored into my back, the glossy wood cool on the nape of my neck. The pain quickened my breath and my heartbeat and giddily, I realised my blood was pooling on the floor.

I took off my shirt, tore a strip of it off, and wound it around the cut. It mustn't have been as deep as I first thought, because the flow of the blood was already slowing. The strip of fabric felt tight and solid, and I knelt and cleaned the blood from the floor—my parents couldn't know I was bleeding, couldn't know what I'd done. I was surprised by the sudden, slight sting of shame.

I swallowed it back with disturbingly little effort. And then climbed the stairs and fell into bed.

I woke up the next morning to the sounds of a house disassembling. I felt hungover—the light punctured my eyelids and my head was heavy and dull and everything in me hurt. I remembered almost nothing of the night before—stumbling out of the pub with Patrick and Goose and going home and then, and then—

I looked down at my arm, at the strip of my grey T-shirt still wound around it. The blood had dried, and it now looked like rust. It had soaked through the fabric and had gotten on my sheets and I swore, knowing I'd need to bleach them unless I wanted sneering questions about my menstrual cycle from my father. As if he'd even hear about it. Or care to mention the blood to me regardless. He was probably already gone.

And so I rose from my bed, ignoring the dull throb in my arm and my head and my all-over stiffness, and made my way to the bathroom. I spilled a few over-the-counter painkillers into my hand—two? three?—and swallowed them back without water. I leaned my forearms against the sink—my head ached and my throat was raw, and when I looked in the mirror at my shadowed eyes and my roughened face, I was startled.

I looked different.

Or, more likely, I was simply hungover. The skin under the strip of cloth itched, and I turned on the shower and rummaged through the vanity drawers looking for gauze. I found some and untied the bandage.

There was nothing there.

I staggered back against the wall, holding my arm out in front of me, turning it, flexing it. I'd been piss drunk, yes, but *that* drunk?

Had I even cut myself?

If I hadn't, then where had the blood come from?

I examined the unbroken skin on my arm once more, and let the strip of cloth fall to the floor. I stared at myself in the mirror and smiled.

That was three years ago.

Everything and nothing has changed since then, and I find myself reaching for the medicine cabinet, longing for a razor blade and not to shave with, when the phone rings again. I wait for it to stop. It doesn't. Goose shows up in my room instead.

"Noah." Goose stands in the doorway, looking unusually unsettled.

"What?" I ask, more sharply than I intended.

"Hate to interrupt your wank, but you've got a call."

"If it's the bloody solicitor—"

"It's not."

"Well, don't keep me in suspense."

"It's Mara," he says.

"Which?"

"What?" Goose looks perplexed.

I narrow my eyes. Is his memory the problem, or is mine? Did we have the conversation in which I drunkenly explained M's existence, or not?

"Where's the phone?" I ask.

"In the kitchen," he says.

I blink, then drift past him.

He calls after me. "You do realise you're naked, yes?"

I look down; it appears he is correct. My hair is still dripping wet. "Seems so," I say, though I'm not sure to whom. I swipe the towel from the top of the door, and knot it round my waist in the hall.

"Mate," Goose says, covering the receiver. "How'd she get this number?"

"I'll ask her."

"You're sure you want to talk?"

I'm not sure about anything. Even if *my* Mara is on the other end of the line—I try imagining it, but my mind empties out. I've no idea what I'll say.

It's not her, though. It won't be her. "Hello?"

"I thought you were going home," M says.

I exhale. "How did you get this number?" I ask, as promised.

"Ask me in person." She hangs up. Instead of silence, a brash, awful sound assaults my ears. Goose walks in to find me wincing, holding the receiver midair.

"Went well, did it?"

"Obvious?"

"Brought you your trousers," he says, handing them to me.

"You seem inordinately concerned about my state of undress."

"Of course I am. What would the driver think?"

"What driver?"

"The one on the street who I believe is waiting for us." He claps me on the back. "I'm still game for Ibiza or wherever, mate, but it appears we'll be going to the Shaw estate, first."

16

ENTRUSTED ME

THERE DOESN'T SEEM TO BE MUCH POINT IN resisting anymore, once we've been found. And so I spend the vast majority of the drive to the manor either being too triggered by familiar sights or overwhelmed by thought spirals—about a surprise reappearance of the professor (he loves those), or about the remote possibility of my own grandmother and Mara's meeting face-to-face—to take advantage of the mini-bottles of liquor that come with the car. I regret it immediately, once we arrive.

The manor was closed to the public for my father's funeral, but it is quite clearly open for business today. There are tourists

(tourists!) clustered in couples and families over the grounds and in the car parks. The driver deposits us in one of them instead of taking us up the private drive to the main residence.

"These were my instructions, sir," he says when questioned by Goose. I'm finding it difficult to concentrate or care. The manor was typically closed to the public when our fucked-up little family made the occasional visit here from London, so the tourists are a novelty and possibly a welcome distraction from the tedium, should we need one.

The house looms over the grounds, haughty and oppressive as we approach it.

"When do you become a proper *lord*, exactly?" Goose asks.

"You know, I'm not sure? Oddly enough, it hasn't been a priority."

"Fair," Goose says, just as one of the volunteers or staff—I haven't spent enough time here to know the difference at first glance—exits the gatehouse and approaches us.

One does not simply walk into the Shaw manor, unless one is a Shaw. Everyone who isn't has to either work there, or buy a ticket. And unlike the funeral situation, where I was prominently displayed and presented as heir apparent, today I might as well be anonymous.

Which is why we're stopped by this well-intentioned, exceedingly polite and apologetic man.

"Sir," he says, facing Goose. "Sir, I'm afraid you're at the wrong entrance."

"We're not, actually," I say, stepping between them and extending my non-fucked-up hand to shake his. "I'm Noah Shaw. Would you please inform Elliot and Sylvia their grandson is here?"

Far from being surprised, however, the man smiles, managing to convey polite disdain and condescension at once. "Identification, please, sir?"

"Alas, lost," I say. "But Albert has known me my entire life. He can clear this up for us right quick, I'm sure."

"I'm afraid I don't know an Albert, sir."

"Albert Stratton? The family valet?" It's exceedingly un-English to lose one's composure, but I began the day at a disadvantage, and I'm edging close to a breakdown as it is. It's unfair, I realise; the man is probably just a volunteer, but nevertheless.

"Sir, you're going to have to go through the regular entrance if you would like to *purchase* admittance." His shoulders rise in a phonily apologetic shrug.

"Of course," Goose says with an equally phony smile. The man hands him a map with a satisfied nod and waddles back to the gatehouse.

Reentering the great hall without Mara is more than a bit sobering, I confess. Goose and the tourists blur into the background, and I feel strangely alone, but not. It feels like Mara's here, somehow, shadowing my steps. I look up at the balcony that rings the hall and for a moment I think I see an afterimage of her in mourner's black, standing with her back to me, in the space where she stood just weeks ago. Or was it months?

Burying one's dreadful parent is always complicated, I imagine, but my father *was* uniquely appalling and the circumstances of his death uniquely complicated, after all.

I remember telling Mara about it, when he went missing, and then when his body was found. She put her arms around my waist, fitted her chin against my chest.

"*I'm so sorry,*" she said.

That was the moment I should have begun to wonder.

A tour group approaches, and a fresh, rosy-cheeked brunette delivers introductory sound bites about the architecture and paintings, a welcome distraction, however brief. I'm half tempted to join them.

Instead, I gamely lead Goose to the East Wing, where the family (what remains of it) resides. I'll need to get him a pass and let my grandparents know we'll be staying for a bit, at least until our shit arrives.

I walk with purpose, but find myself oddly hyperaware of my surroundings. Heads seem to turn in my direction. My footsteps alone seem to ring out on the marble floor.

Most of my memories of this place are a child's memories, with a strange, alien tint. My stepmother was ruthless when it came to watching me, given my propensity for self-injury and my grandmother's fear that I'd damage something priceless in the process, which meant that most of my exploring happened outdoors or after dark. I liked playing about in the ruins, obviously, but my favourite haunt was the falcon mews, back when my grandfather still hunted.

He'd had a gyr named Lucy; a stunning hunter, notoriously crusty to everyone but him. We were visiting for Christmas, once, when I snuck out through the old servants' kitchen, stopping off at the mini-fridge my grandfather kept full of dead mice for her. I grabbed a handful of them and set out.

I must've been ten or eleven—old enough to have learned how to properly tie jesses and fit a hood, but I didn't plan to fly her. I stalked my way through the yew trees until I reached her cage.

She awoke in an instant when I approached, fixing me with steely, intelligent yellow eyes. I opened the mew the way my grandfather had shown me, and offered her a mouse on the glove.

She made me wait for it, not breaking eye contact. After an age, though, she hopped onto the glove and took it. I gave her another. And another. She let me stroke her feathers with my ungloved hand as she ate the last one. Then she looked me in the eye, and took to the air.

My grandfather spent twelve days following her from tree to tree, sleeping when she slept, waiting for her weight to come down to get her back to the glove. He never did. She's still out there, for all I know.

Goose thrusts something in my face. "Here, take this." The map.

"What?" I ask absently. Then, "I don't need it."

"We've just passed that leering, mannish baby statue again. For the third time."

"No, that leering baby was on a goat. The others were on horseback."

"Just take the map, I beg you."

"I just need to find someone who knows me." I look around; we're the only people in this corridor. There's a velvet rope blocking off the stairwell at the end of it.

"Follow me," I say with authority. Then, with a flourish, I step over the sign hanging from the velvet rope, marked PRIVATE.

"The silent alarm will go off, and someone will come along to scold us," I explain. "Then they can deliver us to the lord and lady."

"Or we could check the map," Goose says. "Whilst we wait."

"Never," I say. "It's a point of pride, now."

"You're intolerable."

"I know." The corridor remains empty. "Right. Let's go downstairs." Goose heaves an exaggerated sigh, but does as he's told.

We pass living rooms and state rooms and music rooms on our odyssey, not that I can tell the difference between them. The portraits in each look on us with a reptilian coldness as we walk by. I hate them all, every single one, men, women, children. They manage to look as though they feel entitled to everything both within and without their canvas prisons, down to their collective melancholy mien. Even the children seem absurdly sombre. What monstrous privilege!

With the exception of our footsteps, it's dead quiet one floor below the main, which is possibly why I decide to enter one of the music rooms. Goose arranges himself in a copy of one of the more ridiculously posed portrait subjects.

"We're going to die down here," he says cheerfully. I sit at a harpsichord. "Some unsuspecting NatTrust volunteer will stumble upon our desiccated corpses in a hundred years, hold our skulls aloft, and exclaim, "'Where be your gibes now?'"

I play a few jaunty notes.

"What are you doing?"

I think the voice is in my head, at first, which is why I don't turn around.

"Noah."

My sister's voice escalates in volume and annoyance. She stands in the doorway, nostrils flared. I marvel silently at this.

"What's wrong with you?"

I can't decide if she's actually here, or if this is merely the leftovers of my drug-induced, hallucinatory nightmare. I look at Goose, who is looking from her, to me, and back again.

He sees her too. That's good. "What are you doing here?" I ask her.

"Am I not allowed, now that it's your house?"

"This isn't my house."

"No? I was told otherwise, by Grandmother."

"Right," Goose drawls, backing out of the room. "I think I'll let you two catch up. Quality time." Katie steps aside to let him out, but doesn't come farther inside. She doesn't follow him, either.

I rise from the harpsichord bench. Lean back against the instrument.

"Stop," Katie says.

"What?"

"You'll break it."

I stop leaning.

"What happened to your hand?" she asks warily.

I catch my reflection in an antique mirror. No wonder people have been staring—it's bruised and cut and rather obviously so in the T-shirt I'm wearing.

"Spot of bother in a pub," I say to my reflection. It agrees.

"Over Mara?"

"*Mara?*" That gets my attention. "No."

Katie looks past me, meeting my eyes in the mirror. "Is she here too?"

I shake my head, swallowing hard. "Why?"

She shrugs. The simple gesture is loaded with meaning.

"What?" I ask her.

"Nothing," she says venomously.

"What are you doing here, though, really?" I ask quickly, changing the subject.

"I came back. Like you."

"I'm not *back* back."

"You're here." She arches an eyebrow.

"Ruth said you were going to Florida."

"I changed my mind."

"Are you in school?"

"Do I *look* like I'm in school? What *is* this conversation?"

I don't know how to talk to her, or even what I'm supposed to say. I honestly can't remember the last thing I *did* say to her. She's been little more than a footnote in my life for months.

How is it that I could be so close to Mara's family, that her brothers feel like my own, when my sister is such a stranger to me?

"Is Grandmother here?" I ask stupidly.

"Somewhere," she says. "She didn't tell me you were coming."

"She didn't know."

"I heard about what happened in New York," Katie says, after a pause.

I decide to say nothing, in the hope of drawing her out.

"The fire?"

"Oh."

"Mum was worried." Mum. Ruth, she means. She scratches compulsively at a bit of wax on one of the silver candlesticks squatting on the mantel, crusting her fingernails in the process.

"Sorry?" The word sounds more like a question than an apology.

"You didn't call her."

"I . . . meant to," I say. I *did* mean to, in a vague sort of way. But so much happened between then and now—who'd have the time, honestly?

"Right," she says, turning on her heel.

"Wait." I cross the room in two strides, reaching for her shoulder—

"You don't give a shit!" she explodes, when I make contact. Her angelic face reddens. "About any of us!"

I'm blown back by the display of emotion. Funeral aside, I can't remember ever seeing her cry, let alone scream.

"That's not true." Is it? I feel guilty. Perhaps because I am guilty.

"When's my birthday," she says coldly.

"September twenty-third."

She stands there, the silence unspooling as I do the maths.

"I missed it," I realise.

"Yes, you *missed* it," she echoes mockingly. "And Mum's. You didn't even stay for Dad's *funeral.*"

"I—didn't," I say, feeling ghastly. "I'm sorry, Katie—"

"*Kate*. It's *Kate*." She whips back into the hall, her light chestnut hair bouncing against her shoulders with the force of her strides. She's tall, and fast, but I'm taller and faster. I catch her round the shoulders.

"I'm not sorry about missing Father's funeral," I say. She stops in the corridor. Waits. "I *am* sorry about missing your birthday, and Mum's. And for worrying you both."

Her silence cools. I try and divine some hint of what she's thinking in order to say something that'll appease her, but without my ability, it's impossible to really know. I assume she's still angry.

"We're orphans," she says, and I respond with the next thing that comes to mind:

"How Dickensian."

It is the wrong thing. Her strong brows draw together and her jaw tightens. At fifteen—no, sixteen, I suppose—she looks more like the pictures of my mother than I'd remembered. Whilst I was off with Mara, she was growing up.

And in an entirely different family, in a sense. She has no memory of our mother at all, or so she's always claimed, and to her, our father was perfect. I never really understood how siblings *worked* till I got to know Mara's family. When one of them fought with their parents, the other two would rally behind him (her, usually) in solidarity. Any fight I'd ever had with our father, Katie would check out of. Which I get. I'm older. I should've been protecting her, not the other way around.

But there never really was anything to protect her from, though, was there? She's had everything she ever asked for. My father outwardly adored her. She's always been popular. She's always had friends, made friends. Did the things girls—normal girls—seem to do. She was never a rogue doctor's test subject, as far as I'm aware, nor was she ever menaced by a living human experiment gone wrong. No track marks I can see, never any extended bathroom trips after meals that I remember. Looks healthy. Seems fine.

"I don't understand," I say finally, impatiently. "I don't know what you want from me."

"I don't want anything from you anymore," she says. "You've made it quite clear that you couldn't be less interested, so after you get whatever it is you've come for, just . . . go. Back to New York or Florida or wherever it is that Mara's gone."

The words hurt because they're true. I haven't been interested in anyone who isn't Mara, or anything that doesn't involve her, since we met. I'm a few steps away from the closest family I've got left, and I hardly know her.

"Go," she says, indicating the stairs ahead. "You're free."

I nearly laugh at the absurdity of the words. I couldn't be less free.

"I don't want to go," I say, though it isn't completely true, not really, and she's smart enough to know it.

"Really," she says icily. "You couldn't get away from us fast enough after Daddy . . ." Her words trail off. "What, now that he's gone and you're getting everything, you're here to claim it, is that it?"

"That is *not* true, and not fair. I told the solicitor I didn't want anything, that you should get it—"

"Well, I didn't, and it's not about the bloody *money*, don't be so *appalling*." She swallows. "I don't understand, you hated him, why would he give you—" She catches herself, closes her eyes. "I don't care. I honestly don't. Just take what you've come for and go back to Mara."

"I'm not going to do that."

"Why? Why are you here, then? Not because of the fire, certainly. You could go anywhere, buy a bloody flat anywhere Mara likes," she says.

I say nothing.

"Surely Yorkshire isn't her destination of choice, not when you could buy her the world, now." Her eyes narrow, and I can see her working it out. Her expression—angry just seconds ago—relaxes into a blank mask. "She's left you, hasn't she?"

"Kate—"

"She did. She broke up with you."

After a moment, I say, "I ended it with her, actually."

The mask breaks, revealing a bitter smile. "I'm sure that's what you're telling yourself." She turns around, heads for the arched staircase, putting more space between us. Then, facing me once more, "I can't believe I actually thought for a second that someone told you I was here and you came for me."

"Wait—"

"Don't worry," she says, "I'm not angry."

"No?" I ask, hopeful. Stupid.

"No. Just disappointed," she adds witheringly, echoing our father's favourite line. As she ascends the steps, she says, "By the way? Those trousers are a mistake."

17

LIKE SISYPHUS

S HE'S RIGHT, ABOUT THE TROUSERS.

She's right about the rest of it, obviously. I might be able to catch up with her, but what would I say to her?

There are things about our father you don't know.

I can't go back to Florida or New York, not without Mara.

If I had it to do over, I would leave the funeral again.

That's the truth of it. I'd do it all again, probably. She doesn't know our father was a monster, and I'm glad of it, mostly. She deserves every happy memory she has, and I wouldn't want to corrupt them.

Though it is unfair that I've been cast as the villain for it.

Missed birthdays don't really stack up to everything else I've been dealing with, do they?

I'm a bit torn between righteous indignation and guilt. She doesn't know who our father was, the things he did, and she never will. I try to imagine a world in which I could tell her without hurting her, invite her into the other world I straddle the way Mara invited Daniel.

But she isn't Daniel. She wouldn't *want* to know about my other world. She likes the one she has, and revealing the existence of mine would spoil it.

That's what's so fucked about being here. The fact that I *should* be here, for normal, rational, human reasons, like Kate. Not because I let myself be dragged here by M, or was nudged here by the professor's bloody fucking condolence card with that bit about my inheritance.

I want to escape. I *can't* escape.

My feet carry me toward the music room. I aim for the harpsichord again under the ever-watchful eyes of the portraits—there are so *many*. They can't all be Shaws, can they?

"May I help you?"

"God!" I spin, startled. There seems to be a woman behind me, where Katie—*Kate*—had been standing.

"Mrs. Balfour, actually," the woman says. "Have you gotten turned around?"

"I'm not lost," I say slowly.

"Come along," she says, in a way that brooks no

disagreement. "I'll show you the way back upstairs."

"I'm looking for . . ." For what? I ran into Kate, made a bloody disaster out of that. Goose likely used his horrid map to find the café. What am *I* looking for?

"The loo?" she asks impatiently.

"What? No." Her bland smile vanishes as she gets scrunched up.

"Sylvia Shaw," I say. That's who I came to find. "My grandmother."

I expect the same sort of reaction as the gentleman outside, at first, so the flicker of recognition is a welcome sight.

"You're the son."

"Grandson," I correct her.

"David's son."

"Yes," I say, trying not to sound contemptuous. "Did you know him?"

"Formally," is all she says. "Your grandmother isn't here, at the moment."

"I see."

"Is there anything I can do for you . . . ?"

"Noah," I say, extending my hand.

She smiles, waiting.

"I'm terribly sorry," I say. "I haven't spent much time here, and I don't know everyone's role and title—"

"I'm the curator," she says.

Eyebrows raised. "Really? Splendid."

"Was that you, playing the harpsichord?"

"It was, I'm afraid." I beam apologetically, doing my best impression of the grandson Lady Sylvia tells people I am.

"It was a gift from Lord Robert Arden to your great-great-great-grandfather. Did you notice the decorative roses on the soundboard?" She walks back into the room to point them out. "I think your fingers are the first to touch these keys in at least a hundred years."

"Right," I drawl. "I am sorry about that."

"How did you find it?" she asks, curious. "Was it tuned? I've wondered about these old instruments—we have them cared for, you see, but there's no way to tell whether they still perform as they ought to without playing them, and it isn't worth the risk, of course."

"Of course," I agree, a bit curious myself. Not about the harpsichord—about her. Is she the Argus Filch of the Shaw manor? Summoned by magic whenever a wayward guest violates the "No Touching" rule? "What did you think, of the sound?"

"There's no audio with the visual," she says, pointing to a corner of the room.

Cameras, then. Less interesting.

"It's rather fortuitous, our meeting," she says. "Your grandmother had hoped to introduce us at the service."

I remember that, now. I'd gone looking for her whilst Mara met with that volunteer, Bernard, hoping for more information about Sam Milnes. I try to recall her words, race to catch up with the shadow of her that haunts my mind, but she slips away, taking the memory with her.

Mrs. Balfour might know something, though. A different idea takes shape.

"I'd hoped to find you then as well," I say. "It was a surprisingly busy day."

"My condolences."

I can't quite tell if there's sarcasm lurking beneath her odd affect.

"Are they here, by the way? My grandparents?"

"I'm afraid not," she says. "Visiting friends, in Bath."

They have friends? "Oh," I say, feigning disappointment. "I was hoping to spend time with them. They were quite eager for me to learn about the manor," I add, hoping Mrs. Balfour will step in and offer. She doesn't.

"There was someone I met at the service, who seemed to know quite a lot? Bernard, something or other? I believe he's a volunteer?"

Mrs. Balfour's expression remains carefully blank.

"With the National Trust, perhaps?"

"You'll have to check with them."

"I see," I say, and sigh. "You know, since we're here, would you be kind enough to show me round a bit?"

"I have quite a busy afternoon, I'm afraid, but we can make an appointment to go over the plans."

"Plans?"

"For the renovation? It's all rather straightforward."

"I'm sure it is, but we needn't be as formal as all that." I try and gauge whether to ask about Sam straight out . . . and decide against it. Don't want her clamming up. "I was mostly hoping you could tell me about . . ." My eyes dart, landing on—

"The portraits?"

"Of course, which ones?"

". . . All of them?"

Her eyes crinkle at the corners, and I think she's about to call me on my shit, but then she walks to the far wall. "You noticed the inconsistencies, I gather? You have a keen eye, Mr. Shaw."

"Noah, please. My . . ." God, I almost said girlfriend. Fuck it. "My girlfriend's an artist. She instilled a bit of an appreciation for . . . painting." Should do.

"I see," she says, then crosses the room toward the opposite wall, deftly avoiding the harp and carefully staged chairs upholstered in gold silk to match the gold leaf entablature. "After the fire, the paintings in this room were all restored by a different artist from the one who did some of the others you might've have seen upstairs. That's why some of them appear a bit smudged in places—it was a stylistic choice, supposedly." She backs up to the centre of the room, standing beneath the crystal chandelier as she appraises them. "The effect isn't so dramatic here," she says, pointing to a portrait of a grey-haired woman in a low-necked dress, who does look a bit blurry, actually. Then she turns around, eyes searching the room before exclaiming, "Ah, but there's an excellent example! Come." She walks hurriedly toward one of the two black marble mantels in the room, positioned opposite each other, and points at a picture hanging to its left.

"That portrait of Lord Simon up there, you see?" She gestures to it; the portrait lighting above it is a bit dimmer, giving it a gloomier effect. "There are several others in the house of him as well, but they're remarkably different, though they were painted the same year. The originals, that is."

Lord Simon grimaces over us, obviously tall despite hunching in his wingback chair, and gaunt beneath his formidable sideburns. He holds a cane at an odd angle, making it seem nearly indistinguishable from his limbs.

"Who was he?" I ask absently.

"Your great-great-grandfather, I believe."

Oh.

"How interesting!" I exclaim. "I never knew any of this."

"Happy to help," she says. "But I'm afraid I really must be going now."

"I understand, of course. Before you go, would you mind telling me where I can see the others?"

"Others?"

I indicate the painting.

"Ah yes, of course. There's one in the second-floor library, and another in one of the more popular rooms in the manor. In fact, it's on my way, if you'd like me to show you?"

"Oh, would you? That would be lovely."

She smiles genuinely. I'm in.

Not one for idle chitchat, she makes it a working walk, informing me of the detailed plans for the renovation of parts of the main house as well as the mausoleum. "Old homes, they get tired, like we do. Need a bit of freshening up, now and again. Otherwise they'll collapse!"

"We can't have that."

"No, we certainly can't. Right, then," she says, once we're in the library. This part of the house is tourist-accessible, and we're not alone in the room; a couple is reading the small plaque beneath some artefact, and a few uniformed kids are pulling faces at each other in the leaded-glass windows overlooking the gardens. She walks me over to a painting.

In this one, my great-great-grandfather is square-jawed, muscular, and staring off into the middle distance, standing without a cane and looking every part the British Colonial Occupier. The image is immediately and intimately familiar, like I've seen this picture before.

"The portraits of him were both upstairs, at one point. Most visitors never guessed that it's the same man."

A ridiculous claim; most visitors would be unlikely to single out any of the portrait subjects from the others, and if they did, why would they care? I don't correct her. We must allow people their pleasures, however small.

"Forgive me, I know almost nothing about art. But if the original you showed me before was lost in the fire, how could the artist have restored it, exactly?"

"An excellent question. Typically art restoration is done on damaged paintings, not destroyed ones, but in this case, the artist had a painting *of* the painting to go off. So it's more of a reproduction than a restoration, really."

"A painting of a painting?"

"Yes, the first Lord Simon was rather vain. Had dozens of portraits done of himself, so many that they're primarily kept in different locations instead of on display."

"How odd."

"And expensive. The artist who did the reproduction was going off a painting of Lord Simon and the rest of his family; the painting was hanging in the room where they sat for it."

"But why reproduce *that* painting?"

"I've asked that myself, actually. I think the artist had some sort of a dispute with him, to be honest, which would explain why it's such an . . . unforgiving portrayal."

"Is it possible they were painted in different years?" I ask, head tilted.

"Not according to the valet's records, no."

"Is it possible the valet made a mistake?"

"Well, I suppose anything's possible, but it would be the first. His diaries were meticulous."

"Diaries?"

"Yes. This is an historic property, Mr.—Noah—and even centuries ago there was a certain reverence for the manor, even amongst the servants."

"Fascinating," I say. "Perhaps he grew ill."

"That's likely, Lord Simon did die that same year."

"How?"

"Cholera, on a trip to India. Never made the voyage back."

18

EACH ONE OF YOU CAN LOVE HER

I CAN'T GET OUT OF THE MANOR FAST ENOUGH. When I finally manage it, I find Goose alone, loitering in one of the estate's many gardens.

"Sight for sore eyes," I say.

He cracks a half smile. "Glad you made it out alive."

"Only just," I say. "You?"

"Thought I'd take a moment of reflection in the gardens."

"How's that going?"

"Bloody useless. There's a pop-up café, though, where we can get coffee, at least."

"That's where I was heading to find you."

We start off in that direction. I ought to be reflecting on my meeting with Lord Simon, via Mrs. Balfour (*WHAT DOES IT ALL MEAN* and all that), but it's the encounter with my sister that weighs on me.

"Goose?" I ask.

"Mmm?"

"What was it like, for you? Growing up?"

"How do you mean?"

"How did your family treat you? Your brothers?"

The breeze ruffles his hair before he smoothes it back, loping alongside. "Well, I'm the beloved baby, of course. By the time I was coming up in school, they'd all gone off. Did all right for themselves in the end, though. Oxbridge, and all that."

"And left you to fend."

"A bit. But that's all we can do, isn't it?"

"What's that?"

"The best we can." He smiles.

It's a sad expression. Wounded. They grew up and went, leaving him the only one around to listen to the alcoholic ramblings of his mother, the screaming matches between her and his father. It was less dramatic in my broken family, in a way—when my mother died, my father became a ghost as well. Ruth tried, but she couldn't fix the thing at the heart of it. Without my mother, our family didn't make sense.

I left Kate in that. I've got excuses, good ones, but that's all they are.

I don't want to leave things like this with her. I've fucked up too much as it is.

"Maybe I ought to stay around a bit longer, even after our things get here?" I ask as we approach the café. Idle chatter and the hissing of espresso machines fill the pause in our conversation. "Try to sort things with Kate?" Things can hardly get worse.

"Speak of the devil," Goose says, tipping his head. I follow his gaze.

My sister is sitting at a table by a hedge, and Mara's grandmother is sitting opposite her, wearing tight jeans and an oversized sweater, hands cupping her mug.

Let this be a lesson for you: Things can always get worse.

I approach them because I have to, obviously. Mara's grandmother pretends not to notice me come up, and my sister's facing the opposite way.

"Hello," I say warily.

Kate turns to us, eyebrows raised. "Goose," she says to him, as if our earlier meeting hadn't happened, as if I'm not there. "You're looking well."

"You flatter me."

"Goose?" Mara's grandmother says, brandishing a northern accent, now. "What sort of a name is that?"

"The sort you earn at an all-boys boarding school for behaviour I could never recount in polite company," he says.

Kate looks at M. "This is—Em, did I get it right?"

"Close enough." She smiles. "Lovely to meet you, Goose," she says to him. Then, extending her hand to me, "And you as well . . ."

"Noah," I say. "Shaw."

Mara's grandmother looks back and forth between me and Kate. "I'd guessed, but didn't want to be rude. I was a mate of your dad's, at Trinity. The resemblance is uncanny."

Would it be so terrible, to be able to kill someone with a thought? I wonder. "And how do you two know each other?" I ask Kate.

"Your sister had some questions about the house," M says brightly.

"Em's a volunteer," Kate says.

"Is that right?"

"In a manner of speaking," M corrects.

"What did you read for?" Goose asks her.

"Classics," she says, with an expert touch of humblebrag. "It's not directly relevant, I know, but I've been thinking of writing a book on follies."

"Follies," I repeat.

"The classical statues and structures you might've seen on the grounds. So called because they serve no actual purpose except as a display of wealth."

"I know what they are," I say, the last of my tolerance rapidly waning.

"Oh, sorry! I wasn't sure." Mara's grandmother grins,

pushing her seat back. "I'm afraid I've got to get back to it, though. Glad I could help—lovely meeting you," she says, extending her hand to Goose first, then me.

"Em," I say. "Is that short for Emily? Emma?"

She smiles, with teeth. "Oh, no, my name's not quite so common, but it keeps life interesting to leave some things a bit of a mystery, don't you find?" She winks at Goose. "Not unlike your friend, here."

"Indeed," I say.

She bites her lower lip, still smiling, and then brushes past me, knocking into a chair as she does. "God, I'm *hopeless*," she mumbles. "Cheers!" she says, waving.

It's *almost* convincing.

"Lovely," Goose says after her.

"She offered to take me out someday, tell me about Dad," Kate says, eyes meeting mine as she sips from her coffee. "Said she knew our mother, too."

"I see," I say slowly, considering whether to take the seat that M just vacated. "You think that's wise? Going along with someone you hardly know?"

Kate rolls her eyes. "Don't be ridiculous. It's not as if she's some middle-aged pervert trying to lure me into the back of his van."

Middle-aged, she isn't. "Maybe you ought to at least check with Grandmother first."

"What, now you've decided you're going to act like a big

brother?" She gets up from the unsteady little iron table. "You might not be interested in hearing about what our parents were like back then, but I am. Goose," she says, pushing her chair in. "Lovely to see you."

"And you," he says, as she stalks off.

"Kate—"

"I'll text if I'm kidnapped or something, all right?" she says loudly, over her shoulder.

"I don't have my mobile!"

She keeps walking.

"You're really in it, mate," Goose says, just as I feel something vibrating in my pocket.

A phone I don't recognise? How novel. "Hello?"

"Go to the White Horse pub down the road," Mara's grandmother says.

"New phone, who's this?" I ask politely.

"Act smarter than you look," she says, and hangs up.

I let Goose lead us to the car park. "Where'd you get the mobile?"

"Mara's grandmother," I say.

He taps the side of his nose, once. "You neglected to mention that. When?"

"Five minutes ago," I say. "M is for Mara. You just met her."

IN HER MYSTERY

SHE'S WAITING FOR US IN THE NEARLY EMPTY pub, sitting at the far end of the bar. M looks out of place, but only because she isn't a seventy-year-old man.

She's twice that, I force myself to remember. More than. The three other occupants of the establishment are wrinkled and ruddy and grey; Mara's grandmother's face is unlined, her hair full and loose and shining black. She'd have been in her eighties when they were born.

Goose is staring as well. Out of the corner of his mouth, he says, "You're saying that's—"

"Yes."

"Oh my wow," he murmurs.

M stands from her stool without a word, not even so much as a nod of acknowledgement, and walks past a few empty booths to a back door, her trainers squeaking a bit on the stone floor. She pushes it open, disappears behind it.

Goose seems puzzled. "Do we . . . follow?"

"Think so."

There's a small garden dotted with a few shabby tables, the white paint peeling and a bit rusted. M's standing against one of them, one ankle crossed in front of the other, wearing an expression of exasperation and disdain.

"How old did you say she was?" Goose whispers.

"It's rude to inquire about a woman's age," M says at full volume.

"It's rude to appear where one hasn't been invited," I say brightly.

M ignores me. "Hello again, Alastair."

Goose sighs. "Knew my name all along, then?"

She smiles patronisingly. "I can call you Goose, if you like."

"I like," he says back.

Watching them, I realise I've no patience for this. For her. "What is it you want?"

M takes a deep breath, then breathes out a long, drawn-out sigh. "I want to apologise."

She shifts her weight. She's shorter than I remembered—maybe it's the trainers? In the light, alone, I notice details I missed at the manor; her sweater, three sizes too large. Her lips and skin free from any obvious makeup. She looks small. Young. Not even as old as the thirty-six years she claimed when we first met.

She was outfitted like a Raymond Chandler character, then. A dame in distress, pleading for my help. Today, she's a grad student, eager to get on with her research.

The change feels calculated. Which is why I say, "Apology accepted," and then, to Goose, "Let's go."

I turn around before he can answer, making for the door back into the pub. I fully expect to hear M call out after us; I'm surprised when she doesn't.

Goose catches up to me in a few strides, now back in the darkened pub. My pace is quick.

"What's going on?" he asks.

"Nothing," I say, a bit peevishly.

"Why, though?" he asks, earnest.

"Because there's no point staying." What's changed, since I left her car in the middle of the street? She sent a different car to fetch me at Goose's hospital, somehow knowing where I'd be. She arranged for a plane—*my* plane—to bring me to England, where she wanted me to go. Then she found us again when all I wanted to do was hide.

I'm done with it, being summoned. Done being herded. Done being pushed. Just, done. "She wants something I'm not inclined to give," I say to Goose as we pass the old men at the bar.

"Something about your memories, right?" We walk outside, the air chilled and damp. "Your mum's?" he adds delicately.

"Don't think so," I say. "She mentioned an ancestor of mine, whom she knew." The pub sign above us creaks and sways in the breeze. "My great-great-grandfather. Saw a portrait of him today, actually. At the manor."

"That's *kind* of brilliant, you've got to admit," Goose says. He's stopped in front of the pub. "She barely looks thirty."

"Thirty-six," I say, despite myself.

Goose runs his hand over his jaw. "*How*, though? If she's as old as you say—she'd have been born in *Victorian England*." He looks longingly at the entrance to the pub.

Shite. "You want to go back in."

Goose lets his head fall back. "Come on, mate!" he says, staring at the sky. "It's pretty fucking incredible. Think of everything she must've *seen*."

"Look," I say wearily. "I know this all seems fascinating and special at the moment, but going back in there? It won't be worth it. Promise."

Goose isn't having it, though. "Worth *what*?" he asks, animated. "An hour talking to her? An afternoon?"

I shake my head slowly. "That's how it starts," I mumble.

"What, we can't spare the time?" He shoots me a look.

Fuck. I run my hands through my hair, groaning.

"Let's just go back in, hear her out. If we don't like what she says, we go. Easy. Done."

I *know* better than to agree to it, is the thing. Truly, I do. But he sounds so damn *reasonable*, and rational. It chips away at my resistance. Despite what I know.

Goose bites his lip, his expression pleading. "If nothing else, we ought to go back in for a glimpse of what *our* future'll look like in a hundred fifty years."

"Our abilities are gone, remember?"

"She said she can help get them back, though, *remember?*" he asks mockingly.

I look away from the pub, toward the road that leads to the manor. "I don't know that I want them back."

"Well, I do." Goose lifts his chin.

"You might regret it."

"And you might not." He rolls his eyes. "Honestly, when did you get so *dull?*"

"Fine!" I say, surprising myself a bit. "Fine." Goose flashes a toothy grin. "Christ, you're annoying."

"You're going to thank me." He walks past me, straight into the pub. I'm following *him*, now, as he strides eagerly toward the back garden. M's still perched on the edge of the table where we left her, only now she's smoking. And there's a bottle of liquor on the table as well, along with three glasses.

"He has questions," I say flatly.

She pulls at her cigarette, then takes it from her mouth. Her lips curl into a smile. "I have answers." She extends her leg under the table, pushing a chair toward me. The iron scrapes the stone. "Have a seat."

20

INTO HER CONFIDENCE

SHE HAS GRACE ENOUGH NOT TO LOOK SMUG AT our return, at least. Then takes the bottle and pours out a finger of scotch into each glass, offering them to us.

"I ordered it before you left," she says. "I did mean what I said before. I *am* sorry."

"It's fine," I say dismissively. "Goose?" Might as well get on with it.

"Right," he drawls. "I'm not quite sure how to ask without being rude—"

M turns her smile on him. "Don't worry about it. I'm hard to offend. What would you like to know?"

Goose takes a sip of scotch, considering his words. He leans one elbow on the table, chin in hand. "Your origin story, for a start."

Her smile flickers for a moment. "So would I."

Goose's brow furrows.

"How much has he told you?" M tips her head at me, still speaking to Goose, though.

"Hmm." He sucks in his lips. "Everything, I reckon? Bit hard to say, though . . . we were rather drunk, at the time."

The corner of M's mouth turns up.

"The part I'm having trouble with at the moment . . ." Goose starts. "You're Mara's *grand*mother, Noah said."

"That's right."

"Which makes you . . . how old, precisely?"

"Honestly?" She shrugs, resigned. "I don't know."

Goose's eyes flick to mine. "Noah said . . . you were born in *Victorian* England?"

I'm momentarily tempted to correct him, but M shakes her head. "I wasn't born in England at all. At least, I don't believe so." Her brows draw together, before a conspiratorial grin appears on her lips. "That'd be a plot twist, wouldn't it?" she says to me.

I've managed not to get drawn into things, yet. And plan to keep it that way for as long as possible.

M takes a drag off her ciggy, exhaling the smoke through her nose. "I was found in British India," she says to Goose.

"During Queen Victoria's reign. I don't know when I was born. I . . . seemed young, I suppose, when I was taken." A far-away look comes over her face for a moment, before she turns to me. "By your great-great-grandfather."

Goose's eyes widen, his mouth forming a surprised grin. "Noah saw portraits of him today, didn't you?"

M raises her brows. "Did you? Which?"

I don't answer her, but Goose nudges me with his foot.

"Which what?" I ask her.

"Which portraits? They keep a few of him on display, I hear."

Something about the way she says it catches at me. "You *hear*?" I ask. "Why not just visit yourself?"

"I've seen some of the older ones, once. But I haven't been to the manor in quite some time."

"Why not?" Goose asks.

"I've learned to avoid cameras, at my age," she says wryly.

"Yet you were there today—"

"Outside, not in. And out of view of the security cameras."

My eyes narrow at that. "What are you afraid of?" I ask. "Why hide?"

"I don't hide. I move. All of us do." The smoke from her cigarette curls in the air. "Easier to avoid questions that way, I've learned. Tried to collect the pictures that I was stupid enough to pose for, once, and got most of them, but some have been more . . . inaccessible than others. As for the manor," she goes on, "I thought it wiser to avoid drawing notice for my uncanny resemblance to a nineteenth-century portrait hanging in one of the rooms."

"Wait, really?" Goose leans in.

She nods. "I sat for it with the second Simon and Elliot Shaw, as well as Sarah, Simon's wife." She looks at the table. "She commissioned the same painter who worked with Simon, before . . ." Her voice trails off, but she recovers quickly. "Elliot insisted on Dash being in it—one of Lord Simon's foxhounds," she adds in response to our confused expressions. Her eyes squint, a bit. "Elliot's grabbing his collar in the painting, if I remember correctly? Wouldn't sit still for it. Never liked me, much." Then, to me, "Which portraits did *you* see?"

I shrug offhandedly. "I don't know. Wasn't as though they had titles or anything."

"What was he doing in them?" she asks.

"Sitting in one, standing in another," I say vaguely. It's a bit of a heady feeling, having answers to someone else's questions, for a change. There's power in it.

M knows it. Which is why it's gratifying when she presses, "Was there anything that stood out? Anything at all?"

I could say no. Shrug. Deflect. But her questions have *me* rather curious now, given what the curator, Mrs. Balfour, said.

I take a drink. Make her wait for it. "The curator mentioned there was a fire, and some of the paintings have been restored," I say then, searching her face as I speak. "The ones

I saw had been done the same year, but he hardly looked like the same man in them."

M inhales slowly. "They were painted before, and after."

Goose looks puzzled. "Before and after what?"

M offers a small, hopeful smile to me. "That's what I've been hoping you'd help me find out."

"You knew him, though, you said," Goose says with a narrowed look.

"I *met* him," M corrects. "Once. And my memory . . . there are gaps in it." She closes her eyes. "I remember being in the carriage with him. The feel of the velvet . . ." Her hand reaches up to her throat, as if she's feeling for the pendant that was once there. "And the smell. Sandalwood, and something else; like meat that had been left out in the sun." She gives a single shake of her head. "There's hardly anything else, from before."

"What about after?" Goose asks her.

I knew some things, about after. From Mara. From the letters Simon Shaw wrote, and the ones Sarah Shaw wrote and the journal she kept, even after his death.

But here, in front of me, is the source.

"Simon brought me to the port—Calcutta, though I'm not sure I knew the name, then. He left me with a man I called Uncle. He took me in to live with his family, and I did, for a bit. They fed me. Taught me. Cared for me, like family. They were kind." She looks down. "They were murdered.

"There was an Englishman Uncle had brought me to at

the port, on occasion. He asked Uncle questions about me, in front of me—what I was learning, how I was developing, whether I'd fallen ill. I was measured. Inspected. Uncle was paid each time. After he was murdered, Sister took me to the Englishman." Her jaw tenses. "After *she* was murdered, he arranged for me to be delivered to your family in London."

She stops talking, and only after the silence stretches on for over a minute do I realise she won't start again, unless I urge her on.

"That hardly brings us up to date," I say.

Her cigarette's burned down to ash. She flicks it to the ground and stubs it out with the toe of her white trainer. Then takes a sip of scotch from her glass, making a face as she looks at it. "I'm going to need something a bit lighter if you expect me to cover all three centuries." She leans to her right, looking over Goose's shoulder at the door. "Doubt they have table service, back here." She meets his eyes. "Would you mind, terribly?"

Faced with the prospect of being rude or being excluded, Goose, like a proper Englishman, chooses the latter.

"What would you like?" he asks, only a mild hint of reluctance in his voice.

"A pint would be lovely," she says with a smile.

"Of course," Goose says. He stands, ruffles my hair as he leaves. Rather roughly.

Then, once he's gone, "Did you know about any of it?" M asks. "Anything I said?"

Not entirely sure what she means or what she's after, I say cautiously, "Bits, here and there."

"You haven't *remembered* any of it, though? Anything about Simon . . . ?"

"Why would I?"

She rubs the bridge of her nose. "You're connected to him, I told you."

"I'm connected to my mother, too, aren't I?" I ask sharply, before taking another sip. "Why would I remember someone I've never known, instead of someone I *wish* I'd known?"

M considers my words. "That's one reason, right there. You loved your mother. But some part of you might be worried, subconsciously, about what you might learn if you open that door."

I see myself back in Brooklyn, in the flat, holding my mother's journal:

I don't know if I can bring myself to love him.

Seems a crime to marry not for love, but for purpose, even though I know it won't be forever.

Is that even worse? Marrying him, conceiving his child, knowing that someday I'll die for it?

And then, like poison, my father's voice seeps into my mind, sneering: *Your mother gave up her own life to have you, and you kept spitting on her memory.*

I take another drink. "What's Simon got to do with it?" I ask, momentarily relieved by the scorch in my throat.

"Haven't you ever wondered why your parents ended up together?" she asks.

I didn't need to wonder. I'd been told.

The mental image of my sunlit flat splinters, and a new one spiders together. The stacked trunks filled with my family's history are replaced with mannequin parts as the abandoned factory fills itself in around me, grey concrete and grimy glass:

"The man you call Lukumi, who I knew as Lenaurd, manipulated your mother, recruited her, then introduced her and me so we could breed. You were *planned, Noah.* Engineered. *To be the hero. To slay the dragon. But you fell in love with it instead."*

I can almost feel the softness of Mara's cheek against mine as she rested in my lap on the hard cement floor, ready to die after my father forced her to choose between her life and her brother's. Ready for me to kill her.

And then it's Mara's voice I hear:

The villain is the hero of her own story. No one thinks they're a bad person. Everyone has reasons for doing what they do.

21

HAVE I CURSED YOU

HE SOUND OF MARA, HER VOICE, HER heartbeat, her breath, her *sound*—leaves me aching with loss.

"There's a reason it was *your* parents, specifically, that the professor chose." It's my mother's words that flood my mind next:

I've talked to Mara about it. Says she's dreamt about my death "a thousand ways over a thousand nights" and that there's no timeline in which I'll have his child and live.

She says I might regret it, my choice, once I have that child in my arms.

As the professor says, every gift has its cost.

M casts her gaze down, to her feet. "I did help him. I regret it."

"I'm sure you have many regrets," I say with bitterness. Projecting, of course.

"I do," she says earnestly. "You were told about the archetypes, yes? The professor told me that too," she adds, with barely concealed resentment. "Convinced me that the world needed you, a Hero."

The word parallels my thoughts so closely that I look up, startled, and wonder if she can hear them.

"What's your Gift?" I ask warily. "Your Affliction?"

She looks confused, for a moment, at the change of subject. "I thought you knew."

"Remind me," I say tonelessly.

M's expression shifts. Hardens. "He told me I was the Shadow."

"And what does that mean?"

"What has it meant for Mara, in your experience?"

My back goes up. "You're not Mara."

She's nodding now, in agreement. "Exactly. He told me what I was, and told me what *she* would become, if I didn't die." She looks at her own glass, then, and in one quick movement, drinks what's left in it. "Nearly everything I know I've been told by the professor. He told me what *he* wanted me to believe. What it served him to have me believe. I spent too many years, believing him. Believing *in* him. Not knowing any better."

"Why does it matter *now*, all of a sudden?" I say, on edge still. "And what's Simon got to do with it?" The sound of my father's voice, the memory of what he said, still coats my mind like some toxic film. I finish my drink to dissolve it, pouring another straightaway. I'm fiending for a smoke, too, I realise; Mara hated smoking, so I've mostly stopped carrying them, not that I ever felt the nicotine before. I'd feel it now, though, surely.

M considers her words before speaking. "I meant what I said, when I apologised to you. I made assumptions because I knew your parents, your family, and about you through others. I shouldn't have—I *don't* know you and I don't know my granddaughter . . ."

Her voice trails off and her silence stretches on. I arch an eyebrow. "There's a but, lurking, isn't there."

"If you say that Mara doesn't need saving, that she doesn't need help, then I believe you." She takes a deep breath. "But *I* need help." The words seem to cost her; her shoulders slouch, and she seems smaller. "I need saving." She looks down at the table, picks at the peeling paint with her fingers. "You were right about me. I have many regrets. I've done things that I . . . I've done things," she finishes, her voice lowered.

Hinges creak behind us, and the door to the garden opens, revealing Goose, holding three sweating pints.

"Waited *ages* for the bartender," he says, sounding mildly annoyed. "Ended up hopping the bar myself, thought I'd get some for all of us. Have some variety." He sets the glasses down carefully on the unsteady table. Then, looking back and forth between us, he asks, "What did I miss?"

M offers a brief flicker of a smile. "I was about to pick up where we left off, as it happens."

"Goody," Goose says brightly.

M takes a small sip from one of the pints. "Not long after I was brought to London, to live with your family, I got married. He opposed it." Then, to Goose, she explains, "The professor."

"Right, I've heard of him," Goose says, nodding.

"He was my tutor, then," M says to me. "Your great-great-grandmother, Sarah, had said Simon arranged that, before he died." A muscle tenses in M's jaw. "He opposed the marriage. But Charles was sweet. Gentle. And my skin didn't bother him."

Goose, puzzled, asks, "Why would it?"

"Stop interrupting," I say. I know where her story is headed, I think, and want to get there. Hear her tell it.

She brings her hand to her cheek. "Not a colour you'd have seen at society balls, at the time. Though some found me *exotic*," she says with an edge. "But I had no parents, no family name of my own, no wealth of my own—still, Charles didn't mind." A smile begins at the corner of her lips, and then fades just as quickly. "The professor stopped coming to the house, once we were engaged. I saw him next six months later, on our wedding night, after I woke to find my new husband dead."

Her hand reaches for her neck, her fingers spreading over her collarbone. "He was outside, standing there in the darkness, looking up at me in my dressing gown. He beckoned me outside and I went. I thought . . . I don't know what I thought. That he would help me, I suppose. But he told me we had to leave—my new home, and London entirely." Then, through gritted teeth, she says, "He knew my husband was dead without me saying it and he said—I'll never forget what he said." She closes her eyes. "'The life you lived is no longer available to you. Everything you once had will vanish. You will be shunned, cast out.'"

And then M meets my eyes. "I was afraid to leave London. To leave your family. 'They are not your family,' was his reply. But he never told me who *was*."

She swallows hard and says, her voice low as she recalls the professor's words, "'Your husband is dead because you killed him,' he said. 'You are not what Simon Shaw thought you were.' I asked him *what* Simon had thought I was, then. 'A cure,' he said. And when I asked him what I was if not that, he replied, 'A disease.'"

"Christ," Goose says, almost under his breath.

A tiny, incredulous smile appears briefly on her mouth. "I asked him why he would say that, *how* he could say it, and he said he'd 'seen' it. In my future. Then he told me to obey him.

"I was scared, but angry as well. He'd vanished—left me without a word. He snapped at me, said I wasn't his only student, he'd been assisting another at Cambridge but came, 'as swiftly as he could.'" She glares at nothing, remembering. "Then he ordered me, 'Take nothing from this house. Nothing from this life. We begin your real education at dawn.'"

M's attention drifts back to us. She looks at me, but not my eyes. Her gaze is on my throat. "He gave me my pendant that night."

22

THE ANCIENT TRAGEDY

I KNEW NOTHING THEN, ABOUT THE AFFLICTIONS. Though he called them Gifts, at the time," she says to Goose. "Our lessons together had been about science and history and maths—he taught me everything I knew about the world. And then he showed me a new one, and told me my place in it," she adds coldly. "We are what we believe we are, and *he* told me what to believe, what I was. He was my teacher, my father, and my lover, later. I trusted him implicitly. So when he assigned me my role, I performed it. Until I dared to imagine I could play a different part."

Her words feel familiar, like echoes of my own thoughts.

Mara believed what she'd been told by the professor, after

she got his letter. By my father, after he tortured us, tried to kill who we were.

"*I have no right to want you,*" she said to me.

"*You have every right,*" I insisted. "*It's your choice. It's ours. We don't have to be what they want. We can live the lives we want.*"

And then I took off the pendant I'd worn since I'd found it, amongst my mother's things. I hadn't known until that day what it meant, what it would mean, me wearing it. Once I did, I took it off in front of her. Offered it to Mara in my open palm. Offered *her* my choice.

And I didn't regret it, not once, until she'd taken away mine.

"I was taken as a child to a foreign country, knowing no one but your family and the professor," M goes on. "Then my husband died in our bed and the professor appeared in the middle of the night, claiming I'd killed him and would suffer for it unless I went with him." Her nostrils flare. "When we met I asked you to help me for Mara's sake; I'd assumed she'd been manipulated, like I had been. But she had something I never had. She had you."

M looks at me appraisingly. "You said she is where she is now because she chose to be, and I believe you, now. And respect you for respecting her choice. But *I* never had one. The professor never allowed me that."

Her invoking our first meeting makes me think of something else. "You said my family owed you a debt," I say slowly.

She nods, once. "The professor said that he'd met me in India, when I was younger, not in London as I'd first thought. He said he was paid by Simon Shaw to 'unlock the secret to immortality.'"

My brow furrows. "How? How would Simon have known anything about you, all the way in India? How did he find the professor?" I ask her.

She smiles slightly, knowingly. "That's what I'm hoping you'll find out."

"But how?" Goose asks, clearly baffled. "How, precisely, is Noah supposed to learn what you can't?"

M looks at me, then at Goose.

"Genetic memory," I say, feeling resigned.

"We're connected to those who share our Gifts," M says to Goose, repeating her words from our first meeting.

"All of us?" Goose asks.

She hesitates for a fraction of a second before nodding.

Goose's expression is open, inquisitive. "How do we get that?" he asks. "The memory thing?"

She smiles carefully. "It starts with having an open mind."

Goose sits a bit straighter. "I've got an open mind. Is that how we get our abilities back?"

M arches her brows.

"It was all of us who lost our superpowers, on the bridge," says Goose.

"So I've heard," she says.

How, though? Who would she have heard it from? "From whom?"

"There's a whole world out there. More Gifted every day."

"Yes, why is that, exactly?" Goose asks her, just as I say, "That's not an answer."

"Partly, your father is to blame."

Kells's voice worms its way into my consciousness, the words she spoke in those hallucinations—or memories.

David Shaw recruited me. Sponsored my doctoral research. Your father knows what you are. He knows what Mara *is. His company's been conducting research that probably spawned a clutch of Carriers all over the world.*

"Kells wasn't the only doctor working for my father."

"Not as such, no." Then, "I'm not convinced your abilities are really gone," she says to Goose. "I think, instead, they might've been . . . cut off."

"By what?" I ask.

"How?" Goose says at the same time.

She shrugs one shoulder. "I can't say I know for certain. You might've done it yourselves—our Gifts, they're unlocked by consciousness. Will, and intent," she says. "So whether it's your abilities you're interested in," she says to Goose, "or whether you decide to help me find the freedom that's been denied me," she says to me, "you'd best begin by getting out of your own way." She pours another glass of scotch, slowly. "Face what you've been hiding from."

"I'm not *hiding*," I say, chin lifted. "I'm *avoiding*."

A withering look in response. "You walked into traffic to avoid me," M says. "I won't pretend to know you, but from what little I've seen? You run *from* pain, not toward it, like you think you do."

I raise my mess of a fist as evidence to the contrary.

"Some might say a broken hand is preferable to a broken heart." She looks at me with compassion, but without pity. "You've been through hell. Most of us have, but you had *David* as a father." She tenses as she says his name. "And you lost Naomi so young. And you and Mara are twisted up in a net of the professor's own design. It wouldn't surprise me at all if you've locked away memories that might hurt you," she says. "Somewhere in your mind is the key." She nudges the glass, her own glass, toward me. "You have to want to find it, though."

"How?" Goose asks.

I shoot him a glare.

"As I've said from the beginning, I would start by going home," M says. "By which I mean the manor." She reaches down for her bag. "That's where your family's story begins." She stands, shouldering her tote. "And then you might consider visiting Cambridge? You've got loads of family history there as well."

"All right," I say finally. I'm sufficiently intrigued, now, despite myself. And if I say no, she'll probably never stop haunting me. "On one condition, though."

"Yes?"

"Leave Kate out of it," I say, remembering what my sister said, thinking of her and M together, today. "All of it. Don't contact her again."

M doesn't hesitate before answering, "Done." Then she withdraws an envelope from her handbag. Slides it across the table.

"You don't have to *pay* me," I say, slightly horrified.

"It isn't money."

"Dare I ask?"

The corner of her mouth turns up. "It helped me open my mind, once, when I found myself . . . blocked. It's a bit out of fashion, now, perhaps. But rather popular in the seventies." She shrugs again. "Not a bad decade, all things considered."

She can't mean—

"Stay at the manor tonight," she says. "Rattle some cages. See if anything bites." She turns to leave.

"And where will you be?" Goose asks her turned back.

She looks over her shoulder. "Waiting," she says, and leaves.

Goose picks up the envelope. Hands it to me. "What do you think . . . ?"

I shrug, then slide my finger under the flap, expecting a letter, perhaps, or maybe a map—

"What is it?"

I slide the small sheets of blotting paper out, just far enough so Goose can see. Each tab of—is it acid?—is stamped with the letter *M*.

"Oh shit."

23

MORE AND MORE VISIBLE

I'T'S MY SISTER WHO GETS US BACK INSIDE.

We shamble back up to the manor just as Kate is driving past the line of yew trees that leads back to the house.

"Kate!" I shout. She passes us, but only slightly, and lets the car idle. I knock on her window.

"Thank God. I need your help."

My sister's blue eyes narrow.

"I've been shit," I say, a bit desperately. "I'm sorry. I know I can't make it up to you, but I want things to be different."

"What do you want?"

"I need to get back in," I say, tipping my head at the house.

"It's your house."

"They don't believe me. I've lost my ID." Should've settled it all with Mrs. Balfour, but ended up with other shite on my mind.

"You're pathetic," she says.

"I am, truly."

"How'd you get in before?"

"With the tourists. Had to pay."

She smirks at that. "All right. Get in."

I wave Goose over.

Kate pushes up her sunglasses, drives up to the gate, and smiles at the guard. "Roger, this is my brother, Noah. He's lost his ID, like an idiot."

"Hi," I say. "Lovely to meet you."

"Can you let the rest of security know he's here?" Kate asks.

"Of course, miss."

"Thanks ever so," I say, as Kate rolls the window back up and drives toward the garage. "You don't have to come back in—"

"I do, actually. You'll need to meet Mrs. McAdams, and Victor—"

"Is Albert not here anymore?" The family valet proved indispensable, in Miami, when things got . . . complicated . . . in the past.

"He's on vac," Kate says, pulling into the garage.

"Shame."

Kate walks through the wings with a self-possession I envy. She looks like she belongs here. Which she does.

Once we've made the rounds, she says, "Hold out your hand."

I raise my eyebrows, but obey. She drops a key in my open palm.

"It's to the residence. The staff leaves at seven today."

"Thank you," I say sincerely.

She doesn't acknowledge it. "Farewell, again, Goose."

"Where are you going?" I ask her. M's promise aside, I can't help but wonder.

"Bath," she says. "To meet Grandmother and Grandfather."

"That's hours away."

"I'm staying the weekend. She wants me to start back at Cheltenham, and wanted to spend time with me before I've got to get settled in for class."

"But I only just got here."

Despite our earlier exchanges, the corner of her mouth twitches into the beginnings of a smile. "You'll manage. Mind the ghosts, though." To my surprise, she kisses me on both cheeks before saying goodbye.

"Well," Goose says. "I'm sure that's fine."

"Which part?" I ask. "Kate?"

Goose glares at me.

"You don't mean—you don't believe in *ghosts*," I say.

"I absolutely do."

I lean back on my heels. "How did I not know this about you?"

"Your unrelenting self-obsession, perhaps?"

"Perhaps," I say. "So." I pat my pocket, where the envelope rests. "What is the plan?"

He squints at the sunset through the tracery on the windows. "Well, it's too early for acid."

"I'm sure that's not a thing. Though perhaps we *should* wait till the tourists leave."

"So we don't end up playing strip cricket in the gardens?"

I hold up a single finger. "One time."

"One *memorable* time," he says. "What do you think Patrick and Neirin are doing just now?"

"I don't know." I run my hands through my hair. "Once you're wrapped up in all this, the rest of the world sort of drops off."

"It is rather a lot, isn't it?"

"Which part, my ex-girlfriend's hundred-and-fifty-year-old grandmother encouraging us to do hallucinogenics or . . ."

"That part, yes. And the part before that, about us being a different species."

"Bit of an exaggeration."

"Is it?"

"Fair." I look up and around. "Where should we go?"

"Kitchen," Goose says. "Always."

We startle the housekeeper upon finding it. "Goodness, you scared me half to death."

"Terribly sorry," I say. "Mrs. McAdams, is it?"

"Yes, sir."

"Oh, Noah, please, I insist."

She smiles. "I was just about to lock up—the cook's already left for the weekend, but I'm sure we can rustle something up for you."

"Oh, no need, we'll be fine," I say.

"We're very resourceful," Goose adds.

She looks doubtful. "I'm afraid we didn't know to expect you, so there isn't anything prepared."

"Truly, we'll be quite all right."

"I *love* to cook," Goose says.

"Really?" Mrs. McAdams looks doubtful, but says, "Lovely. Well, then," she adds, hands on her hips. "I'll leave you to it! Choose any bedchamber you like, someone will be in in the morning to pick up after you."

"Yes, ma'am."

"Enjoy your evening, lads."

"Oh, we will." I smile charmingly.

"Mrs. McAdams," Goose calls after her. "So sorry, one question."

"Yes, dear?"

"I heard something on the way in about ghosts?"

"Ah, is that what you're after?"

"No," he says, just as I say, "Yes," to annoy him.

Her blue eyes widen with mischief. "Which one were you

hoping to spot? The Grey Lady, perhaps? Or the boy?"

"Neither," Goose says, just as I say, "Both."

"Well, I've never seen them myself, but supposedly this is a good spot for it, if you go in for that sort of thing." She gives a little shake of her head, her short red curls bouncing. "There's a book in the gift shop, published by the Trust. Features all the great haunted houses in Britain. There's an entry on this one, as it happens. Shop'll be closing up now, but there might be a copy in the lord's library, I believe."

"Thanks," we say in unison.

Goose opens the fridge once she leaves. "Hmm," he says disapprovingly. "I'm going to need to fetch that book before it gets dark."

"Why?"

"Want to know which rooms to avoid."

"You really are mental."

"Pot, kettle."

It's dark by the time we finish our makeshift supper (tea, sandwiches), and a brief search of my grandfather's study yields no paranormal publications, so Goose decides we should burgle the gift shop.

"It's locked, she said."

"Nothing's ever really locked."

A memory clicks into place, from my other life, again; Jamie breaking into Dr. Kells's office, saying something similar. "You and Jamie really would be quite the match."

There's a pause in the conversation, and Goose sucks in his lower lip. "You think so?"

I was having a go at him, honestly, but now . . . I search his expression. "You really fancy him, don't you?"

"Wouldn't you?"

"I find him rather insufferable, actually."

"You don't," Goose says. "That's just your dynamic."

"Fair point."

Goose scratches his ear. "So, did he ever mention me? Back in New York, or whatever?"

I smile smugly. "He did, in fact."

"Why do you torture me so?"

"He said he likes you. *Likes* likes you," I mock.

"Oh God," he groans, hands in his blond hair.

"What?"

He looks up, through his forearms. "Think I'll ever see him again?"

That catches me, for obvious reasons. "Yes," I say. "I'm sure you will."

Goose senses the conversational shift. "He's Mara's best friend, yes?"

I nod slowly, shifting my gaze from Goose to something, anything else.

"Think they're together?" he asks.

I pretend to take an interest in the patterned fabric of the drapes by one of the desks. "What, like right now, you mean?"

"Yeah."

I let myself think about it, but only for a moment. "I hope so."

Sensing my melancholy, Goose takes my arm formally. "Come, friend. Let us away."

The gift shop is on the opposite end of the manor. Most of the lights are on, but the fire's out in the great hall and, I assume, wherever else they keep the fires lit during the day, for the tourists. Rationally, I know the following:

1. Ghosts do not exist.
2. The security guards are on the premises all night.
3. Ghosts do not exist.

Nevertheless, we grow quieter the farther we walk into the manor, as our footsteps seem to grow louder with every step.

"Can you imagine living here?" Goose asks, as I immediately say no.

"I did think I'd feel more at home here, though," I say after a moment, to help fill the silence.

"What, not at the manor, surely?"

"No. England."

"Do you?" he asks. "Feel at home at all?"

I shake my head. "No," I say quietly. "Further away." I don't think I can get back to home. That feeling I had in Brooklyn, like I belonged somewhere for the first time in my life? That wasn't New York—it was Mara. I can't remember feeling at home before her, or since.

And I can't imagine ever feeling at home, here. Can't imagine anyone feeling that way about this place, ever; it's more like a museum.

A disturbing one, honestly. We pass all the portraits and busts and likenesses of my supposed relatives again, and I wonder what it must've been like to grow up here. To be the child of a lord and lady? Running through these corridors— was running even allowed? How did they amuse themselves? Imaginary friends?

And Simon—did he grow up here? The manor's been in our family long enough that he must have. Which room was his?

These are the thoughts that circle and spin as we wander the unhallowed halls. They make my mind itch.

"Goose," I say, stopping abruptly. "Let's just do it."

"What?" he asks, then narrows his eyes, which rest on my pocket. "*Here?*"

We're on the west side of the manor, a narrow corridor on the first floor hung with tapestries that smell faintly of chemicals and time.

"Why not?"

"Why not drop acid given to you by someone you hardly know in a likely haunted manor? You're right, how silly of me," he says in a flat voice.

"You were the one who encouraged it."

"*Hardly*," he says. "'Let's hear her out,' I do believe I said. 'Give her an hour. The afternoon.'"

"So you were wrong, you're saying. You regret it."

"Not at all," he insists, holding up one finger. "It was quite fascinating, actually. And I'm all for you . . . opening your mind, or whatever." He looks around. "Just, perhaps, not here?"

I take the envelope from my pocket. "Might as well just get it over with."

"Mate, we've known each other since reception. You've never really dropped acid before, not in any way that counts, anyway. Trust me, better to be somewhere cozy, first. Comfortable."

"I don't think this is going to be fun for either of us," I say. "No matter where we are."

Goose raises his hands, shaking his head. "Not me, mate."

"You're not partaking?"

"Are you mad?"

"What?"

"Even if that LSD is *average*, and not some extremely potent toxic shit developed specifically to drive you out of your mind, I wouldn't do it here."

"Because of the Grey Lady?"

"Go on, mock me. See how you feel after your nightmare-fuelled trip. Besides," he says. "You need a Virgil. Someone to guide you on your quest."

I slip open the envelope. "Or at least someone to make sure I don't get lost and drown in the fountains."

"Or play nude cricket."

"Exactly." I take one tab, holding it on the tip of my finger.

"*Cenaturi te salutant,*" I say breezily, lifting my hand.

Goose takes my wrist. "Mate, you sure? Do you trust her?"

I don't. But I care less about that, now, than I did.

I look at the tiny *M*. "No," I say out loud, and place the tab on my tongue.

24

THE WATERS BE TROUBLED

GOOSE WATCHES ME WARILY. "I'M MILDLY alarmed."

"Only mildly?"

"Well, if you go into cardiac arrest or something there are guards around here, somewhere. How does it taste? Bitter?"

I shake my head. "Sweet, actually."

"Strange. Least it's probably not cut with anything too appalling."

"It's not as though it came from some street dealer," I say as I walk ahead. "If she wanted to poison me, I'd be dead, I'm sure. Though then whatever memories she's after would die with me. Anyway, when did you become such an expert?"

"Well, whilst you were off adventuring in the New World," Goose says, walking tall, "it was insufferably dull for those of us left behind. Come, we should settle you somewhere cozy."

I look up. The ceiling's been moulded into geometric patterns with reliefs of the family heraldry and decorative medallions in each. "Where would that be?"

"Probably back in the residence," he says. "Less . . ."

"Oppressive?"

"That," he says, facing a staircase, then turning round to face me. "Shall we go back, then?"

My head *does* feel a bit fuzzy. "What floor are we on?"

"Main, still, mate."

"Hmm," I say, considering the stairs behind him. "Up or down?"

"Neither," he says sternly.

I don't know where Lord Simon's room was, but all the most interesting stories tend to take place—

"Below stairs." I brush past Goose, then begin the descent.

"What a terrible idea."

The walls and ceiling are old stone, polished and smooth. Different faces are carved into reliefs, in a row of niches on the opposite wall.

"Who do you think they were?" I ask idly.

"I'm sure there's a guidebook in the gift shop. We could pop back up—"

"No. This feels right," I say.

"Mmmhmm."

"Don't be so judgemental."

"I didn't say anything."

"You were *thinking* things," I say, forging ahead. Some of the doors are open to the rooms inside—I glimpse a few modernly furnished offices, and a tracery of wires by the wall of one of them, leading to a bell.

"It's like being locked in a museum after hours," Goose observes.

"It *is* exactly being locked in a museum after hours."

Goose rubs his arms. "It's cold down here."

"Pussy," I say, charging forward. "Look, there's a staircase just there." A small, narrow one, bisecting the corridor. "Let's see where this leads, shall we?"

"Right."

Wrong. The stairs lead to another corridor, walls bricked and dark.

"What are we looking for, exactly?" Goose asks.

I trail my fingers over the old brick. "Ghosts," I say. I smile at him, flashing teeth.

"You're *definitely* feeling it," Goose says. "Whatever *it* is."

"I think so," I say, turning toward an old bedchamber. "I feel like touching everything."

"Maybe it was Molly."

"I should be so lucky." I glance at the wall: a light switch. How very fortunate. I flick it, and sconces light up along the wall, along with a low iron chandelier that seems dangerously close to the bed's canopy.

The room's made up in an older fashion than the bedrooms upstairs, and anchored by an elaborately carved bed featuring tiny people and animals twisting together on the four posts.

"Too expensive for servants' quarters," I say, bending to examine one of them.

"Probably extra furnishings, over the years. They probably rotate it all with whatever's upstairs."

"Sounds right." I run my hand over the sheets. There's a crosshatched design embroidered into them, only showing at a certain angle. "Goose," I say. "What . . ."

"Branches," he says dismissively.

"No, look." I unfold the coverlet, scattering dust. I hold the sheets up. "Is that—feathers?"

He squints. "Maybe? Why?"

"No reason," I say, untruthfully. We're looking for signs, after all, aren't we?

There's an enormous dresser on the other side of the wall, with a few pewter platters displayed above it. "What do you think?" I ask him, looking at it.

"About?"

"What's inside?"

"Probably storage. More of this, perhaps," he says, pointing at the serving dish. "Linens, that sort of thing."

I approach it, and gingerly tug on one of the iron drawer pulls. An assortment of stuff, just as Goose suggested.

"Anything interesting?"

I shake my head, even as I continue to look.

"Shit!" Goose backs into me.

"What?"

"Did you see that?"

I shoot him a flat look. "Really?"

"No, mate, seriously. There." He turns, pointing back at the doorway. "I saw something back there."

With a heavy sigh, I leave the drawer and walk back to the hall. On the opposite wall from the bedchamber is a free-standing mirror.

I approach it, and notice there's a tag in the corner, for some reason. LOOKING GLASS, 1806, TYNE & WEAR, the tag reads. "You saw our reflection in the corner of your eye. *You're* the one who's supposed to be guiding me through this trip, remember?"

"I don't remember it on our way in," Goose says sceptically. "The mirror wasn't there—"

"It didn't just *appear*—"

The drawer slams shut. Neither of us is anywhere near it.

I shake my head anyway. "This is cruel, even for you, Goose."

"It's not me—"

I'm shaking my head, backing out into the corridor. "It doesn't work like this," I say. "Everything that's happened to us, even if it seems like it falls outside of the realms of logic, *does* have a logical explanation."

Something thuds back in the bedroom.

"What was that?" I ask.

"Who gives a fuck, seriously," Goose says, so close I can feel his breath on my skin. "Let's leave."

"I'm going to look." My feet don't move.

Move, I order them silently.

It works.

"Can't we just go? We can watch *Coronation Street* and get fucked up."

"That is nobody's idea of fun," I say, watchfully approaching the bed. There's a creeping, nameless dread as I bend to look beneath it and—

"No monsters," I announce with embarrassing relief. But there is *something* down there—

"It's a book." The cover has fallen open. I walk over to the opposite side of the bed and kneel. "A Bible."

"Hallelujah," Goose says. "Let's fucking go."

I squint at the woodcut illustration of a tree that stretches across the inside cover and realise there's script—

"It's a tree!"

"Goody."

"Look," I say, holding it up like a prize. "A family tree."

"Yeah." Goose's face is ashen. "Everything's fine now."

"All right," I say, tucking the book—the Bible—under my arm. "We can go."

"You're bringing *that*?"

"It'll be useful."

"More useful than the Internet? No." He reaches out to my forehead, places a clammy palm on it before I swat him away.

"How do you feel?"

"Fine. Normal," I say, walking ahead. I take the stairs even farther down.

"Where are you going?"

"Back the way we came," I say over my shoulder.

"This isn't the way we came," Goose says at almost the exact same time.

"Fine, you lead the way."

He starts to, but when we've descended long enough for there to have been *two* floors, he says, panicked, "I've no idea where we're going."

"I thought you didn't take any drugs?"

"I didn't!"

"Then how are we still descending?" I ask, just as the stairs come to an abrupt end, before a rough wooden door.

"I don't want to see what's behind that."

"What if we go back up, but there's *no way out*?" I tease him. He closes his eyes and the pulse in his throat jumps.

"Shit, you're really scared."

He opens his wide green eyes. "You're not?"

"Not really," I say, and put my hand on the door. "Ready, steady—"

"Go," Goose says.

The syllable hangs in the air for a beat, before I push the door open.

25

THE SILENCE BE BROKEN

A FEW STEPS, AND THEN THE DOOR HINGES creak as it closes behind us, leaving us in the dark. "Thought you were holding it open," Goose says. Our voices echo, as if the ceiling is improbably high.

"Thought *you* were," I say. "You were following me."

Goose flicks open his lighter. "Better," he says, holding it before him.

The glow is far too small to illuminate much except the damp stone wall nearest to us, but there's an iron sconce with two half-melted candles in it.

"Light that, would you?"

He lifts his lighter to the two candles, catching the wick. A warm glow stretches far enough ahead to illuminate heavy ochre drapes along the wall, velvet furred with a layer of dust.

"Where are we?" he asks.

"Don't know," I say. "This should be a cellar, I'd expect—we're far below ground, aren't we?"

"Don't know. It's not as though I studied the map," Goose says, piqued. "Or inherited this place. What's that smell?" he asks, nose wrinkling.

"The candles," I say. "Tallow. Animal fat." The wicks smoke and the flames gutter.

"Wretched."

I step toward the drapes and pull them to one side, revealing part of a wide window, arched. My finger touches the glass, which impossibly looks out onto elaborate gardens, hardly visible in the night. A gust of wind lashes raindrops against the diamond panes, startling me. The candles barely give off enough light to see, and the shadows they throw are worse. I step backward into Goose.

"How can this be," I mutter. A window onto the grounds when we should be *below* ground? Maybe the drugs *are* taking hold. "Are you seeing this?" I ask Goose, to be sure.

"Yes." I almost wish he'd said no. At least then I'd know it *is* the drugs and not—whatever the fuck this is.

I have that sense, again, as if there's an audience in my

head, as if we're being watched. I agreed to this to open my mind, but it feels like I'm losing it.

Mara's voice echoes in my skull:

I'm afraid I'm losing control. You can't stop it. All you can do is watch.

As I walk, it feels like she's here, shadowing my steps in the darkness. If I were to strike a match I imagine I'd see her illuminated beside me, ghosting my smiles, mocking my words.

"Not helpful," I say to the voice.

"What's that?" Goose asks.

Fuck. "Nothing." I run my hand through my hair, tugging on it. The book I've carried with me from the bedchamber falls to the floor.

I look down; the front cover is open to the woodcut illustration of the tree. The faint script that the Shaw family names has been written in grows bolder on the branches. I crouch down on the floor to look more closely.

"Wait," Goose says, but I ignore him, unable to look away as more names appear on the page—Richard Samuel Shaw, Catherine Anne Shaw, William John, Grace Augusta. The tree sprouts new branches beneath my fingers on the paper, and then the branches somehow, impossibly, spread onto the floor as new names appear, not in ink, but in the planks of the wood itself. They're obscured by the mouldy, elaborate rugs beneath our feet.

"Help me," I say to Goose, and both of us grab the edge

of the largest rug, embroidered with blooming flowers in dull, faded colours. The dust threatens to choke us when we sweep it aside and we cough, fists to our mouths, still crouching, though, because the names keep appearing *in* the wood: Oliver Elliot, Samuel Thomas, Charles, Eliza.

Goose and I walk in opposite directions, lifting the rugs beneath our feet and dragging them aside as we follow the branches.

"Mate, you're here," he says, staring at the floor. I look up, turn my head. "Your name, and your sister's."

Just as I take a step to go look, dark tendrils creep beneath my feet, curving and folding over each other, forming another branch, and then letters, and then a name:

Samuel Milnes

Christ. We *are* related, then. "Goose," I say, staring at the floor. "Come look—"

The shadows keep growing, though, forming an outline of a rope that hangs from his branch. A noose is looped around the neck of the limp body beneath it, wearing the clothes Sam wore when I saw him, when he jumped to his death at my father's funeral.

"Are you seeing—"

"Jesus fuck," Goose says, just as the shade rises. Sam's body is translucent, nothing more than grey smoke. His eyes are open and hollow.

"What the *fuck*—"

Sam's mouth opens, and a cloud of winged insects swarms from the hole. Goose swats at them furiously. The door slams behind us, and a gust of dead air blows the shade away.

I haven't been able to hear the sorts of sounds that I shouldn't in days—weeks, perhaps, but the racing, thundering sound of our heartbeats fills my ears now.

"This is *completely* fucked," Goose whispers. A flash of lightning beyond the window illuminates the ruins of the old abbey, confirming that somehow, we're still in the manor. But where?

Wrong question, Mara's voice teases. *When are you?*

The stale breeze sweeps leaves onto the floor, and, impossibly, breathes life into a great fire, roaring and crackling, barely contained in its hearth.

A long table is in the centre of the room, set with bone china and flowered porcelain on a tablecloth of vines and skeletal leaves. The panelled wooden walls bear elaborate carvings of grotesques, and the elaborate arcading on the ceiling is nearly indistinguishable from the vines that have risen from the ground to overtake it. The room has no windows, but antlered chandeliers hang from iron chains, weeping cobwebs. It is a dead house, wholly silent—not even our footsteps echo on the floor. A flickering glow moves just beyond our line of sight, through a doorway. I follow it.

The room opens into a hall, the great hall, of this same house. The balustrades cut from stone, the twisting banisters, the classical figures above the lit fire, the printed wall coverings, the ornate plaster moulding—all the same, but for the rot and corruption. Once-red paint is browning, the plaster is crumbling, the carpets are damp with mould. The glass eyes of dead animals beheaded and mounted on the walls have clouded over with dust, and a thick fog blankets the gardens beyond the windows, which are nearly thatched with vines and ivy.

I feel something crunch beneath my feet—the face of a porcelain doll, painted, clownish, even more wretched with age. When I look up, Goose is no longer beside me.

I try calling out for him, but before his name leaves my throat, a glow appears ahead, descending through the air.

A man holds a candlestick aloft in the near distance, casting light on the gilt-framed portraits that hang from bright red painted walls—not yet rotted through to reveal the wood and brick beneath. He moves swiftly down a staircase—away from the foyer, toward the East Wing of the house, if indeed it is the same house. I follow him through Gothic arched doorways, and when he shifts the candlestick to his other hand, the light reveals him to be a candlelit copy of the man in the portraits; the young, vigorous version.

He looks in both directions, as if checking to see if his footsteps have been heard, before coming to a stop at a plain wooden door. He sets the candlestick down and withdraws a key from his pocket, turning the lock.

When he opens the door, the professor stands behind it.

Part IV

Before

Remembrance of things past is not
necessarily the remembrance
of things as they were.

—Marcel Proust

26

SEEMS AN IMPOSSIBILITY

St. Thomas' Hospital
London, England 17▪

T HE FIRST TIME THE PROFESSOR AND SIMON meet, Simon doesn't know who he himself is, or at least he can't articulate it.

He awakens in a room filled with beds, lined up in little rows, each filled with the dead and dying. With so many bodies crowded together, one would think there would be noises, but the room is mostly silent save for the groans of the unfortunates who still have the strength to express, but not the self-control to contain, their agony.

There's no telling whether it is day or night, as the room has not a single window open. Simon is scarcely aware of the shadows that enter the edges of his vision, but their voices, somehow, are clear.

"It is highly irregular to grant visitation to this ward," one man says.

"I understand," says another. His voice has a rich, deep, Etonian quality to it. "But as I explained to the president and the Court of Governors, I am here on business of the Crown."

The first man huffs a bit. "Yes, well, the Governors are hardly physicians, are they?"

"Nevertheless."

The first man sighs. "We have two foule wards here, strictly segregated to prevent further contagion. Though we have strict procedures in place, I hope you were informed of the potential risk to your own health in coming here."

"I was."

"Is this an inspection, then?"

"No. But I would like to know more about the hospital, if you would be so kind."

"Very well, then. You've noticed, I'm sure, that given the hour, it is the night-watches now that primarily take care of our patients, making regular rounds of the wards to give proper and careful attention to those who are most ill."

"And how many patients are there, exactly?"

"I would have to consult our records, I'm afraid, to be absolutely certain, but my guess would be about three thousand in-patients, though it is our policy not to admit incurables."

"Incurables?"

"If, after three months, a patient has not responded to the best efforts of our surgeons and physicians, he is dismissed."

"Dismissed to where?"

"Back into the care of his family, if he has not yet succumbed to his illness."

"And if he has no family?"

"I would encourage you to consult with the Governors about that, or perhaps the Crown. I am merely a physician, sir, and this is a hospital. We are in the business of curing the sick. And at that, we do the best we can. Considering the vast number of patients, the rate of mortality here is quite possibly the lowest in all of Great Britain, due to the expert care and attention we devote to even the poorest of the poor."

"Who nevertheless must pay admittance fees, yes?" the second man says.

"Our resources are not infinite, I'm afraid. Where did you say you were from again, sir?"

"It's Professor, actually. And I didn't say," the second man says, coming into focus. He has dark skin and darker hair, hanging in loose, thick curls to his shoulders. He is at once familiar and yet, somehow forgettable. His suit is expertly tailored to match his tall, rangy, muscular frame—the physical opposite of the short, rather squat-looking physician beside him.

"I see," the physician says, sounding a bit exasperated. "Are you a professor of medicine?"

"No."

"Then if I may ask, what, precisely, is your area of expertise?"

"I am a man of many interests."

"And where do you teach currently?"

"Currently, I have taken temporary leave from my position to serve the king."

The physician's frustration is palpable, now. "May I have a look at that letter again, please?"

The professor withdraws an envelope with a broken seal.

"And what sort of patients are you hoping to examine, Professor?"

"I am looking for one patient in particular."

"Well, as I said, I do not have anything at all to do with the administrative matters of the hospital, but I am certain that come morning, one of our takers-in can help you identify him."

"There should be no need for that," the professor says. His footsteps echo on the stone floor. "I will know him when I see him."

"I'm afraid I do not understand—"

"You don't need to understand," the professor says. "As I said, I am here at the king's directive." His pace increases as he wanders amongst the beds; the physician has to trot to match the length of his stride.

As he approaches Simon's bed, the professor's face comes into even sharper focus. It is unlined, but there is a wisdom in his eyes that betrays his apparent youth. He bends at the waist, examining Simon with interest.

"This one. Tell me about him?"

"Oh," the physician says sadly. "I'm afraid he isn't expected to last the night."

Simon's gut twists, but he cannot even cry out.

"What are his symptoms?"

"Wasting, fatigue, shortness of breath. Possible deafness, or muteness, perhaps—he does not respond to questions, in any event. We thought addressing the miasmic concerns might aid him, at first, then one of our surgeons suggested he might be in the later stages of a . . . fouler illness, though he lacks the traditional symptoms. He cannot seem to speak, or remember who or where he is. It was suggested by one of the other physicians that he be sent to the Lock Hospital, but as you can see, he would not survive the transport."

"So he is incurable, then," the professor says.

"It appears so, yes."

"Who paid his admission fees?"

The physician appears perplexed and abashed at once. "I cannot say that I know, sir—Professor."

"I do realise the inconvenience," the professor says. "But I'm afraid my own instructions require an answer to that question."

"As I said, in the morning—"

"The matter cannot wait," the professor says.

The physician's face reddens, and he looks down again at the letter the professor has given him.

"Very well," he says finally. "I shall call upon the Court of Governors at once. I do not know how long the matter will take." He turns on his heel before adding, "You may stay here with him, if you can bear the smell."

"Thank you," the professor says, offering the physician a warm smile. "Your help has been very much appreciated."

The physician leaves, muttering to himself. The professor stands tall, his hands clasped at his back, smiling at the physician until he closes the door to the ward behind him.

"Dalrymple," the professor says to no one.

For a moment, the ward is completely silent. Even the moaning has stopped. Then the door opens with a creak, and footsteps approach, quick and shuffling. A round man with a plump, reddened face appears, looking quite out of breath.

"Professor?" he asks.

The professor inclines his head at the man in the bed.

"Oh, dear," the man named Dalrymple says.

"Go on."

"His name is Simon Shaw. Old family, old money, though it is dwindling as of late. I am not sure how many pounds they have left."

"And what of his life?" the professor asks. "How much of *that* is left?"

"Twelve hours," says a third voice, a new one, resonant

and dignified. Simon cannot yet see the speaker. "Possibly eighteen."

"James," the professor says with a slight smile. "How was your trip?"

The owner of the third voice appears in Simon's field of vision, and says, "More pleasant than I expected, considering everyone I meet here assumes I am a slave."

"And have you disabused them of that notion?"

"When it suits me," James says, glancing down at Simon. "A rather unimpressive figure, if I may say so, Professor."

"For now," the professor says. "What can you do?"

James surveys the ward. Slowly, he walks away from Simon's bed and toward a different one, currently occupied by two grown men. One has bruised-looking skin, the other is sweating and shivering, twisted in his damp sheets.

"Who is this man, Dalrymple?" James asks.

"Which one?"

"The shiverer."

Dalrymple shuffles over, but recoils upon reaching the shared bed. "Oh, my, my, my. Violent temper, that one."

"His name?"

"John William," Dalrymple says.

"He is recovering," James says to the professor. "From his current outbreak."

The professor arches an eyebrow. "How much time does he have?"

"Sixteen years," James replies. "Possibly eighteen."

The professor nods once. "All right, then."

But James shakes his head.

"He has no family," Dalrymple interjects helpfully.

"And is working his way up to murder," the professor adds. "He'll spend the next sixteen years thieving, whoring, and beating others, unless . . ."

James sighs. Glances back at Simon, curled up in his bed.

"And that one?"

"He has a role to play."

"For good or ill?"

"Both, as with most men. But he cannot play it without you." The professor walks over to James, placing his hand on his shoulder. "You know I would never ask if there were any other way."

James searches the professor's eyes. "What are you asking for?"

"Time," the professor says. "As much as you can give him. For him to become who he is meant to be."

27

I AM NOT WORTHY

Simon Shaw awoke the next morning in one of the three foule wards of St. Thomas' Hospital in London to find himself with his memory, his health, and his power of speech restored.

He awoke screaming.

28

SUCH WORSHIP

North Yorkshire, England

HE DAY OF LORD SIMON'S WEDDING TO SARAH Hargrove brought with it unseasonable warmth, sunshine, and two uninvited guests.

The presence of the two men was all the more notable due to the small size of the affair. Simon's own father had died more than forty years ago, and his mother thirty. Simon himself was fifty-five years of age. The two men knew it. His bride did not.

Simon still looked like a man in his thirties—he checked, quite obsessively, every time he passed a mirror—but he didn't feel like it. His bones ached, for one thing, and he dreamt of lost teeth and hair. Any cough or sneeze plunged him into a secret terror which he would disguise as melancholy or ennui to the servants or whomever else he had to deal with. He'd taken to having portraits done of himself every time he imagined his age was beginning to catch up with him, so he could soothe his fears by comparing them. He earned a bit of a reputation for vanity as a result.

That hardly prevented him from receiving far more than the usual amount of attention a wealthy, unmarried lord of his (apparent) age could expect in London society. And he enjoyed it, perhaps too much. Simon tended to fall in and out of love (and lust) easily, and there had been a few incidents over the decades, the most serious of which involved one of his mother's lady's maids. Simon would have married her, but his mother forbade it. He received a letter six months later, informing him of his son's birth.

The letter was from the professor.

If you do not make better use of your time on Earth, you may well find yourself short of it.

Simon made arrangements to provide handsomely for the boy and his mother—he wasn't a *monster,* after all. But he burned the letter. And decided to study medicine, after that. Just in case.

Every now and again, he would receive a letter from the professor—sometimes writing as Abraham Locke, other times as Augustin Langley, and still other times as Armin

Lenaurd—curiously, the initials were always the same. The letters were always short, and always useful, if cryptic.

You might consider an appointment with—
Your presence would be most welcome at—

An appointment led to a role in the East India Company, and as such, an opportunity to reestablish his family's fortune. His presence at a ball nearly a year ago resulted in his introduction to Miss Hargrove—Sarah—whom he adored more than his own life.

But he hadn't seen the professor in person, not since the day he walked out of St. Thomas', to the astonishment of the physicians and surgeons and nurses who attended him. The professor was standing outside the gate, past the green, in front of a waiting carriage. Next to him stood the African, whose name Simon could never remember.

Simon had thought it had been a dream. A nightmare. The professor informed him of the truth, and the hair rose on the back of his neck at hearing his voice again.

"Simon Shaw," the professor said to him, "you owe James, here, your life."

Simon didn't hesitate. He bowed to James immediately. "I am forever in your debt, sir. And I will remain exceedingly grateful all my life."

The professor smiled at that. "I expect that you will. And

you can expect to hear from me again, about that debt."

Simon had got into that carriage forty-three years ago and had seen neither man since. Not until today.

The ceremony began quite ordinarily; Sarah, a vision in her white muslin dress, with tiny white flowers braided into her blond hair, seemed blissfully happy both before the wedding, and during. She beamed as the vicar opened the Book of Common Prayer and began to recite his lines.

Simon let the words drift past him as he lingered on Sarah's face. She was exquisite, but more impressively, she was *good*. A good person, modest and charitable. He knew he didn't deserve her.

"Secondly, it was ordained for a remedy against sin, and to avoid fornication—"

One of Sarah's sisters giggled and was quickly hushed by her mother.

The vicar cleared his throat. "That such persons as have not the gift of continency might marry, and keep themselves undefiled members of Christ's body.

"Thirdly, it was ordained for the mutual society, help, and comfort, that the one ought to have of the other, both in prosperity and adversity. Into which holy estate these two persons present come now to be joined. Therefore if any man can shew any just cause, why they may not lawfully be joined together, let him now speak, or else hereafter for ever hold his peace."

That was the moment, naturally, in which James and the

professor entered the chapel, one after the other.

The shock alone might've killed Simon. The heads of their dozen guests turned to the door. There were murmurs, but the vicar registered his surprise with a double blink, before gamely continuing to recite:

"I require and charge you both, as ye will answer at the dreadful day of judgement when the secrets of all hearts shall be disclosed, that if either of you know any impediment, why ye may not be lawfully joined together in Matrimony, ye do now confess it."

Simon ought to have looked at Sarah, then. That was what he wanted to do. But he glanced at the professor and James instead. Their faces remained impassive.

Only when he realised that they weren't there to stop the marriage, apparently, did he exhale and dare to look at his bride.

Ye will answer at the dreadful day of judgement when the secrets of all hearts shall be disclosed, that if either of you know any impediment, why ye may not be lawfully joined together in Matrimony, ye do now confess it.

What would she do, if he confessed the secrets of his heart? The secrets of his life? She thought him twenty years younger, and Simon had been as careful as he could to conceal his true age, but someone, someday, would surely notice, wouldn't they? What would she think then? What would she do?

The vicar was speaking to Simon directly, now. "Wilt thou have this Woman to thy wedded Wife, to live together after

God's ordinance in the holy estate of Matrimony? Wilt thou love her, comfort her, honour, and keep her in sickness and in health; and, forsaking all others, keep thee only unto her, so long as ye both shall live?"

Simon looked at Sarah, only Sarah, as he spoke the words, "I will."

It was Sarah's turn, then, and her bouquet of lilies trembled a bit as her bare shoulders shook—from nerves, or an attempt not to cry—as the vicar asked her the same question, and she gave the same answer.

"Who giveth this Woman to be married to this Man?"

Sarah's father joyfully performed his role, and Simon took the opportunity to glance, again, at James and the professor, still sitting in the back pew of the elaborate chapel.

Why were they there? What did they want?

The vicar cleared his throat, bringing Simon back into the moment. He exhaled slowly, before saying, "I, Simon Henry Shaw, take thee, Sarah Elizabeth Hargrove, to my wedded Wife, to have and to hold from this day forward—"

For how much longer, though?

"For better, for worse—"

What if they were worse?

"For richer, for poorer, in sickness and in health—"

Sickness. Simon had to force himself not to let his eyes stray from Sarah's.

"To love and to cherish, till death us do part—"

But when? When?

"According to God's holy ordinance; and thereto I plight thee my troth."

Simon was surely sweating through his waistcoat by the time he was finished. He relaxed only slightly as Sarah repeated her vows, taking his right hand with hers.

The words seemed to come so easily for her; her smile never wavered, her voice never faltered. What on God's Earth did she see in him?

The vicar took the ring from its resting place and handed it to Simon, who took Sarah's left hand in his, and placed the ring on her finger.

"With this Ring I thee wed, with my Body I thee worship, and with all my worldly Goods I thee endow: In the Name of the Father, and of the Son, and of the Holy Ghost. Amen."

"Amen," everyone said in response, as the vicar directed Simon and Sarah to kneel.

"Let us pray," he said.

Simon's relief was overwhelming. The prayers went on for years; Simon's knees ached, but surely that was normal, wasn't it? He could feel the tiled floor through his breeches.

The next words that issued from the vicar's lips recaptured his attention: "God the Father, God the Son, God the Holy Ghost, bless, preserve, and keep you; the Lord mercifully with his favour look upon you; and so fill you with all spiritual benediction and grace, that ye may so live together in this life, that in the world to come ye may have life everlasting. Amen."

Life everlasting.

James and the professor both looked the same, exactly the same, as they had decades ago, and Simon was quite sure they were not young men then, either.

What was their secret?

After the ceremony, and the prayers, and the signing of the register, congratulations were exchanged and all of the assembled guests began filing out of the chapel and back toward the manor for the wedding breakfast. All save two.

On his way out, Simon managed to manoeuvre his way toward the men.

"Congratulations," the professor said to him. "I come bearing gifts."

Simon swallowed hard. "What is it?" he asked with dread.

"Lord Simon!" Sarah's mother approached, and gave the professor and James an appraising look. "I would be so honoured if you would introduce us?"

"Certainly," Simon said, a frozen smile on his lips. "Professor, may I introduce you to Mrs. Hargrove."

Mrs. Hargrove's eyebrows arched in surprise. "Professor ..."

"Lenaurd," he lied.

"How exotic!" she said. "And is this your ..."

"This extraordinary gentleman is James," Simon added quickly, because that was the only name he'd known the man by, and such an introduction was sure to be less offensive than whatever Mrs. Hargrove was about to utter.

"Mr. James," Mrs. Hargrove said. "How is it that you've come to know our Lord Simon?"

"We are colleagues."

"Oh! You work for the Company as well?"

"Not at all," the professor said. Simon took that opportunity to add, "The East India Company brings together many distinguished gentlemen from all over the world. I am incredibly fortunate to have made the acquaintance of men of their caliber."

That seemed to satisfy Mrs. Hargrove, for the moment. "Well, I very much look forward to hearing all about your adventures abroad, Professor Lenaurd and Mr. James. I expect you'll be joining us for the breakfast?"

"Unfortunately not," the professor said. "We have some business nearby that we must attend to, but we wanted to offer our congratulations in person." The professor said to Simon, "I'm sure we'll be seeing each other again soon."

The men departed without another word, before Simon could ask them when he would be seeing them, and why, and how they looked the way they looked whilst others aged and faded and died.

He tried not to think about them as he sat next to his wife, in the home they now shared, surrounded by her family. He tried not to think about them for the rest of that day and night. He was only successful that night.

Simon awoke the following morning feeling like a new

man, truly. His worrying had been for naught. He was in perfect health. He had a beautiful new wife. He was the most fortunate man alive.

He dressed for his morning ride and had the groom lead his favourite horse from the stable, a grey mare named Shadow. The horse reared after seeing a lady's hat tossed into the wind, and she threw Simon from the saddle.

The fall broke his neck. He had eighteen minutes to live.

James and the professor arrived in five.

29

A NEW INVENTION

Before

SIMON ENCOUNTERED THE PROFESSOR TWICE more in his inordinately long life. One visit preceded a bout with tuberculosis. After the other, a carriage accident left him nearly dead.

Nearly.

The incidents themselves were always hazy, shrouded in shadows, as were his miraculous recoveries, but they left dread in their wake, and it was dread Simon felt upon seeing the professor at one of the doors to the servants' quarters at his Yorkshire estate. Dread, but not fear. The years had replaced it with anger. Envy.

"What the devil are you doing here?" Simon murmured.

"Curious choice of words."

Simon's eyes slit to half-mast.

"That's not happiness to see me," the professor said. "Won't you invite me in?"

"Come in," said Simon, holding the door open, flicking a nervous glance over his shoulder. The professor stepped inside, his shoulder-length hair in loose curls, wearing a dark suit. Just as before.

"Well, how long has it been?" the professor asked cheerily.

"You know exactly how long," said Simon, picking up the candlestick again. "You could count the days if I asked you to."

"I have counted them, Simon. The days and the years," the professor said without pause. "I'm afraid there won't be another," he added. "But you knew that already, didn't you."

Simon looked away, to the floor. His shoulders stooped. "I feel it. The time."

"Yours is coming to an end," the professor said, and a look of fear ignited Simon's eyes. He stepped back, the candlestick still in hand. He was scarcely dressed, still in his night robe, which hung loosely from his frame.

"The time you were given was temporary," the professor said, advancing. "You have lived a longer life than you were meant to."

"It's not enough," Simon muttered.

"It never is," the professor said.

Simon rounded on him, held the candles up to illuminate the professor's eerily ageless face.

"And yet here you stand."

"We're not the same," the professor said. "You know that."

"You told me—"

"I said that you had a gift, Simon. And you do—the gift of a great name. The gift of noble birth. The gift of privilege. You wield an enormous amount of influence, which I needed, and which you agreed to use in exchange for—"

"More time," Simon said, his voice hollow and desperate.

"A bargain well struck, don't you think?"

"How much do I have left?"

"No more than a year, if that."

Anger flashed on Simon's face. "*Intolerable.* My wife, my children—"

"Your wife is a young woman. You are a man with one foot in the grave, Simon."

Simon blanched. "And what are you? Not a man at all, I venture."

The professor raises his eyebrows. "I am very much a man. A different breed, though, if you will."

"Are you calling me a mongrel?"

"No, I am calling you ordinary," the professor said. "But you have lived an extraordinary life, my friend."

"Is that what I am? Your friend?"

The professor smiled.

"The man . . ." Simon's voice trailed off as he thought, searched his memory. "What was his name?" It lurked somewhere in the shadows of his mind, infuriatingly out of reach.

The professor merely arched an eyebrow at all this.

"The *African*," Simon said eagerly, hopefully, now that he remembered that detail at least. "Is he still alive?"

The professor inclined his head. "His name is James. And yes."

"That's it, then." Simon nodded to himself. "I will go to him at once, as you've come to me before. Where can I find him?"

"I'm afraid that won't be possible."

Simon set the candlestick down on a tall chest. "Why ever not?"

"Even if he were . . . available—which he isn't," the professor said, his voice clipped, "those years—*your* years—came from somewhere. Some*one*." The professor adjusted the cuffs of his suit, then looked at Simon evenly. "There must be balance, my friend. Death is inevitable, for all of us."

"Some of us earlier than others, though," Simon huffed.

The professor's expression remained placid.

Simon's temper got the better of him, finally, and he whipped around to face the professor, and his fate, with bitterness. "And what have you been doing with the gifts I've given you?"

"Making arrangements." The professor stepped farther into the hall, looking around. "The Raj will collapse," he said casually. "Most of the colonies will fall, as they should."

Simon looked stricken. "What? When?"

"Divest yourself of the East India Company," the professor said. "Reinvest in yourself."

After all the professor had him do? After all these years? "That is *madness*! Do you know the lengths I went to help—" Simon shook his head, disbelieving. "The lords would have me murdered if I withdrew my support."

"The Company's power is waning. You may yet still consolidate yours." The professor looked at Simon Shaw directly. "And in doing so, it is possible you may find the time you desire."

This stopped Simon. He went silent for a moment, before asked, "How?"

"Asking the wrong questions will yield the wrong answers," the professor said maddeningly. "You ought to be asking *where*."

"Why ask when you're about to tell me," Simon growled. "That's why you're here, in the middle of the damned night, scratching at the back door like one of the hounds, is it not?"

The professor was unfazed by the insults. He might even have expected them. "There is a child in India rumoured to have the gifts you wish to possess."

"Why not go yourself?" Simon asked, his tone wary, but keen.

"I shall join you there, after a time, but I am only one man, and I am needed elsewhere, first."

The bitterness returned. "I'm needed here, with my family."

"Your wife still has so much life ahead of her, yet."

"No."

"She can marry again."

"*No!*" He slammed his fist against the wall.

"The Company, the Crown and Empire need you."

"*Blast* them," Simon swore. "Surely you don't mean me to inform them of this *scheme*?"

"No," the professor said, unperturbed. "They are not yet prepared for this . . . development. It would put many at risk."

Simon's eyes narrow. "Many . . . of you?" The professor did not reply. "How many others are there?" Simon asked, too greedily. "What gifts do they possess?"

The professor seemed to grow taller before Simon as he spoke. "Before you withdraw your investment in the Company, you will tell the lords and officers that there has been a discovery of a most secretive nature just off the Bengali coast. You yourself will lead an expedition, so as not to diminish the royal forces."

"They will want their officers along."

"They will not have enough to spare," the professor said. "Trust me."

"Then what need is there to inform them at all?"

"If you return—"

"*If?*"

"If you return, it will be with even greater wealth. You cannot afford any accusations. Besides, your wife will worry."

"You've thought this all through, I see."

"I always do."

Simon's tired body sagged against the wood panelling on

the walls. "I *do* feel it," he whispered. "My wife insists I'm going mad, but my bones . . . they're turning to dust inside my body. My beard grows in grey."

"Is that why you've shaved?"

Simon looked away, embarrassed.

"Vanity," the professor said in a low voice. "All is vanity."

It hardly took more than a moment for Simon to recover. "It'll take months to arrange," he said, as if he'd won a small victory.

"You don't have months."

"But the winds, the weather—I doubt we'll make port before the monsoons begin."

"All the more reason to leave quickly."

The fear was back, but he couldn't show it. "This will come at great personal risk, you realise."

"I do. But think of it this way—you may die before you get there. You may die whilst you *are* there. But you will definitely die if you stay here."

A sigh escaped Simon's mouth. But something the professor had said . . . "The child has the gift?" he asked the professor with hooded eyes. "Immortality? Like you?"

The professor weighed his words. "I am not immortal. But yes. The child is like me."

"And where am I to find him?"

"You will write to me at every stage of your journey," the professor said, "and I will make arrangements for some of my trusted associates to join your expedition and track the child."

"How old is he?"

"I do not know his age, or sex."

Simon's jaw set. "Is he without a family? Am I to pry him from his mother's arms?"

"Perhaps," the professor said, his eyes flickering with amusement. "Would you find that objectionable?"

"What do you *take* me for? A monster?"

The professor lifted his brows. "Even if that child would give you the time you desire? You *and* your loved ones?"

"Even then," said Simon, but his voice betrayed him. Then, quietly, "What am I to do with him?"

"Raise him as your own."

Simon looked on, blinking in astonishment.

"The child must take your name," the professor said. "Of that, I am certain."

Simon paused at this. Considering. "My wife," he said, his voice quieter now. "I will need to prepare." Then, "You could have given me more warning," he snapped.

"If I had known, I would have."

"I thought you knew everything."

For the first time, the professor looked unsure of himself. "Not quite. Not yet."

Simon lifted his chin. "Then how are you certain of my future?"

"Men are defined as often by what they are not as by what they are. It is what we don't have that drives us," the professor said. "Learn what a person wants, and you can map his future."

Part V

After
North Yorkshire, England

Face the facts of being what you are, for that
is what changes what you are.

—Søren Kierkegaard

LURED BACK

I'M JOLTED AWAKE BY AN ACRID SMELL AND SEARING light.

"Sir? Sir!"

An older, anxious-looking stranger hovers above me, kneeling. My palms are on the floor, and I try to raise myself up but the world tilts beneath me.

"What the fuck just happened?"

"What the devil are you doing here?" the stranger, now identifiable as a guard, asks. The words spark something in my mind—a memory. Simon. The professor. I struggle to hold on to it when the man asks, "Been here all night?"

I crane my neck to the side and see Goose, also sprawled

on the floor of the bedchamber in the servants' quarters, looking equally dazed. The ochre velvet drapes, the window looking out onto the ruins, the inlaid floor—all gone.

"I'm Noah Shaw," I say slowly. "Lady Sylvia's grandson."

"I thought I recognised you," the guard says.

"Recognised me?"

"From your portrait."

"What portrait," I say slowly.

"Went to a piss-up last night, did you?" he says, rising to his feet. "Came here for a giggle, passed out?"

I swallow, my mouth sour and stale. "Something like that."

The guard sighs. "Chundered anywhere, have you?"

Goose sits up, holding his head as if it's made of glass. "No, sir. We're professionals."

The guard offers a hand to me. "Right, then. Up you go."

I stagger to my feet. "Christ."

Goose is next. "Hell."

"You'll want to be hydrating. Get some protein into you."

"Mmm," I say, noncommittally. "Can you tell us how to get back to—" I look around, trying to remember what happened before—

Before.

"The book," I mutter, scanning the floor. We're in the room where we first found it, aren't we? Did I drop it whilst exploring?

"What's that?" the guard asks.

"Nothing," I insist. "We got turned around a bit."

"No worries, I'll get you back to the East Wing."

"Thank you."

We follow him; the trip is mercifully uneventful but unfortunately lengthy. The light outside is dawn-dim—daylight hasn't broken, yet, but it will soon, bringing tourists with it.

"All I want is a room somewhere," Goose sings quietly.

I laugh, despite everything. The guard shakes his head. *Kids these days, amirite?*

After a century, he finally deposits us at the residence and leaves us with more well-meaning hangover advice in a modernly appointed, comfortable living room. Once Goose and I are alone, though, it's massively, brutally awkward.

"What did you see?" I ask him first.

He shakes his head. "I don't even know—"

"You do," I say, with a fervour that surprises me. "Tell me."

After a pause, he says, "A fucking ghost." He stares at a fixed point on the wall. "A bloody fucking ghost is what I saw."

"You didn't take anything? What M gave us?"

"No."

"You're sure."

"Yes."

That's what I've been relying on, I realise—that we were both high out of our fucking minds.

I grasp at that crumbling explanation anyway. "Maybe—"

Goose shakes his head, stricken. "Don't try coming up with an explanation. There isn't one."

"Maybe M slipped you something at the pub?" I ask, still reaching. In the scotch, maybe. Why not?

His eyes narrow, still staring straight ahead. "Who cares. We still saw what we saw."

He's not wrong. I felt exhausted when the guard left us, collapsing onto a velvety grey sofa like a discarded doll, but now the aftereffect of whatever's been marauding through my system is pinching my consciousness, keeping me awake and wired.

"He was your cousin," says Goose, with a faraway voice to match his faraway look. "What was his name, again?"

"Sam," I say quietly. "Sam Milnes."

"Bad end for Sam," he mumbles, scraping his fingers over his pale stubble.

"He's the one who hanged himself here," I say. "Day of my father's funeral."

"You saw it?"

I nod, head aching with every movement.

"With your ability, I mean?"

"Yes."

Goose's eyes meet mine. "So he was Gifted too, then, right? Isn't that how it works?"

That's how it used to work. "He must've been."

"What was his ability, you think?"

I haven't thought about it. I've *avoided* thinking about it. Even now, when I remember him—especially now—it's mostly horror I feel, and cold. How his fingers were blue when we found him—me and Mara, together.

And how quiet it was near him. A black hole of sound that not even Mara's heartbeat penetrated.

Then I left her to retrace his steps. To follow him, out onto the ledge.

It was Mara's voice that brought me back.

"I don't know," is all I say to Goose, swerving from that train of thought. "It didn't seem . . . relevant . . . at the time."

Goose looks over from his perch, strung up and tense, sitting cross-legged in an oversized ivory armchair. "Maybe it's relevant now. Maybe it's why he ended up dead."

I shrug, disengaging from the question, the memory.

Goose doesn't seem to need my encouragement, though. "There are only three reasons ghosts are barred from the afterlife," he says, ticking them off with his fingers. "One, they've got unfinished business. Two, they need to be avenged before they can move on. Or three: They're pure fucking evil."

"I'm tempted to ask why you know so much about this . . ."

"I'm entitled to my phobias, all right? And I don't want to end up like him."

He's shaken, more than I've ever seen him. "That doesn't seem likely," I say. Reassuringly, I hope.

He presses the heels of his palms into his eyes. "Look, mate, I appreciate the effort, and I know you've seen more shit than I have, but let's be honest—you're as bloody lost as I am here."

"Fair. Though I will say, of all the people I've seen who've died, he's the only one I've ever seen . . . like that."

"The only ghost, you mean."

Or shared hallucination. Or induced dissociative episode. I was prepared to expect Simon. But not Sam. "Right," is all I say.

Goose sits up straight, gripping the armrests with both hands. "What if that was *his* ability?"

". . . Being a ghost?" I ask, despite myself.

"No, idiot, when he was alive. Like, mine is amplification, supposedly, yes? What if his was something broad, like . . . communication? And being around me let him communicate with *us*, the living?"

The idea is . . . a lot. But then, so is everything else.

There's one thing, though, that I can't seem to get around. "Our Gifts are gone, though." Or had I heard his heartbeat, before? I can't be sure. I can't trust it.

Goose shakes his head. "You heard M, that could've been temporary. We might've cut ourselves off from it, she said. Maybe Sam unlocked them for us."

I consider it. I listen.

No sound. Nothing. I can't hear Goose's heart beat, or his pulse race, or his lungs expand and contract. There's only us, talking.

Still, I glance at my hand. I've gotten used to the throbbing, the omnipresent ache of tiny fractures knitting together wrongly. I open it, spreading my fingers. The pain is white and searing.

I close my fist quickly.

"Why not?" Goose asks. "Will and intent, the key to everything, she said."

She did.

"Well, I want it," Goose says. "I'm not avoiding it."

Not like me, he doesn't need to say.

Instead, I ask, "So that's what we're going with, then?" to be sporting. "You're a medium?"

Goose shakes his head vigorously. "Total fucking nightmare. Like literally, my fucking nightmare."

I raise my hands in defence. "It's *your* theory, mate. I was going to suggest you and I might be secret cousins also, given the genetic memory factor."

Goose leans back, tilting his head up to stare at the chandelier hanging above us. "I mean, everyone in England is possibly secretly related to each other, so, sure, I suppose."

"I only thought it might be *slightly* more consistent, considering the Simon and professor bits."

Goose cocks his head to the side. "Simon and professor bits?"

"The hospital? His wedding?"

Goose scrunches his brow. "Whose wedding? What?"

"That was Lord Simon we saw," I say. "Just after the book, the Bible with my family tree fell, and the branches started growing, off the page onto—"

"Yeah, *that* I saw. The names in the floor, and Sam hanging—God. *Fuck.*" He recovers himself. "Wait, so, you saw something else after that?"

I nod. And then I describe it to him, my throat going dry as I do; the old parts of the manor, overgrown and dusty and rotting, then the room glowing with light and life for just long enough to illuminate the door, at first, and then—

M's words echo in my skull.

You've locked away memories that might hurt you. Somewhere in your mind is the key.

I shake my head to rid it of M's voice. "The professor fancies himself an . . . architect, was his word, at one point," I say. "A chess master, basically. I think he can see the outcomes of certain events, but claims he himself can't do anything to affect them. So he manipulates others into doing it." Goose was gone when M talked about my parents. I can't remember if I ever explained that bit to him before. "He manipulated my mother into marrying my father," I say bitterly.

"Why?"

"So I would be born."

Goose shudders. "Vile."

"Yes."

"And it was your great-great-grandfather with him?" He looks around, as if Simon might be standing over his shoulder.

I nod again. "In one of the—"

Memories, a voice whispers in my mind. Mara's voice, again. My Mara.

"Visions," I finally say, ignoring her.

"So it worked," Goose says. "What M told you to do. You did it."

I saw how Simon learned of M. And saw that the professor found him, not the other way around.

But the professor had sent *Simon* to India, after M. He'd told M the opposite. Why?

And how was it, if Simon wasn't Gifted, as the professor said, that I could see his memories at all?

And what did Sam have to do with it? Why did he appear to us—both of us—at all?

"Simon said that someone, a man, gave him . . . more time. More life." I try to find the words to explain what I saw—

Remembered.

I bat the word away. "I didn't just see them in the manor, though. I saw Simon wake up in a hospital with no memory of how he got there, and heard the physician say that he wouldn't last the night. Then, someone else came in and . . ." The details are fading with every word I speak, mercifully. I can't remember the man's name. "The point is, if there's someone out there who can extend the years of someone's life, that means . . . they or someone else would have the ability to cut them short," I finish.

Goose clears his throat.

"What?"

"I mean, I hate to state the obvious . . ."

I raise my brows.

"Isn't that what Mara can do?"

I shake my head immediately, and not just because I don't want to talk about her. Or think about her. "No. Her ability—it's not what I saw."

Goose looks pointedly away.

"Honestly. Mara's *my* opposite." Healer, destroyer. Hero, Shadow. "The man I saw wasn't giving life or ending it, he was . . . exchanging it? Transferring it?"

"Well, if every action has an equal and opposite, et cetera . . ."

"Exactly. That might be why the feather and the sword are the professor's symbols . . ."

Goose cocks his head. "What, like Leo's tattoo?"

I nod. "And the pendant," I say, reaching for it. My thumb brushes the rough grooves in the design. "We looked it up, once, what they meant."

My heart races as I remember—

Can I see yours? she asked months ago, in a different house in a different country, in what might as well have been a different era.

As if I could've said no to her, then. I slipped the black cord I used to keep it on over my head, and placed it in her small, warm hand.

"Egyptian goddess, Ma'at, wore the feather of truth in early paintings," Goose says, bringing me back to now, to here. He mistakes my look of surprise. "It was an A-levels question."

I nod, as if that's why I know about it. "Weighed a man's heart against it—if his sins were heavier, he'd be eaten by a beastie."

Goose strokes his chin. "Then what's the sword for?"

"Think she held a sceptre, not a sword, in the original. Sword's the modern interpretation—justice is swift and fierce. Or something," I say, hoping we can move on now, back to A-levels and England and away from Miami and Mara.

Goose leans forward, stretching his legs out, elbows on knees. "But then there was what your dad was doing, right? That doctor he had working for him, using you all—"

Using *us*. The ivory walls of the living room bleach out into white, and instead of windows looking out onto gardens I'm in Horizons again, looking at Mara through glass, at her face when Kells told her I'd died. I remember the way she sounded there, her hollow voice and empty eyes, and what I did and said to her to stop it—

Get out. Kill them all.

Kells used us, and I used Mara.

She was drugged. Compromised. More vulnerable than I was, and I used her. She woke up alone, in Horizons, had been told I was dead, and then did what I told her to do to get herself and Jamie and Stella out. She killed them all, and then I threw her away.

"Mate? All right?"

Clearly not. I run my hands through my hair, gripping it too hard just to feel something else. "Bit fucked up, is all."

"We ought to sleep, probably," Goose says, though his eyes are wide, and his face is still ashen.

Part of me wants to agree. But the other part is afraid to close my eyes. I don't know where I'll be when I wake up.

31

REMNANT OF THE PAST

E COMPROMISE. INSTEAD OF BED, WE head to the kitchen. We cajole the staff into allowing Goose to cook, and though they protest at a bit, at first, it's mostly for show. They seem glad to have the morning off, as there's no one but us in the residence anyway.

Goose is taking the security guard's advice to heart and is assembling omelettes for us.

"So," he says, surveying his ingredients. "The professor. His symbols. Feather, sword, opposites." He moves a few jars of spices into a cluster. "Then we've got your father, and that doctor."

He's determined to work this out, to fit it all together, bless him. "The professor talked about needing balance in the force, or something. And on that Horizons list, they differentiated between ones they labelled 'originals' and the 'induced,' according to a protocol developed by the professor, as it happens, under an alias, of course."

"Wait, induced? Like, synthetically?"

"Not *like*. *Exactly*."

"Copies," Goose says quietly. "Your friend Stella said that, before . . ."

Before.

I open the refrigerator, hoping there's a way to assemble Bloody Mary ingredients, because this conversation requires more alcohol.

"So we've got the originals," Goose says, holding up a raw onion, and placing it on the counter. "And then the copies, basically, that your dad made." He prods the withered, caramelising version in the sauté pan.

"Right. Here's what I haven't twigged yet, though. My father *loathed* my . . . Affliction, or whatever, so why would he want to re-create it in anyone else?"

Goose shrugs. "Lots of reasons. Seems profitable, for one."

Goose wasn't there for the part when my father seemed completely fine with me holding a gun to my head, ready to pull the trigger.

"*Do it then, if you're that selfish,*" my father said.

"*If I am, it's because you made me that way,*" I said back.

"*Spoken like a true spoiled brat . . . I thought you were ready to be the man your mother hoped you would be, but I see you're just a child, who would burn all his gifts because he can't have the one he wants.*"

I can't say it. I wish I'd never heard it. "Not that he's above authorising human testing," I say. "But something doesn't fit, yet."

Goose twists around. "Not just authorising human testing. Authorising testing *on his own child.*"

The words sharpen the memories I've been desperate to forget.

"*Deborah had theories about how to find others like you, and theories about how to cure them, but nothing promised to help you, until she found your Mara. Mara ended up teaching me as much about you as you did about her. More perhaps. I had no idea how your ability worked. How you heard things, what you saw. But it was hubris,*" my father said. "*If there is a way to arrest the anomaly, we haven't found it. You might be the key to it, Noah, but we'll never know as long as she's alive. And you can't stay away from her, and she can't help what she is.*"

She can't help what she is, he said. Was he right?

If he was, after all, then I helped make her what she is.

Get out. Kill them all.

I have stayed away from her, though, at least. My father was wrong about that.

When I find my voice, it's hoarse. "My father wouldn't have been above trying to replicate the thing he'd eventually be trying to eradicate," I say slowly, hoping that's enough of an explanation for Goose without having to recount the rest of it.

It seems to work. "Remember what I said, about unfinished business?" He doesn't wait for me to answer. "Sam killed himself here, at your father's house, on the day of your father's funeral. He's your cousin, we now know, but maybe your father did something to him, too?"

His company's been conducting research that probably spawned a clutch of Carriers all over the world.

Maybe my father got started somewhere closer to home.

As the onions sizzle, Goose says, "Maybe it's the copies who are dying, like Stella said, and the fact that Sam happens to be your cousin's just a red herring."

There've been plenty of those. "A possibility," I say.

"What did it say next to Stella, on that list?"

I try to remember. I try not to remember. "'Suspected original,' I think."

"Suspected isn't confirmed, though, is it."

"No, it isn't." He sighs. "If only my name were on a list somewhere," he mumbles tiredly. "I'd like to know if I'm going to vanish one day and reappear in your cellar, haunting your family manor."

"Mate," I start.

"No, no, it's fine, don't worry about *me*," he says. "In some ways, you and Mara are awfully bloody lucky, you do know that, right?"

I nearly laugh, but there's bile in my throat. "Kind of playing it fast and loose with the word 'lucky,' aren't we?"

"Least you don't have to worry about possibly being on a hit list, somewhere. Don't get me wrong, your whole *situation* isn't exactly enviable, but at the very least, you're as original as it gets."

I'm about to retort, but the words catch in my throat as an idea shakes itself free.

"I'm not, though, am I?" Not the first in my family bloodline with an ability. "There was my mother, and Simon." He may not have had the same sort of Gift, but he had a role to play, the professor said. M knew them all. "What's M's role?" I ask aloud.

Goose is slicing mushrooms when he says, "She wants to know where she came from. Her own history. Isn't that what she said?"

"She did," I say, thinking. "She also said my family owes her a debt." The professor and James mentioned a debt, but that's all I seem to remember about it. "And when she first appeared, she said Mara's life was in danger. Told me I needed to remember Simon in order to save her." *Slay the dragon, save your girl.* "From the professor, I assume she meant. And then when I told her Mara didn't need saving, she said she could help me get my abilities back."

"Hmm."

And when that didn't work—

I'll keep Alastair in my thoughts.

I'd nearly forgotten that, in the midst of everything else. I glance at Goose, uneasy. Have I told him what M said, already? Should I tell him now?

"She's the reason I went to the hospital to find you," I say. "She cycled through all of her reasons for needing me to be here, in England, at the manor, one after the other. None of them worked. And then she said she'd keep you in her thoughts." Which brought me to the hospital, where the car was waiting for us.

Goose looks up. "You think she lied?"

"I'm sure of it," I say. "Less certain about *what.* But I'm not convinced we know what she's after, yet."

"Learn what a person wants, and you can map his future."

The professor spoke those words to Simon, words I hadn't remembered until tonight, until—

Until Sam opened the door.

"Who benefits from Sam's death?" I ask. "And the seemingly random suicides of a handful of interconnected teenaged strangers."

"Maybe no one," Goose says, cracking an egg into a bowl and scrambling it. "Maybe it's just something that happens to the copies."

I've heard that—or something like that, when Daniel told

me about his original trip to the archives. Kells's experiments on baby twins, with Jude and Claire being the only survivors. She'd been trying to induce abilities in them but they all died anyway, eventually.

Goose rolls his shoulders. "But I can see you don't find that satisfying, so."

"Because it's not a handful, is it. The professor said there needed to be balance, but—"

"*Partly, your father is to blame,*" M said.

"My father fucked with the balance, and now there are more of us than there should be."

"Should be?"

"More than there's *supposed* to be. If *more* of us keep cropping up? Eventually the world will be overrun."

"A Marvel scenario, definitely," Goose says, lacing his fingers and stretching overhead.

"Which the originals wouldn't want," I go on, ignoring him. What did M say? She doesn't hide. She *moves*. "If you've been around for centuries, then you need secrecy to survive."

"You think the originals are destroying the copies?"

I sit still, thinking. "Could be." Everyone wanted to find us, at one point. There was Kells, of course, rounding us up in Florida on my father's behalf. But also, didn't Leo and Sophie claim to be searching for others in solidarity, or whatever? They even made that map at that safe house of theirs, leading anyone who saw it to everyone on it.

The map. Sophie. A memory scratches at the door of my consciousness, asking to be let in.

"*Imagine all of us walking around with a candle,*" she said at that disastrous dinner party Goose threw back in Brooklyn.

"*And then the light snuffs out. It just started . . . happening. People going missing. So we started tracking it. . . . People came and went from the brownstone—but pretty much whoever came to the safe house would stay when they got there. Everyone told us where they were from, what they could do—we started piecing together whatever we could. When Felicity and the others went missing, they fell off the map. Literally. There's nothing I can do.*"

And then Sophie said, "*We can't do this by ourselves. We all have to work together—*"

I hear Mara's voice in my mind again.

"*But you're the hunter,*" she said to Sophie.

When I stepped into M's car, I'd scarcely given a second's thought to Leo and Sophie and whatever the fuck they might be doing now. I haven't thought about suicide, much, either. Mine or anyone else's.

Have I stopped caring about them because I stopped feeling them?

Appalling, if true. The rising tide of shame tells me it is.

I'm tempted to ignore it, but watching Goose putter around in the kitchen . . .

Least you don't have to worry about possibly being on a hit list, somewhere.

A hit list. When I first saw the map hanging at Sophie and Leo's place in Brooklyn, the map they'd made, knitting connections among Gifted they'd come across, it seemed supremely stupid. What if someone had found it, used it to find others, not to help them but to—

Hunt them.

And when I asked Sophie who first fell off her map, she said—

Sam. *"I think Sam was the first."*

A cold finger trails the nape of my neck.

She didn't know him, she insisted. I rifle through my memories, searching for her words—

"A friend of Leo's, her name's Eva—he was her friend. I never actually met him, and he died in England. You were there. With Goose."

"I think I have an idea," I say, as Goose folds the other ingredients into the eggs. "Someone who knew Sam. Who might not live far away."

"Go on."

"Sophie and Leo made that map, marking up places the other Gifted had cropped up, and where they came from."

"Oh, right." He dusts his hands off on his jeans. "Took up most of the wall in that shabby room."

"Jamie and Mara took pictures of it. Mara sent them to me, hundreds," I say, and as I speak I realise with growing horror what we're about to have to do.

Goose's eyes widen encouragingly. "Even if your mobile isn't here, your pictures would sync to the cloud, wouldn't they? Surely *someone's* got a tablet or a laptop here."

I try to walk it back. "Even if not, Sam Milnes—remember that grave, in Whitby?" Allegra Milnes, was the name on it. "It can't be that hard to find someone who knows him." Or knows *of* him. Like that man, Bernard.

A door's thrown open in my mind, illuminating the memory that has hidden itself from me. I glimpse Mara below stairs, black-frocked, and bright-eyed. I hear her voice in a breathless gush:

"I started going on about how upset I am about your father, and what happened at the funeral, and then I go shivery and whisper, Sixth Sense *style, that I saw the whole thing. He licked up everything I offered him, and then begins telling me, 'in strictest confidence,' how 'The boy is the great-great-grandchild of a house maid that served your great-great-grandfather.' There are pictures of him somewhere, a portrait in the house. There's all of this stuff that goes back centuries, he said. Your family kept everything."*

"Did he happen to add anything helpful, like, for example, where?" I asked.

"Yeah, no. He talked about servant records and family trees and shit being here, in the house, but where *here, he didn't know. But he did give me a name."*

"Need I ask?"

"Sam Milnes. Familiar?"

I said no.

"He's apparently also the great-great-grandson of the old groundskeeper, but his G3 was fired as soon as they discovered the lady's maid was pregnant, and moved south to do something else, I don't remember, and Sam's dad is a chef at a pub about an hour away from here. Not at the funeral."

"His father wasn't? Mother?" I asked.

"Nope. No one in his family. I asked specifically."

"Bad blood?" I wondered.

"Bernard mentioned something about a rumour that he wasn't the groundskeeper's kid, that someone in the family knocked her up, then sent both of them packing to hide it." She shrugs one shoulder. *"Or some other shit happened so long ago that no one cares about it anymore."*

I relate all of this to Goose, rather desperately, as he chops up some chives and sprinkles them on our omelettes, which I've no appetite for any longer. "So, we could log in to literally any computer anywhere and access your pictures which contain biographical and possibly geographical information to find the person who knew the living version of a ghost we've seen who has unfinished business with us," Goose says, placing one plate on the marble counter. "Or we can go back to Whitby, look up the name of the woman whose grave you punched, who's been dead for so long we'd have to use microfiche in an ancient library somewhere to see if any news articles come up about her and your family, and track down Sam's father in whatever pub he's working in, and work backward from there? Those are our choices?"

Fuck. *Fuck.*

Goose blinks silently.

"Fine," I say miserably. "If our shit's not here yet, we'll ask Kate for her laptop instead."

As it happens, our shit *is* here, much to my surprise. I didn't have my own room in the manor—I hadn't spent enough time here to claim one—but upon reencountering Mrs. McAdams, Goose has the presence of mind to ask her about our things, and she shows us to one of the guest rooms with several boxes and trunks I recognise. Painfully.

"They arrived the other day," she says cheerfully. Victoria Gao kept her promise.

I survey the mess. My mobile must be somewhere, in it. I'm far too much of a coward to look.

If I find it, I'll know whether Mara's texted or hasn't. Emailed or hasn't. Whether there's been silence for the last several days or weeks or lifetimes since I read her words and heard her voice. I've crossed an ocean to get away but she's taken up residence in my head.

Goose recognises his own bag right away, though, and upon noticing my apparent paralysis, asks me for my username and password.

"I won't linger anywhere I shouldn't," he says in response to my obvious wretchedness.

I tell him, and he does not give me shit about it, for which I am forever in his debt.

Can't bear to watch him scroll through pictures, though. Can't even look in his direction.

"Found the map," Goose says.

I exhale the breath I've been holding for a year. "I think we're looking for an Eva."

"That makes it easy."

"Well, start in England."

"Thanks for that most obvious advice."

I finally muster the strength to stop being a pussy and turn to watch him. His eyebrows are scrunched up. "There aren't many Gifted in the UK, it seems."

"Or not many who crossed Leo and Sophie's path in Brooklyn, anyway."

"Point," he says. Then his eyes narrow. "There's a Ceridwen Evangeline in Cardiff."

"Evangeline, Eva—close enough?"

"Close enough for me," Goose says. "No offence, but I'm ready to get out of this fucking house."

"So soon?"

Goose returns a flat stare.

"So, off to Wales, then?" I say.

Goose shakes his head. "No, she'd be my year, or a year ahead. On gap or at uni." He turns back to his phone. "Shame, I suppose we'll have to creep her social media."

"Shame, indeed."

It takes Goose less than a minute before he finds her. "Pack your things, friend. We're off to Cambridge."

Fancy that.

32

UNFATHOMABLE BEING

"THIS IS WHAT YOU'RE MISSING," I SAY TO Goose, as the bus from the train station drops us on King's Parade, which seems to be swarming with an alarming number of swotty-looking freshers.

"Not missing," he says peevishly. "Not technically, not yet. They've just come from their gap yahs promoting literacy in the third world—"

"Or, alternately," I say, "experiencing a spiritual awakening in—"

"Machu Picchu," Goose picks up.

"After a stint working a bar in Australia and joining their mates in—"

"Thailand," he cuts in. "For a Full Moon Party."

"Which they can't remember because of the hallucinogens they tried in Cambodia—"

"There was a lot of *banter*, though—"

"And made for the best Insta-story *ever*."

Goose laughs, then tips his head at one of the younger-looking boys with an overloaded rucksack. "Do him."

"Firsts in all A-levels at . . . Harrow," I start. "He'll spend Freshers Week reinventing himself, buying decks off a second-year and discovering a love of house music. Easy." I scan the hordes before spotting a laughing brunette holding court in a squad of other girls. "Her?"

"Looks like she says the word 'yay' a lot and is *so* there for her friends."

"Savage." I narrow my eyes, before landing on a target. "That one's going to vlog his drunken exploits manning a trolley on Caesarian Sunday."

Whilst we're snarking, neither of us notices the boy who walks up to us until he's already slipped envelopes into our hands.

"Think we've been mistaken for gownies?" Goose says.

I hold up the envelope, my full name in printed script. Goose's matches.

"Life comes at you fast," I say.

We open them at once.

King's Library

Midnight

I flip mine over. "That's all there is."

Goose nods in agreement.

"Thoughts?" I ask, already suspicious.

"Could be from a Westminster bloke who recognised us?" Goose asks. "Freshers Week, there'll be soc initiations, formal hall . . ."

"How charmingly naïve," I say with a sigh. "More likely, someone knows we're coming. M did suggest we come up, after all."

Goose examines the invitations. "She's never bothered with formality before."

"True," I admit. "Might be the person we've come to look for knows we're here, looking?"

"How?" Goose asks, then answers himself. "Right. Superpowers. I forgot."

"The professor has a habit of knowing where and when to appear to maximise his fuckery."

"This is the chap who knows the future, yes? Of the world. And human history. And he's decided to spend his time printing invitations for us?" Goose asks witheringly.

It does sound stupid, out loud. And yet.

Goose inspects the college gates. "Colleges'll be locked tonight. Especially King's—I've heard the porters are terribly strict, because of the tourists."

I examine the gate more closely, and the green beyond it. None of it's accessible to the public.

"We'll have to apply our considerable charm. Might do to stop and shop for formal dress?" Goose says, eyeing a store across the street. A mannequin dressed in white tie stands guard in the window.

"Why would we?"

He holds up the invitation. "These are posh. They're *engraved*, even. Wouldn't want to look out of place, would we?"

"We don't even know what it's for," I say, rather vexed.

"A party? Or a soc? Or hall?" Upon registering my expression he gives an exaggerated sigh. "Or it's a trap and we're being invited to our own beheading." He turns over the invites again. "Quite elegantly, I must say."

I rake my fingers through my hair, wound up.

Goose *met* M. Heard *everything* I told him. Saw what Stella did to herself on the bridge and heard about the others.

But that's the problem, isn't it—he's only *heard* most of what has happened to us, Sam's ghost aside. He met M, was entranced by her, but did he believe what she told him, truly? She was interesting, no question, and she told a good story.

Goose does love a good story. Always up for an adventure.

That's what this is, mostly, for him. A story he's caught up in. Nothing gained, nothing lost. Not yet.

I can't exactly blame him. I *was* him, once.

When Mara first told me about herself, I believed her because *I'd* heard her myself. Heard her voice in my mind, anguished and angry, trapped beneath the asylum she'd brought down with her thoughts:

Get them out.

But when she confessed the rest of it? Her certainty that she'd hurt me, that *she* was my weakness? I dismissed it. She'd been in my bed, in my arms, vulnerable and exposed. On her birthday, she said she'd kissed me and I denied it. She said she'd hurt me, and I told her she was dreaming—

"All right," I say to Goose in a rush. If I think about her that way, that night—abandon all hope, ye who enter there. If I remember that dream, I will never want to wake up. "Let's go."

Two hours and two thousand pounds later, it's late afternoon and we've got hours to kill yet, and now also bags to carry and nowhere to put them.

"Know anyone from Westminster we can crash with?" I ask Goose.

He nods. "Not sure where they're staying, though—but it's Freshers Week. We could just, you know, go along?"

"Meaning?"

"Find a gullible-looking fresher, lie about not having got our IDs yet?"

"And then ask for . . . who was it that you know who goes here?"

"Nate Hollis's here, I think."

I shake my head. "Oxford, I thought."

"Shit, you're right. Spencer, though!"

I scarcely remember him, but what I do remember . . . isn't flattering. "That twat? Managed Oxbridge?"

"Father's a big Tory donor, I think."

"What year was he, when I left?"

"Sixth form, so, he'd be a fresher then."

I sigh. "We don't even know what college he's in, do we?"

Goose shakes his head.

"Why don't you have more friends?" I whinge, before saying, "Fine. All right, I'm starving—let's forage. We'll sort it out then."

We scan the cobblestone streets in search of something promising and simple. The streets are all ancient and tangled, and what storefronts there are, off the main drag of King's Parade, are so inconspicuous it's as if they're trying to hide.

After walking for ten years, we finally happen upon a green façade and a sign that says GREEK RESTAURANT—more importantly, unlike the other restaurants we've spotted, it's thoroughly swarming with students. More likely to find an easy mark, here.

Walking in, we order on the first floor, fighting for space with all of the people crammed together, waiting for a table or even a chair.

"In hindsight," Goose says, looking forlornly at our shopping bags.

"Yeah. Stupid."

"You pups lost?" a girl says to us, her face half hidden by dark blond hair. "You look rather desperate."

"Oh, we are," I say. "Definitely."

She pulls a sad face. "Mummy and Daddy haven't come along to see you off?"

"I'm an orphan," I reply gravely. Goose covers his mouth to hide his grin.

The girl looks appropriately abashed. "I'm *so* sorry, that was shit."

A guy comes up beside her, holding a steaming something wrapped in foil. "Always putting your foot in it, Audrey."

"I really am sorry," she says, before turning around.

"Wait," I say. "Apology accepted, if you help us."

She lifts her eyebrows. "Help you . . . ?"

"We're looking for our mate . . ." Goose begins, and I know he's debating which name to ask for. Which name would she use here herself? "Ceridwen," he goes with. Most distinctive.

She shakes her head. "Don't know her, sorry."

The guy squints. "Wait, Ceridwen Rees? At Emma?"

Emma? Goose and I exchange a look. "Yes," he says.

The girl with him—Audrey, I suppose—narrows her eyes. "How do *you* know a Ceridwen?"

"Met at a swap last year," he says casually. "When I had time for those sorts of things."

I've been in America too long, and out of Westminster for longer. I try not to look utterly lost.

"Know where we can find her?" Goose asks.

"What would she be wanting with you lot, I wonder."

"I'm her cousin," I say.

"He's an orphan," Audrey repeats.

"Heard that bit, yeah. Don't know what to tell you—you've texted already, I'm sure?"

I nod. "No response, and we've got all this shit . . ."

"Right," he says. "Well, you're ours for the day, I suppose." He extends his hand. "Kai Singh, Tit Hall."

Audrey extends her hand as well. "Audrey Burrow, Jesus."

"Noah Shaw," I say.

"Goose Greaves," he says.

They look on expectantly.

"Colleges?" Audrey prompts.

"King's," I say, because my mother went there, and it's all I can think of.

"Pembroke," Goose says.

"You shouldn't have any trouble getting into Pembroke—porters'll let you in with your email."

"Right," I say slowly as I invent a lie. "Thing is, all our luggage was lost on the flight. Haven't had a chance to replace it." Goose begins shifting the shopping bags to hide the gym bag he brought.

"Flight?" Kai asks dubiously.

"From New York," I say, preparing to lay it on very, very thick. "My father's funeral," I add solemnly.

They both look squirmingly uncomfortable. Kai tries to recover by saying, "I've got a mate at Emma who can get you in. He might know her—they've got a *splendid* bar."

Emma . . . *Emmanuel*. And Tit Hall must be Trinity Hall. In another world, if I were another person, this could be my life.

"Expensive but splendid," Audrey chimes in. "What's all that?" she says, glancing at the bags as our order's called out. There are so many students they take turns passing our food to me through the crowd.

Goose looks at them, then at Audrey. "Clothes?"

Audrey narrows her eyes. "You aren't prepared at all, are you. Where'd you go to school?"

"Westminster," we both say.

"How posh," she says mockingly. "And no one told you anything?"

"I've been . . . preoccupied," I say. "But we'd be *so* grateful for your help."

She looks at Kai, who smiles. "Of course, mate. Follow us."

33

WITH PRINCIPLES

THEY OFFER TO HELP CARRY OUR SHOPPING bags to Emma and we eat as we walk, hand-waving our reasons for not going straight to our colleges to drop everything off. Kai's texted his mate, Jack, who's waiting for us at the student gate.

"Aren't you a sorry bunch," he says, opening it for us.

"Now, now, Jack," says Kai, "the children are our *future*."

"How unlucky," he says. "'Less either of you is a rower?"

Goose chimes in happily. "I am."

Jack pats his shoulder approvingly. "What school did you go to?"

"Westminster."

"Could be worse." He shrugs. "You any good?"

"Not too shabby."

"We'll forgive the fact that you're a public school twat, then. You?" Jack asks, as he signs us in with the porters.

"Not a rower, alas," I say.

"He's a communist," Audrey says.

"Oh, *King's*? Dreadful. Do not, under any circumstances, join one of the political parties."

"It's a sign you aren't being invited to *real* parties," Audrey adds.

"All right, mate," Kai says. "Enough shit chat. You know where Ceridwen is?"

"Have you texted her?" Jack asks unhelpfully.

"No answer," I say.

"I can bring you by her room—her flatmate could let you in, if either of them is there. If *neither* of them is, you can come round to mine."

"Thanks," Goose and I say together.

We pass the wide, emerald-green Front Court, which is completely empty. The clock tower looms over us, and the windows in its dome are dark. I feel watched as we walk beneath it.

A mad thought. "Where is everyone?" I ask.

"What do you mean?" Jack asks.

"Seems rather . . . uninhabited?"

Kai and Audrey laugh. "You can't walk on the grass, and

everyone's squirrelled away at Gardies and the bars hiding from freshers."

"That's where we found these two," Audrey says.

"What, Gardies? Maybe you're not so hopeless after all," Jack says appraisingly.

"It's the only place open after ten," Kai explains.

I blink. "You're not serious?"

Audrey laughs. "Your college bar's where you'll spend most of your time."

"Or Cindies. On Tuesdays and Wednesdays, at least."

I raise my eyebrows.

"A club. Has a different name now—"

"Since the nineties, basically."

"But everyone still calls it Cindies. Everyone who goes is charmingly naff, though."

"If you're a hipster and can afford it, there's Fez on Thursdays—"

"And Life, which, if you can overcome the stench of Jaeger and vomit—"

"Wait, wait," Goose says, holding up a hand. "You're saying the only place to go out after ten here is a Greek takeaway, or a club?"

"There are five," says Jack.

"Clubs, that is," Kai says.

"And, yes," finishes Audrey. "Look, this isn't—where did you just come from?" she asks me.

"Brooklyn." Sort of.

"Right. This isn't Brooklyn. We make our own fun."

"Everyone basically stays at their colleges, except for swaps," Jack says.

"And bops."

She tsks at our quizzical, disappointed faces. "Swaps are where a group from one college will organise a drinking meet-up with a group or soc from a different college."

"And bops are piss-ups. Fancy dress, usually."

"You'll basically be spending the next three years within a half-mile radius," Audrey says.

"But it'll be the best three years of your life," Jack assures Goose. Rowers. So chummy.

Neither of us says a word, since we don't even go here, but I can't help mentally comparing it with, say, Daniel's NYU. Even Daniel was rarely on what passes for a campus, there. The college is scattered amongst throngs of restaurants and cafés and offices and buildings stretching from the Battery to Midtown, and the fifty thousand students have New York as their playground, to ravage or retreat from in anonymity, if they want it.

Jack leads us through an old stone staircase, and admittedly, it *is* gorgeous—spires and chapels dripping with culture and history and the ghosts of shit-droppingly famous people from bygone centuries.

But it feels . . . close, roaming the corridors. As if the

ceilings might cave in. And I have that feeling, still, only just managing to avoid looking over my shoulder to meet the eyes I feel on the back of my neck. "Doesn't it get to feel . . . claustrophobic?" I ask.

"Maybe if we went to Girton," Jack says, and Kai mimes gagging. "But otherwise, no, not really." He raises his hand to a door.

"Wait, *this* is the dorm?" I ask.

They look at each other, then at me.

"He spent his last two years in the States," Goose says quickly.

All three of them look sceptical, still, and I kick myself inwardly.

"I was sent down from Westminster for shagging the headmaster's daughter," I say, hoping to justify my ignorance sufficiently. "My parents both went here, and after the funeral . . . it felt right, coming back," I add quickly.

This, they seem willing to accept. Though they may not entirely believe me, I've found that one can almost always count on the English to be too polite to say so.

Jack knocks on the door, with the rest of us a bit crowded in the corridor. Just as I think I hear a sound coming from inside, the door cracks open, and a girl's face peers out. She smiles widely, but it doesn't reach her eyes. "Yeah?"

"Ceri, you got a guy in there?" Jack says, pushing the door.

The girl holds it fast and rolls her eyes. "Piss off," she starts, as Jack says, "Your cousin's here."

Her brows pinch together. "I don't have—"

"I'm Leo's friend," I say before she can finish that sentence, trying to edge my way in front of Jack, so she can see me just in case her ability means that she might recognise us. Part of me hopes it docs, that she's the reason I'm feeling so paranoid. "He sent me to find you."

Jack, Kai, and Audrey all turn to one another. "You swotty little sixth-form shits," Kai says, as Jack roars with laughter.

"You don't even go here," Jack says. "*Classic.*"

I ignore them, because Ceridwen's expression changes once I've invoked Leo.

"Thanks, Jack," she says quickly. "I've got it."

"What're you doing with these *children*," he says. "Cougar town?"

"That's right." She rolls her eyes. "Bye, Jack." Then, to us, "Come in," she says. I try and slip past Jack, who's blocking the doorway, and the door to the flat opens wide enough to reveal an overturned chair—and the closing of a cupboard door.

"You *do* have a guy in there," Jack says. "Saucy."

"Mmm, yup, now fuck off, seriously," she says. "Come *on*," she says to me. I squeeze past Audrey and Kai and Jack.

"Sorry," Goose says to them as he follows me into Ceridwen's flat. "Thanks for the advice, though."

"Thanks," Ceridwen says before shutting the door on the three of them. Her flat isn't at all what I expected—one of the walls is stone, like the rest of the building, and the windows are leaded glass and lovely, but the furniture is prison-issue, and you can't swing a kitten in here.

"Where's Leo?" she asks immediately.

We had time to plan for this, technically. What we'd say. And yet.

"About that . . ." I start.

"He didn't actually send us?" Goose has decided to get right to it, I see.

Her expression shifts, from anxious to guarded. "And who are you, exactly?"

"Goose Greaves," he says, extending a hand, which Ceridwen regards warily. She crosses her arms over her chest instead of shaking it.

"How did you find me?"

"We *do* know Leo," Goose says, and I let him keep the lead since he's taken it. "We met him in Brooklyn, a few weeks ago. A mutual friend mentioned your acquaintance."

"Still doesn't explain how you found me. He knew me as Eva," Ceridwen says, still keeping her distance.

"Goose . . ." Is an expert Google stalker, turns out? Crept your social media? There is no good answer here. "We found you through a different friend of yours, actually," I say, veering dangerously close to the subject of Sam, fully aware that there's no good answer there, either—at least, not one we want to lead with. So I deflect. "You didn't trust Leo enough to tell him your first name?"

"He couldn't pronounce it," she mumbles, adding a slight eye roll that breaks some of the tension. "When did you last see him?" she asks Goose.

We exchange a glance. How long *has* it been, since the bridge?

"A week or so, I think," I say. Flashbacks to Regency England really fuck with one's sense of time, turns out. "Maybe a bit longer?"

Her eyes close. "He said he and his girlfriend were heading up to Cam to meet me."

Goose and I exchange a look. "From New York?" I ask.

She nods. "He texted from the airport, there, saying he was on his way that day. Said he needed to talk in person, that he didn't trust texts." She lets out a breath. "That was the last I heard from him. You?"

Goose and I share another awkward look. "We . . . didn't exactly part on the best of terms," he says, which is clearly a mistake, because Ceridwen then refocuses on me.

"What did you say your name was, again?"

"Noah." I offer my own hand, which she also doesn't take. "Noah Shaw."

There's a noise in the cupboard. Ceridwen's eyes flick toward it.

"We can come back later," Goose offers, "if this is a bad time?"

"Maybe—" she starts, just as the cupboard door opens.

The person who steps out looks so much like Jamie that I think it *is* Jamie, at first. Bit taller, though, with less hair.

"Shaw?" he asks me, in an American accent.

"Yes," I say.

He stalks toward me with purpose, meeting my gaze straight on. Without looking at Ceridwen, he says to her, "Lock the door."

34

SINS OF THE FATHERS

RIGHT," I SAY, BACKING UP, ONLY JUST BARELY avoiding Ceridwen as she brushes past me to do as instructed. The lock clicks behind us. "I just want to start by saying I've no idea what Jamie's told you, but I swear I never touched his sister."

"Who the fuck is Jamie?" he asks, still advancing.

"You're not . . . related?" I ask.

"Is he black?" the guy asks. "Because we don't all look alike, you know."

Off to a cracking start. "Of course not," I say, as Goose says, "You actually really do look like him."

"Should I kick them out?" Ceridwen interrupts. "Call the porters?"

The guy narrows his eyes at us, then says to Ceridwen, "This asshole's father's responsible for my childhood."

That escalated rather quickly. "If it's any consolation, no one hated him more than me."

The guy raises his eyebrows, then rolls up his sleeves.

"I don't think there's any need to get physical—" Goose starts, but then Jamie's double just holds his fists up in the air. Exposing the scars on the undersides of his wrists. Vertical.

I exhale slowly. "I've done the same. I understand."

"Yeah?" He tilts his head. "Was it hard for you, growing up the son of a billionaire? Let's see your scars."

"Mmm. The thing about that," I begin to say, realising that neither he nor Ceridwen has outed himself or herself yet. But there's no point being coy, and someone has to go first. Might as well be me. "I—both of us," I say to Goose. "We're—Gifted."

"Gifted?" he repeats witheringly.

"I can heal," I say with as much dignity as I can muster. It isn't much. "Myself and others."

"Cool," he says flatly.

I have literally never felt less cool.

I notice him noticing my still-split knuckles and likely still-fractured fingers.

"My ability's . . . dormant at the moment," I go on.

Silence.

"Or gone. I don't really know." My audience is nonplussed. "Any of this registering? At all?"

Goose decides to chime in, having apparently witnessed a sufficient amount of my humiliation.

"We came here to ask you about Sam," he says to Ceridwen. "So we can stop whatever happened to him from happening to anyone else."

I would've given him the throat-cut gesture if I could've done. We're sure to be kicked out or have our asses kicked, or both.

Except . . . that's not what happens. Ceridwen's eyes fill with tears, but she blinks them back. Takes a few steps over to a small dresser before turning back to consider me and Goose. Her silent friend is leaning against the wall, watching us carefully.

"You knew him?" Ceridwen asks Goose.

Goose has the audacity to look to me for an answer. Such a shit.

"I was there," I say as slowly as I can, watching Ceridwen's eyes widen. "When he died."

Her jaw clenches, and her grip on the dresser tightens. "How? How did he die?"

I'm about to say, "*He hanged himself,*" when I realise that, whilst technically true, that's not what Ceridwen's asking. She knew him. She knows that.

"He was murdered," I say instead.

A tear escapes her eyes, rolls down her cheek. "I *knew* it," she says softly. "We came up in school together. I was a year older, but our little sisters were friends, so." She wipes her cheek with her sleeve. "He'd never have killed himself. Never." She sniffs, silent for a moment. Then, to me, "Did you try to heal him? Is that how you knew?"

I catch Goose's eye. We *really* should've had a plan.

"I saw it," I say. "I—"

Felt it.

"I watched it happen," I say instead. "It's—it *was* one of the things I could do."

"One of your *Gifts*," her friend says, faintly contemptuous.

"Lucky me," I say, matching his tone.

"Not a fan of that one?"

"Not a fan of any of them, to be honest," I reply, and notice a slight shift in his expression. A spark of interest.

A moment passes before he indicates my hand. "Looks painful."

I shrug.

"How'd you do it?"

"Punched a tombstone," Goose says cheerfully.

"Too bad you lost that healing factor."

"Is it?" I ask him.

Ceridwen smiles slightly, for the first time. "Sounds like you, Isaac."

A name. Finally.

And a familiar one, at that. "Leo mentioned you," I say, my eyes narrowing. "Said you went looking for a cure for this . . . what we've got." I finish. The word rustles up something M said to us, but before I catch hold of it, Isaac peels himself from the wall. Walks toward Ceridwen's bed, where a blue rucksack rests against one of her striped pillows.

"Ceri, I should go."

She shakes her head vigorously. "Nonsense. *They* can go."

"Did you find it?" I ask him. "A cure?"

He's silent.

"Look," I say, treading as carefully as I can. "I know you've got no reason to trust us. Especially if you knew my father."

"Did *you* know your father?" he asks me. "If you didn't, you're an idiot. And if you did, you deserve what he got."

"I am an idiot. But trying not to be."

"Keep trying," he says, and he sounds and looks so much like Jamie I can't help but ask, "You're sure your last name isn't Roth?"

"Very sure," he says, and pauses. "It's Lowe."

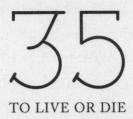

TO LIVE OR DIE

"W ELL," I SAY, ENDEAVOURING TO KEEP MY jaw from the floor. "That changes . . . everything."

"You understand why I'm not a fan of your father's work, then."

"I do," I say, still shocked. "But how did you get away?"

Goose raises his hand. "I'm actually having a hard time following."

Isaac looks at Ceridwen, then me. "Shaw's father hired the woman who adopted me when I was a baby. The woman who *experimented* on me when I was a baby."

"God, Isaac," Ceridwen says. "I didn't know."

Isaac doesn't say anything in response. Instead he considers *me*, searches my face. "What do *you* know?"

I inhale through my nose. "That Kells was a monster. That my father encouraged her to be." I look at Isaac, truly unable to imagine what he might've endured at their hands. The only context he fits in is with Jude.

Just thinking that name rounds my hands into fists. My broken one throbs comfortingly.

"Try not to take offence at this question," I say next, because Isaac is right—I am *absolutely* an idiot. "But how are you *normal*? I've met the product of one of Kells's experiments, and ... he wasn't." A laughably inadequate description.

"I was from an earlier set," Isaac says. "Of twins," he explains to Goose and Ceridwen. "My twin didn't make it, but since I survived, she figured she got the protocol right."

"Yeah, she didn't."

He shrugs.

"This is mad," I say quietly. "How did you escape?"

"She took me out for ice cream, once. I ran away. I was six."

Christ. "I'm so sorry," I say.

"I don't need your pity."

"And you don't have it. Obviously you've done all right for yourself."

At that, he arches an eyebrow. "How would you know?"

"Because you're still here."

By some miracle, those words seem to resonate with him.

"They didn't make it easy, but you're right. I survived," he says, almost to himself.

"How?" Ceridwen asks, with awe and respect.

"Got thrown into foster homes a couple of times, always managed to wriggle out. When you have the kind of adoptive parent I had, you learn not to trust adults pretty quickly," he says acidly. "So I lived on the street, pretty much. The homeless community was kinder and more trustworthy than most other people I've met. There were some people who looked out for me. Helped. I taught myself to read, and"—he shrugs—"here we are."

"Incredible," Goose says. "I couldn't've done it."

"You'd be surprised what you find out you're capable of," Isaac says. Then looks Goose up and down. "But no, you probably couldn't have done it."

"So how'd you fetch up here, at Cambridge?" Goose asks.

"I don't go here," Isaac says. "I came to warn Ceri."

Goose and I exchange a look.

"How do you two know each other?" I ask quickly, not quite sure how to transition to our . . . theory.

"I started the New York safe house," Isaac says. "Leo took over when I left."

"To find a cure," I repeat.

"Which I never found," he reminds me. "But I found other things." I notice him glancing at my pendant, peeking out from my shirt collar. Could be useful.

"You've met the professor?" I ask.

"Took him twelve years to find me," Isaac says, a hint of pride in his voice.

A plan begins to take shape. "Are you in his little club now as well?"

Isaac cuts me a look. "If you're asking whether I have one of those"—he nods at the chain around my neck—"the answer's no."

"What is that?" Ceridwen asks me, but it's Isaac who answers:

"Another version of the symbols on our tattoos," he says to her.

Leo mentioned that someone else had designed them. Said Isaac was the first one to get it.

Ceridwen shoots me an enquiring glance. I hold out the pendant for her to examine it.

"What does it mean?" she asks.

"We've been wondering the same thing, actually," Goose says.

"Do you have one also?" she asks him.

Goose shakes his head. "No tattoos, either, I'm afraid. What do you suppose *that* means?" he asks Isaac, suddenly the group elder.

Surprisingly, Isaac begins untucking his shirt. He lifts it up to his ribs—along one side is a tattoo, identical to Leo's—a curving feather, the spine of it fashioned into a sword.

"The professor told me about the symbols when he found me." He looks down at it. "The feather, the sword. How they represent justice. He told me some stories, about my *real* background, he claimed. He knew what I could do, and suggested I use my gifts for good. Told me he was trying to make the world a better place, and needed my help to do it." Isaac's expression darkens. "I was tempted, for a minute, but then I thought, if he knows so much, why didn't he find me sooner? If he knew so much, how could he let me be taken and raised by a sadist?" He straightens his spine. "I decided if he couldn't have made the world a better place for one eighteen-year-old kid on his own, I didn't think his was a cause worth joining." Isaac crosses his arms over his chest. "So I reinterpreted the symbols he told me about. Got the tattoo. Started squatting in the brownstone. Leo tracked me down not long after that, and then he started finding others who felt the same way we did."

"Which is?"

"I believe in justice. I just think we have to make it for ourselves."

He and Mara would get on well.

Something he said catches me, though. "Did you say . . . *Leo* tracked you down?"

"Yeah." He nods. "Why?"

"I thought he created illusions," I say. "A girl, Sophie—she was the one who found others like us."

Isaac shakes his head. "Nope, you've got it backward."

"My mistake," I say slowly. But it isn't. Sophie described, quite lengthily, how her ability worked. Why would she lie?

"Why didn't you go back?" Goose asks. "To New York?"

"I had a different . . . perspective, from Leo."

I think back, remembering our conversations in Brooklyn, in that house. About Mara, returning to our flat, drunk with power. Flashing me that wicked smile, that feral look as she pressed her hands against the wall of the clock tower, daring me to—

"He wanted to develop his Gift. Get stronger," Isaac says, mercifully interrupting my thoughts. Long enough for me to slam the door on them, on Mara, though she won't stay there for long.

"And you?" I ask him. "What do you want?"

"I want to be left alone."

I turn to Ceridwen, then. "What about you?"

"To live my life," she says, looking away from us. "Stay at Cam. Keep my friends." She turns to Isaac. "We haven't done anything wrong. We shouldn't have to hide."

"I don't hide, I move."

I don't hide, I move. M said that too.

"Do you know anyone named Mara? Or Em?" I ask. She aimed me here, in their direction, after all.

"She black too?"

"No," I sigh. "Never mind."

"Ceri, it's your choice—if you want to come, I'll help you. If not . . ."

"I just don't see how I could."

Isaac looks at her, disappointed. "Then I did the best I could. I've got to go."

"Why?" I ask, trying to delay him a bit, till I sort out why they're here, and why *we're* here. "What's the rush?"

He sighs. "Leo and Sophie said they were coming a week ago, right, Ceri?"

She nods.

"But they're not here, and you are."

Goose blinks. "What, you think something's happened to them?"

"Honestly?" Isaac shakes his head. "Otherwise I'd've gone to New York before coming here." He looks meaningfully at Ceridwen.

"Is that your Gift?" Goose asks. "Sensing danger, or something?"

"No. Just common sense."

"So what's happened to them, do you think?" Ceridwen asks him.

"I think after the past six months, Leo's finally started listening to me."

Ceridwen turns to me. "Isaac thinks we should all be off the grid. Never spend too much time in one place. And never spend too much time with anyone else like us."

Isaac shrugs a shoulder. "Like I said, common sense. It's smarter to avoid groups, if you want to avoid attention.

Speaking of," he says, lifting his rucksack off the bed. "I really do need to go."

"But there's no one else here," I say, looking around. "You think we're being watched?"

He raises his eyebrows. "You think you aren't?" Then, "I wouldn't say 'watched,' necessarily. But 'sensed'? Definitely."

"All of us?" Goose asks.

He considers this before nodding once.

"So you think you're in danger as well?"

"We're all in danger, all the time."

"Fun guy," Goose says to Ceridwen, who manages a grin.

Isaac runs his tongue over his teeth. "How old are you?" he asks Goose.

"Eighteen," Goose replies.

"And you?" Isaac asks me.

"Nearly eighteen," I say.

"Right. Most of you are. How old am I?"

"No idea."

"Twenty-one," he says to me. "Three years may not seem like a lot, but trust me—your gifts, or whatever you wanna call it? They only *start* with healing. You've got some rough years ahead of you, if you make it that long. Not everyone does."

"And why is that?" Ceridwen asks. "Has anyone figured that out?"

I nod. "I think there's a difference between the . . . artificial version of the gene, for lack of a better word, and the original version."

Isaac slow-claps. I ignore him.

"How do we know which one we've got?" Ceridwen asks nervously.

"If you didn't grow up in a lab, that's a start," Isaac says.

"A start," Goose says. "But not really conclusive, is it? *I* didn't grow up in a lab."

"Nor did I," says Ceridwen.

"And we're still here," Goose chirps.

"Sam isn't." Goose shuts up.

"You didn't happen to have any . . ." How to put it? "Issues, growing up?"

"What sort?"

"Were you in treatment for anything? Depression, anxiety?"

Something closes down behind Ceridwen's face. "That's really none of your business."

Isaac sighs, frustrated. "The *doctor* who adopted me, she wasn't the only one, using people for research. Although she might've been the only one who experimented on babies." His jaw tightens, and he aims a glare at me. "His dad paid other people in other places to test kids he thought would be close to manifesting. Teens with mental health issues. So they wouldn't be believed."

She shakes her head vigorously. "I don't remember anything."

"That doesn't mean it didn't happen," he says quietly. "You know that as well as I do."

Goose looks back and forth between them. "Wait, what precisely is it you both can do?"

Ceridwen looks to Isaac for reassurance.

"Tell them." He gestures at Goose. "If you want."

"I didn't really know that I could do anything until Leo found me. But I can cancel out other Gifts."

"Oh my wow," Goose says quietly. Then, "You're my opposite. I make them stronger. What are the odds?"

"Odds have nothing to do with it," Isaac says, then runs his hand over his mouth. "It was designed that way."

"But not everyone was *designed*," I say. "Goose never spent any time at a mental hospital."

"Did he need to?" Isaac straightens. "You guys were here. Growing up in the shadow of the piece of shit who started all this. How hard would it have been to . . ."

"Manipulate his genes without anyone noticing?" I cut in. "You're seriously asking that question?" I shake my head. "Kells was *still* trying to sort out how our abilities worked when I was in Horizons, not even a year ago. And her next experiment, after you? His name was Jude, and he was a fucking *nightmare*. *Completely* out of control."

"Yeah? What happened to him?"

I hesitate.

"His ex-girlfriend," Goose answers, ever so helpfully.

"Sounds like an interesting story."

"That depends on whether you like happy endings," Goose says.

Isaac shoulders his rucksack and leans in to kiss Ceridwen on each cheek. "I prefer no endings at all," he says, before he walks out on us. The three of us stare at her closed door.

"You know," Goose says, "he never actually said what his Gift was?"

Ceridwen's eyes are fixed on the spot. "Isaac makes people forget things. Or helps them to remember."

36

EITHER/OR

GOOSE AND I EXCHANGE A VERY MEANINGFUL look. One that does not go unnoticed.

"What?" Ceridwen asks.

"That's literally why he's here," Goose says, tipping his head at me.

"Wait," she says, shaking her head. "I thought you were here to find *me*. Because of Sam. And what you . . . saw."

I nod. "But I also just found out we're related—"

"How?"

"Cousins," Goose says.

"No, how did you find out?"

I could tell her half the truth? The bit Bernard conveyed to

Mara, the rumours about Sam's actual ancestry.

Or I could confess the whole truth; the family tree Sam showed us that confirmed them.

"It's . . . complicated," I say, buying time whilst I decide.

"Try me." Ceridwen folds her arms across her chest.

Goose decides for me, as it happens.

"He's a ghost," Goose says indelicately. "Who haunts Noah's family home."

Ceridwen's expression doesn't change. As the silence stretches on, she finally says, "What are you on about?"

"Unfortunately, exactly what Goose just said."

"No," she says. Closes her eyes.

"He showed us something—"

"He's *dead*," she says, the pitch of her voice rising. "I was at his *funeral*."

"I know—"

"Then what *is* this? Some sort of sick—"

"Listen," Goose says, his tone as serious as I've ever heard it. "I'm newer at this than the rest of you. I don't know how this shite works. But we both saw him." He indicates me. "Together."

"What did he look like, then?" she challenges me.

"He looked like he did when I found his body," I say, then warn her. "Think, seriously, before you ask me to tell you more."

The spark of anger dies out in her eyes.

"What was his ability?" Goose asks her.

"He . . ." Ceridwen starts, then bites her lip. "He could . . . put thoughts in your head? Leave imprints there, with what he wanted to say." She swallows hard. "Messages."

Goose raises his brows.

"I think he wanted me to know that we're related," I say. "He showed us a family tree."

"What? In your house somewhere?"

"In a book," I begin. "It's . . . hard to describe." Without sounding mad. "But then the images he showed me opened a door into something else, something only I could see. Memories I'd . . ." Inherited? "Forgotten," I settle on.

The word is barely out of my mouth before Ceridwen swerves around me to throw open her door. She starts down the corridor at a trot.

"What's happening?" Goose asks out of the corner of his mouth as we hurry to catch up.

"Dunno."

"Our stuff's back there—"

"Really?"

Ceridwen rounds a corner to the right, and then another. She glances over her shoulder, once, and shouts, "Keep up!" Then vanishes down a staircase.

Two flights down and we're beneath the arcading. The Front Court and gate are on one side. On the other, a dark garden surrounded by a smaller cluster of old stone buildings with leaded-glass windows.

We're the only people out. Something splashes in a nearby pond, and then I hear Ceridwen's voice up ahead, to the right.

"I need you," she says. "I need you to do this for me."

"Ceri—"

Isaac's voice. I stop Goose, and motion for him to be quiet.

"Please."

"I can't miss the last bus."

"It's not the last."

"The last of the night."

"So stay with me, and take my bike in the morning."

"He won't want it."

"I think he does. Just talk to him. *Please*," she says again, and then her tone changes from plea to command. "You owe me."

Silence. Then two pairs of footsteps on grass, one light and soft, the other quick and heavy.

Isaac and Ceridwen walk out of a courtyard side by side.

"Ceridwen says you have a memory problem," Isaac says to me. "Is she right?"

I nod.

"Fine. Let's talk."

He refuses to go back to her room, though, so the four of us meander our way through one of Emma's several gardens as Isaac keeps an eye out for a place to sit.

"He's quite particular," Goose says.

"Walls have ears," Isaac says. "Especially in places like this."

Before either of us can ask what he means, he says, "Watch out for the ducks."

"What—"

Goose stumbles, setting off a racket of wings and quacking. "Bloody hell."

"Told you," we hear Isaac say from somewhere up ahead. His voice sounds muffled, his footfalls heavier. "Right," he says, and then I see him, but just barely. He's standing in a small copse of trees, off the path and far out of the glow of lampposts.

"How clandestine," I say, looking above us at the sky, dark as spilled ink. "I'm not sure anything I have to say merits this level of intrigue."

"I told you he wasn't interested," Isaac says to Ceridwen.

"Wait," I say. "All right. What is it you want to know?"

"What do you want to tell me?"

"You really do sound like him," I say.

"Your friend?"

A single shake of my head. "The professor."

I didn't mean it as an accusation, exactly, but the air shifts, and Isaac's tone changes. "I'm not like him."

I could let it go, but I don't. "You're always moving," I point out. "You show up wherever and whenever you like to offer cryptic warnings and dire predictions."

"I've *learned* from him, sure. But I'm not like him."

It's Ceridwen who asks him, "What've you learned?"

I think the only reason he deigns to answer is because *she's* the one who asked. He bites his lip before saying, "Some of the things I've tried to pass along to you. Don't stay in any one place for long. Don't touch anyone you don't trust."

"Don't trust anyone at all?" I ask.

"I trust some people," he says, his eyes on Ceridwen as he speaks. "Not many, though." Then, "The professor's the oldest one of us, I think. How do you think he got that way?"

"Knowing the future probably helps."

Isaac cracks a rare grin. "In some ways, yeah, sure. But think about it—what would you do if you knew the future?"

"That would depend on what it looked like," I say.

"What if you thought you could create it?" I can feel his eyes on me in the dark. "What would the future look like, if you believed *you* could shape it?"

"We can, though," Goose says. "Everything we do changes the future. Every action has a reaction."

Isaac's nodding. "But you don't know what the reactions will be, and you can only control how *you* act."

"Isn't it the same for the professor?" Ceridwen asks.

Isaac and I answer at the same time. "No." We look at each other.

"He uses people," Isaac says first. "Gives them a taste of what they want and dangles it in front of them until they dance." He glances at my pendant. "That's what that means," he says to Ceridwen. "Shaw's a puppet."

I stiffen. "You don't know anything about me."

"Ceridwen said you're having memory problems," he says evenly.

I should say yes, but instead I say, "So?"

"Too many or too few?"

I avoid his eyes. "Both."

"He got a message from Sam," Ceridwen says. "*After* he died."

A beat. Then, "Thought you said your abilities were gone."

"I'm not sure mine is," Goose cuts in. "I saw Sam, too."

Ceridwen looks at Isaac. "Could he be alive, somehow, you think?"

Isaac looks at me expectantly, though I'm certain he knows the answer.

I exhale. "I didn't just see him die. I *felt* him . . ."

Shit. Least I caught myself before adding anything too gruesome?

"I'm sorry." I shake my head. "There's no way."

"So why track down Ceridwen?" Isaac asks me. I'm still stung by the puppet insult, though, so it's Goose who answers.

"You said his Gift let him imprint a thought in someone's mind, right?"

She nods. Then amends, "Not just from person to person. He could imprint them on things." She turns to us. "Tell Isaac what you told me. About the family tree."

I do. I recount the scene, and Isaac makes Goose do the same.

"Well, you didn't witness a memory," Isaac says finally.

"How do you know?"

"Because the details would be different. Little things, stuff people don't even think about. It's subconscious. Hard to lie about."

"So?"

"So I think you're right. It was a message, not a memory."

"What was the message saying, though?"

Isaac lifts his chin. "That depends on what you saw next."

"I saw my great-great-grandfather."

"Why?"

Because I'd been asked to? Because I finally allowed myself to? "How should I know?"

"Why do you *think*?"

"You sound like a therapist." I let out a breath, not sure how much to reveal. We hardly know him, after all. "Genetic memory, I suppose?"

"That's a *how*, not a *why*."

"He's on a mission to confront his past," Goose narrates, "so he can find a way to . . . move forward."

At that, Isaac raises his brows.

"A Bildungsroman situation," I add. "Deeply unsublimating."

"So you decided to come back to England to confront your past," Isaac says drily. "All on your own."

He's said he'd never met a Mara, or an "Em." Best not bring her up just yet; stick with what he already knows. "The professor left me a note, at or after my father's funeral, basically congratulating me on my inheritance. And then in the envelope was a ripped-out page from somewhere—an encyclopaedia, maybe, who the fuck knows—about priest holes."

"Wait," Ceridwen says. "Priest holes?"

"The family manor was constructed before the Reformation."

Her mouth falls open and her eyes narrow as she realises, "You're *that* Shaw, are you? I've been to your manor on a school trip. State school," she adds snarkily.

I sigh.

"So you think—or, wait, this professor chap thought there was something hidden away in the priest holes in your house? What did you find, when you looked?" she asks us.

I didn't. I ignored his subtle attempt to get me to look, and spent most of my energy ignoring M's unsubtle ones. Instead, "We didn't exactly get that far . . ." I begin, looking to Goose for help. "There was a bit of a detour."

"Also, completely thrown by the ghost thing, to be honest."

"Had to get the fuck out of there after that happened."

"*Had* to," Goose echoes. "To be fair," he adds, "you were fucking pissed at the time."

Ceridwen glares at both of us. "Should have led with that, maybe?"

"Pissed?" Isaac asks.

"Fucked up."

"I know what it means. On what?"

"Honestly, I don't even know."

His eyes narrow slightly, but he tells me, "Go on."

I shrug. "Then I saw the unillustrious Lord Simon Shaw in a hospital, barely conscious. The professor showed up and saved his life."

After I say the words, I realise just how still Isaac is as he listens to me. "Try again," he says.

"Pardon?"

"You're lying."

"I'm not—"

"How did the professor save Simon Shaw's life?" he asks again.

"I—" I'm fighting to remember the details, suddenly. Blurred shapes and shadowed voices . . . "There were two men with him." Tall? Short? One of each, I think? Their names are just out of reach. "One of them did something to him." I can't remember what it was, anymore. Not at all. It feels like a staircase in a house I've always lived in is now missing one of its steps, and I only noticed because I've stumbled through it.

"You said Simon talked about needing more time," Goose cuts in. "He asked the professor for the man who could give him more life."

His words pluck a familiar string somewhere in my mind, but the note's too far away to recognise.

"Different memory," I say. "They talked about going on

some kind of voyage, to discover something . . ." Some*one*? "In India."

"India," Isaac repeats. He swallows hard. "That's interesting."

Goose arcs an eyebrow, giving me a sidelong glance.

"Is it?" I ask. "Why?"

"The professor thought I could learn something there myself. Find someone."

"Learn what?" Goose asks.

"Find who?" I ask perfunctorily, because I'm certain I already know.

"You've heard the gods and monsters bit, right?"

I nod, Goose nods, but Ceridwen's shaking her head, rather angrily. "Why don't I know what you're all on about? Why am I the only one who doesn't know?"

"Far from the only one," Goose says. "I only heard weeks ago."

"But *you* knew," Ceridwen says to Isaac.

"We didn't know each other all that well, when I was in New York."

"Well enough," she says, and if this were a normal night and we were with normal people, that would be the moment that Goose and I backed away slowly.

As it is, though. We bite our tongues.

"I didn't trust—" Isaac catches himself before saying a name, but it would've been Leo's name, I'm sure of it. "I didn't trust everyone there."

"I was there," Ceridwen says. "What's changed?"

"Me," Isaac says.

Clever, clever man. Cleverer still, he changes the subject, from one that's clearly about them and *only* them, back to one that includes me and Goose.

"The professor has a few speeches he recycles," Isaac says, his voice softening when he looks at Ceridwen. "In one of them, he says there's a monster for every god, a demon for every angel, a villain for every hero."

Hero. I can't help but hear it in my father's sneer, and remember what he believed it meant I should do.

"Then he name-checks a philosopher—Jung and Euhemeris are particular favourites—and presents the idea that we, the Gifted, are the gods and monsters of myth and legend. All of the stories were written about people like us, with abilities normal people didn't have the language to explain."

"Maybe there's an obvious answer I'm missing," Goose says, "but how do you know he has speeches? Were you . . . recruiting for him, or something?"

Isaac shakes his head. "The opposite, almost always. My *blessing*," he says nastily, "is that I can restore memories, and delete them." He inhales. "My curse is that when I do, I either gain someone else's, or lose one of my own."

"Shit," is all I seem to be able to say.

"Hard luck, mate," Goose mumbles.

"Or that's how it started, anyway. It used to be worse, actually, when I had less control over it. That was when the professor found me. It was after I'd moved to Brooklyn, met some of the others already. The professor came calling and hinted at the idea that if I could trace some of those stories and legends back, it might help me find someone who could, as he put it, 'heal you of your Affliction.' And when someone shows up offering you the thing you want most, how can you say no?"

That's what Mara wanted, once.

"Fix me," she commanded. "This thing, what I've done—there's something wrong with me, Noah. Fix it."

The look on her face broke my heart. *"I can't,"* I said.

"Why not?"

"Because you aren't broken."

I was wrong. We were both broken.

"That's what you wanted most?" Ceridwen asks, wrenching me back into the present. "That's why you left?"

"They don't get it," Isaac says, but not to Ceridwen, or Goose. He looks at me, speaks to me, as if I'm the only one there. "They're not constantly aware of their blessings, the way we are, so they don't feel their curses as keenly."

Ceridwen doesn't approve of that answer. "That's not fair—"

"Go on, Shaw," he says. "Explain it."

I look at him questioningly, until I realise what he means. Then I say, "No."

"Okay, I will. When Sam jumped off the bell tower at his father's funeral, Noah didn't just feel the noose as if it were around his own neck. Or his bones snapping like they were in his own body. Or the air being squeezed out of his lungs like someone was wringing them out like a wet rag."

Ceridwen goes completely pale.

Isaac doesn't stop. "He felt the fear and terror Sam felt before he jumped, and kept on feeling it until he died."

I feel like hitting him, is what I feel like. "How do you know," I say, my voice low.

"I didn't. I guessed. I was proving a point."

"You're an arsehole," Ceridwen says.

I agree.

"True, but irrelevant right now."

"Is it?" Goose asks.

Isaac shrugs. "All right." He looks at Ceridwen. "Ask him yourself, then. I'll do it, no matter what he says."

Ceridwen blinks, surprised.

"Ask me what?"

She takes a deep breath. "Do you want to remember? Or do you want to forget?"

MORE VISIBLE

I'M NOT SURE I UNDERSTAND THE QUESTION."

Isaac shoots Ceridwen a pointed look.

She chooses her words carefully. "You said you came here to find me because of Sam, right? He showed you something, something Goose didn't see, and he wouldn't have shown you what he did if it wasn't important. But just now, when Isaac asked, you couldn't remember the details." She looks at Isaac, then me. "He can help."

Isaac's already shaking his head, though. "She's right and wrong. I *could* give you your memories back, the details. It'll be rough, but I could probably do it. What I can't do is help you." He pauses. "Because I don't think remembering will help you."

"Oh?"

"I've only ever heard someone describe a memory the way you did once. And that's because an original was in it. From what you've told me it sounds like there were three of them in there, at least."

Four, if you count M.

"They're crawling all over you."

An unsettling thought, and description. "It wasn't *me* they were talking to, though—"

"Doesn't matter. Most of the Carriers I've met—"

"That's the word Kells used for us," I say, eyes narrowing. "Carriers."

"Yeah, she was a scientist, and to her that's what we are. To the professor, with his mystical shit, we're Gifted, or whatever. It doesn't matter what they call us, it matters what we are. And what we are is different. From them, from everyone else, and from each other." He takes a deep breath. "Most people like us, they've never heard of him, let alone met him, the professor. He shows up in person, or sends a letter, or skulks around offscreen to manipulate us like pawns on a chessboard we don't even know we're walking on."

"I don't disagree."

"That chain around your neck," he says, tipping his head at it. "Why'd you put it on?"

"It was my mother's," I say, without hesitation.

"Try again," Isaac says, irritatingly.

"I found it in a box of her things, after she died—"

"Not what I asked. Stop wasting my time."

"Look, I don't know what you're on about but—"

"*Why* did you put it on?"

"What are you, a human lie detector or something?" Goose asks.

"No, I've just had a lot of practice listening to people. Enough to know when they're not telling the whole story."

"Fine," I say. "The whole story, that's what you want?" Isaac looks back placidly. "My father moved us to the States a couple of years ago. Miami." I'm hyperaware of the fact that I've only ever told this to Mara before, and now I'm telling a former schoolmate and two strangers. "Ghastly house, there was only one suitable room in it, so I claimed the library as mine and then began to—" I catch myself, close my eyes. Try to remember what I told Mara exactly. "I felt like I had to unpack," I say. It feels like Mara's here, on the grass, looking up at me as she once did from the floor of my room. I'd give anything to have her back.

But the Mara I'm remembering now isn't the Mara that exists.

A mourning dove calls out softly from somewhere close by. I shake my head once. Soldier on. "I was exhausted, had planned on passing out when we got there, but I just headed right for this one box. Inside it was a small chest full of silver, but I started setting it aside, taking the chest apart. Under a set of knives, I found this," I say, reaching up to my neck to touch it, the pendant. "I started wearing it that day."

I glance at the rest of them, who seem satisfied. But Isaac's watching me in a way I don't like.

"I took it off a few months ago," I say, aiming for casual and likely failing. "The professor sent me a letter, and in it he included one from my mother as well. She wrote it before she died."

That I remember without effort, and every word feels like a wound.

Do not find peace. Find passion.

I had.

Find something you want to die for more than something you want to live for.

I'd done that, too.

When you find someone to fight with, give her or him this.

I swallow hard. "She wrote things, about what she thought I should do with my life, how I should live it." I've shown the letter to Mara, only, and can't believe I'm about to repeat those words to *this* audience. "Told me to 'fight for those who cannot fight for themselves. Speak for them. Scream for them. Live and die for them.'"

Your life will not always be a happy one, but it will have meaning, my mother wrote.

I skip that bit. "Then she wrote, 'when you find someone to fight with, give her or him this.'" I indicate my chest, where it rests above my heart.

"Did you?" Isaac asks.

"Find someone to fight with, or give it to her?" I ask. He just stares in answer. Goose can't meet my eyes—my display of emotion is hideously embarrassing, no doubt. Ceridwen's mouth is parted slightly; she's hanging on every word, though.

"Yes, and no," I say. "She got a letter from the professor too. Warning her to stay away from me, essentially." Not essentially. Exactly.

You will love Noah Shaw to ruins, unless you let him go, he wrote to her.

Whether it is fate or chance, coincidence or destiny, I have seen his death a thousand ways in a thousand dreams over a thousand nights, and the only one who can prevent it is you.

It's becoming harder and harder to force the words out of my mind into my throat into the air.

"Let me take a stab at that interesting story you alluded to," Isaac says.

A blessed interruption, though an unfortunate choice of words.

"Your ex—she's your opposite?"

"Common enough trope," I say indifferently. "Star-crossed lovers, all that."

Isaac sighs. "Yeah, they eat that shit up."

"She kept repeating the professor's words. *'He would help create a better world. Without you, he can.'* Maybe that's why she did it," I say without thinking. Twelve lives for my worthless one. Twelve families ruined. She'd said she had nothing to do with what happened to Sam, Stella—and I would have believed her without question, before. Before she became the person my father or the professor or I encouraged her to be.

I notice Isaac's raised brows and say, "She did something I . . . couldn't forgive." My body tenses. "I told her I never wanted to see her again. And I haven't."

"But there it is," Isaac says, looking at my pendant.

I exhale through my nose. "The professor told us if we put it on, he'd 'know of our decision,' whatever the fuck that means. I took it off because it all felt like a manipulation." My jaw tightens. "I didn't want to be used, a tool in his fight or a pawn in his game or whatever tortured, overused metaphor you prefer."

My words to Mara shove their way into my mind, again.

We don't have to be what they want. We can live the lives we want.

"I thought if I took it off, I wouldn't have to be who he'd decided I should be. But I realised he'd been playing me— both of us—the whole time. So I decided, fuck it. I'd go along, then spoil his game when I got the chance."

It's all true. It just isn't *everything* that's true, missing the M narrative. But it might be enough.

"So," Isaac says, gathering himself up. "This is you playing along?"

In a sense. I nod once.

"He's still playing you," Isaac says. "And not just him," he says, discomfitingly.

Did he know about M after all?

"All those originals leaving footprints in your thoughts? You're a wanted man, Shaw."

I shrug one shoulder. "Knew that already. The professor said I fit the Hero archetype, or whatever. *Destined for greatness*, were his exact words, I believe."

"Harry Potter," Goose says. Whilst going back and forth with Isaac, I'd nearly forgotten Goose was here.

"With a death wish," I add after a beat. "And better hair."

"I believe there's a case to be made that Harry *also* had a death wish," Goose says. "To be fair."

"So what are you saying, exactly?" Ceridwen asks Isaac, ignoring Goose and me.

"I'm saying you can't do what he wants, or even the opposite of what you think he wants, without playing right into his hands."

"What if he's not the only one?" Goose asks, and it takes everything I have not to kick him.

Isaac shrugs. "Doesn't change anything. They're older than you and smarter than you and stronger than you. You think you're all 'Damn the Man! Save the Empire!' But they're the Man *and* the Empire."

Goose and I exchange a glance. "Are . . . we supposed to know what that means?"

Isaac rolls his head back and groans. "You can't beat them, is the point. Whatever the thing you want most is, that's what they'll use to get what they want from you."

"Why don't they just take it?" Goose asks. "I mean, if they're as powerful as all that."

"I don't think they can," Isaac says. "Or I bet they would. But as for you," he says to me, "you've got a decision to make. What is it that *you* want?"

Where do I start?

"I don't want anyone else to die," I say.

"Everyone dies. You can't change that, and neither can I. Next?"

"Fine, I'll be more specific. I'd like for other Carriers or Gifted or whatever the fuck you prefer to call us to stop committing suicide *en masse.*"

He stares for a second, then says, "I don't know why what's happening is happening, but I know that I can't fix it."

Ceridwen's shaking her head. "No, you don't. You don't know that there isn't a memory buried in his mind that'll unlock why this is happening," she says. "Sam didn't want to die. You said you went looking for a cure, right? Maybe he tried to show Noah something, point him in that direction—"

"Here's what I can offer you," Isaac says to me, ignoring Ceridwen. "And it's *all* I can offer you. I can fill in the gaps in those memories of yours. I can unlock the door to that house. But the key might also unlock other rooms inside it that you'll wish you'd never seen. Things the people you're connected to might've done that you'll get to experience, relive, through their eyes, with your awareness." His voice takes on an edge. "Think about those people. Those things. That legacy. Then think about the things you've seen and felt and whether you wish you could scrape them from your memory."

Like what it felt like to break my bones on the ruins, when I wasn't old enough to understand why.

Or cut myself when I was fifteen, when I thought I *did* understand why.

Or the look on my father's face when I held a gun to my temple and he didn't blink.

Or Mara. The way every memory, every thought, everything I see and feel circles back to her, always. Reopens the wound I cut, prevents it from healing.

"How can you be sure I won't forget other things?" I ask. "Like how to speak or tie my laces?"

Isaac shrugs. "Messing with memories can change your personality, yeah. But isn't that the point?"

It's Goose who looks uneasy, now. "Sounds a bit risky, mate."

"It is," Ceridwen says. "Whatever he takes from you, it'll be gone forever."

I look at her, then at him, wondering fleetingly if that might have come between them.

"How specific can you be?" I ask unhelpfully.

"I mean, pretty specific. Almost *Eternal Sunshine* specific."

"Watched that with my older brother, once," Goose says. "Correct me if I'm wrong, but that movie didn't end happily, did it?"

"No," Ceridwen says flatly. "It didn't."

"It was ambiguous," Isaac adds, a touch defensive.

Ceridwen faces me, about to say something, but Isaac cuts her off. "Maybe there is something bouncing around in that head of yours that'll magically put an end to all of this. Maybe the professor wasn't just using you, and me, and everyone he's ever met, and he really does need us to rid the world of evil. Maybe he's the good guy. Maybe we *are* all heroes. But if someone gave me the choice, whether to remember everything I've been through in order to bring me here, to this moment, or whether to forget?" There's pity in his eyes. "I would rather forget. For whatever that's worth." His eyes search the clearing for a moment, before he lifts his rucksack to his shoulder. "But you have to learn shit like that for yourself. I'm stuck here till morning, so you have till then to choose."

"Isaac—" Ceridwen says.

"One last bit of advice? Make sure your choice is *your* choice. Not the professor's. Not anyone else's. Because you're the one who has to live with it. Not Ceri, not your friend here, and definitely not the professor. Not any of them. You can't beat them. Remember that."

"So what do we do?" Goose asks.

"What I do," he says. "Avoid them. They can't win if you don't play."

38

OUT INTO THE WORLD

Isaac takes Ceridwen aside for a moment before leaving us, and we give them their distance.

"Think we can still make that party?" Goose asks quietly.

"You're not serious."

"Well, if you're going to have your memory erased, might as well have one last bash." His tone's careless, but he won't meet my eyes. Then, "You're not really considering it, are you?"

"Might do," I say just as casually, which is just as much of a lie. Then I do what I'm better at—I deflect. "I'm not sure a party's a good idea, to be honest," I say, watching Isaac whisper to Ceridwen out of the corner of my eye.

"But having a stranger mess around in your head is?"

"You think *he'd* approve?" I tip my head at Isaac. "Of accepting an invitation we don't know the origins of?"

"Mate literally said 'walls have ears.' Wouldn't look to him for social guidance. Probably we were recognised by Spencer or Nate or even Jasper, right? Remember him, the J-Crew?"

Rower, used to prank the younger years with a small gang of fellow Slytherins. "Stupid name," I say. Now all I can think of is the clothing company.

"It'll be fun," Goose says. "We can prank them back, once we're inside."

If it's them. "And if it's not them?"

"You sound a bit paranoid, mate."

I do. And feel it. Have been, since well before we arrived, before we left New York, even. And I've been wrong and right to—we *have* been herded to England. But the professor did it first, before M, who lied in the beginning but made no secret of the fact that she wanted me here, and why. And she seemed to loathe the professor more than I did, more than Isaac. That's been the common thread, which makes Goose right, as well, in a sense.

The professor knew, impossibly, improbably, where to find me and Mara on her birthday. He knew of Simon's existence, and found him. Both of them worked together to shape the moment I'm in, to shape my existence. I swore to myself I wouldn't play the professor's game, whatever it is, that I'd destroy his eight-dimensional chessboard instead.

Which has led me to Isaac, whose only advice is to avoid them. To live like him, always moving, always hiding. No risk, no chance. I get why he lives that way, why he prizes survival above all else.

Goose couldn't be more different. He prizes *fun* above all else. And unlike Isaac? He's *happy*.

Unlike me.

Ceridwen's on her way back to us before I can reply. "So," she says with forced lightness. "Looks like you're spending the night as well."

"Don't worry about us—" I start.

"We wouldn't want to trouble you—" Goose says.

"Nonsense, we can grab some takeaway from Gardies, then head back." She indicates the rooms at Emma.

"Actually," Goose says, "we were invited to a party at King's later on—"

"You're welcome to join us—" I say.

"It would be splendid if we could dress in your room, though," Goose finishes.

Ceridwen looks at us sceptically. "Dress?"

Once back in her room, she eyes the fruits of our shopping experience earlier in the day. "*Where* exactly did you think you'd be going tonight?" she asks. "The nineteenth century?"

"Bit much?" Goose holds up a waistcoat.

"A bit, yeah."

"Seemed like a good idea at the time," Goose says. "Thought perhaps we'd be invited to Formal Hall somewhere." Ceridwen starts laughing. "No?"

She shakes her head. "Not how it works, sorry."

Goose pouts. "We got invitations and everything."

She tilts her head, and Goose hands them to her. "Midnight? At King's? Sorry, no, you've been invited to a soc initiation, probably. Or a prank."

Wonder what her take on it'll be. "You don't think it's odd that our full names are there?"

Ceridwen shrugs a shoulder. "Likely you were spotted by someone you know whilst milling about with the freshers. Hopefully it's someone who likes you. Otherwise you're in for a bit of a night."

Goose is wearing a rather smug smile.

"Will you come along?" I ask Ceridwen, who's already shaking her head. She sits on her bed, folding a leg beneath her.

"I appreciate the thought, but my binge-drinking days are behind me."

"You're not in a soc?" Goose asks.

"I am—it's the done thing," she says with a crooked smile. "But I've already had my initiation, which wasn't as stupid as whatever you're surely about to do. You likely won't remember me or anyone by the time it's over."

"I think we've found paradise," Goose says solemnly.

If I'd never heard of Mara, if we'd never met, if my parents had been fucked up in the normal way, and if the professor had never existed? Goose is who I'd be like. Who I'd *want* to be like.

"I think I might agree," I say back.

Once we're both suited ("At least you're not wearing red chinos," Ceridwen says, upon seeing us), Ceridwen offers to show us the way to King's. "Not that it's difficult to work out," she says, "since it's literally the centre of the bubble, but one mustn't forget one's manners."

Once we head out, Goose says, "God, those Tabs really weren't joking when they said there's nothing open at night."

Our footsteps echo on the cobblestones—we're literally the only people in sight, though a peal of laughter rings out from a street or two away.

"You honestly don't even notice it after the first week or so, not with the college bars and swaps and things," Ceridwen says. "Though I imagine it is a bit jarring if you've just come from New York."

We're standing in front of the gate to King's, and Goose stares up at it. "There's literally nothing like this in America."

There really isn't. I'd gotten rather used to how *new* everything seemed in Miami, especially, and even New York. But standing in front of a chapel constructed by Henry VI is quite the reminder.

"It is rather extraordinary, isn't it?" Ceridwen says, then

looks at her wrist. "It's not midnight yet. Want to look around?"

I nod, and Ceridwen takes off at a slow stroll. We follow, and I imagine my mother here, walking this same path, or having breakfast in Hall, or sleeping in a room less well appointed than Ceridwen's. Instead, it's that journal entry of hers that comes to mind—

If it weren't for the professor, I think, I might've done it already. God knows there's a ready supply of drugs, even (especially) at King's.

She was writing about suicide, of course. I swerve away from the rest of her words and the thought of her here and try to place myself back beside Ceridwen and Goose, who seems to be asking her for advice.

"Don't ride the Jesus horse," is the sentence I catch.

"Is . . . that a euphemism for something . . . ?" I ask.

"No. The horse, at Jesus. Don't ride it."

"Right," I say, still out of it. "Forgot that one." I gaze back up at King's College Chapel, feeling as though I couldn't be farther from Miami or New York, in every possible way. "It's all very *Christian*, isn't it. Seems rather exclusive, no?"

"Don't think they were big on inclusivity in the Middle Ages," Ceridwen says. "The term that's beginning this week is still called Michaelmas. The next one is Lent, then Easter."

"Christ."

"Also a college," she adds with a grin. "Not to be confused with Corpus Christi. Which, again."

"Wait, is there a Jesus *bar?*" Goose asks.

She laughs. "Not only is there a bar, but Jesus has a somewhat peculiar obsession with cock, as it happens. Cocks on the logo, bronze cocks—"

"Like some bizarre compound of sexual innuendo and poultry," I say.

Goose turns to me. "I need to go here, absolutely."

"Despite the lack of nightlife?" she asks teasingly.

"You lot make your own fun, I'm told. And luckily, we're used to that, aren't we?"

Ceridwen flashes him a half smile. "You should come up next year," she says to Goose. Then, to me, "You as well."

My eyes take in the stonework on the gate, the turrets and arcading on the college. Mara talked about going to uni, and I would have followed her anywhere. Can't really imagine her here, though.

But then, I couldn't have imagined myself without her. Yet here I stand.

"Hard to imagine a future in which I go here," is all I say.

"Then you've got a rather lacking imagination," she says. Then, her tone shifting, "We might be different from most everyone else in some ways, but we don't have to live like it. It doesn't have to define you, unless you let it."

What would it feel like, to really believe that? "We really do appreciate everything."

She lifts her shoulders in a careless shrug. "We're family, of a sort," she says. "Got to look out for each other, haven't we?"

Two guys in red chinos approach us in the darkened street, and Ceridwen rolls her eyes. "Bloody hell," she mumbles. Then, to us, "Right. You lot have fun. I'll let the porters know to let you in, if you remember your names when it's all done." She flounces off, drawing the attention of the approaching chino-wearers, before they turn to us.

They both look like they lost out at auditions for *American Psycho: The Musical*.

"Alastair Greaves?" one of them asks.

"Literally no one calls me that," he says, extending a hand. "Noah Shaw?"

"Present," I say, as Goose stifles a laugh, but only just.

They withdraw something from each of their pockets—kerchiefs, I suppose. "Turn around."

I look witheringly at Goose. "This is really how I'm going to spend my last night as myself?"

"If you drink yourself into oblivion you won't need any of our new friend's help." He grins.

"You owe me," I say to him as I turn away from the Tory Twins.

"You'll thank me later," he insists as both of us are blind-folded.

"*Ecce ego mitto vos sicut oves in medio luporum!*" they say loudly, in unison, before an unseen hand prods me forward.

I'm jostled into Goose's shoulder and hear him say, "Caught

'*wolves*,'" before we're told to shut up. We're marched forward and, after several metres, downstairs.

We've climbed down dozens of stone steps by the time Goose says, in a low voice, "I've just worked it out." One of the Tories knocks in a peculiar way on what sounds like a wooden door.

"Please, keep me in suspense," I say, when I hear footsteps heading back up the stairs. I used to know perfect abbey Latin, once. Seems the eidetic memory bit's been lost with my other abilities. Shame.

"*In medio.* Among," Goose says, as ancient iron hinges creak. "Behold, I send you out—"

"As sheep among the wolves," another voice answers—an incredibly familiar voice, and completely jarring, given where we are.

The blindfold's pulled from my eyes, and Jamie's standing in front of us, holding the door open.

39

ALWAYS A RIDDLE

As I stare, wordless and blinking, I wonder for a fraction of a second if Jamie and Isaac look and sound much more alike than I remembered, and if it's the former who's standing in front of me.

But then Jamie does a little tap dance in the arched doorway, and then spreads out his arms. "Ta da!"

"*Brilliant*," Goose says, applauding. "Jamie Roth! Who'd have guessed?" He turns to me.

Hearing Goose acknowledge him puts me back on somewhat solid ground. "Well done," I agree, looking over Jamie's shoulder at what appears to be a party going on behind him.

"Thanks! Come on in," Jamie says, sweeping his arm.

"You were literally the last person I expected to see," I say a bit dreamily as we walk over the threshold.

"Literally?" He mocks my accent. "The last?"

"We are still in Cambridge, yes?" I ask him as I touch one of the stone walls. If this is an illusion, it's impressive. If Sophie and Leo show up, I suppose I'll know once and for all if we're fucked.

"Usually people don't start feeling up inanimate objects until they've had one of my cocktails, but go ahead. And yes, we're still in Cambridge, Dorothy." He takes something from a silver tray being passed by a waiter in a tuxedo. "This," he says, holding up what appears to be a fig smothered in something, "is fucking delicious."

Goose bites his lip. "Want. Immediately."

"As you wish," Jamie says, holding out his elbow to Goose.

"What are you doing here, though?" I ask warily.

"Brooklyn was boring without you," he says. "So I texted your sister to find out where you were, and she said here. And then I thought, why limit myself in applying to American colleges only? Why not explore opportunities abroad." He winks at Goose.

My eyes narrow. "How'd you get Kate's number?"

He makes a cringe face, then explains to Goose, "We went out a while ago, for a very brief second. I'm a changed man." Then, to me, "You really forgot?"

I had, actually. It's strange, seeing him here, and seeing him without Mara—the two of them have become paired, now, in my mind. I resist the urge to look for her, but only just.

I skirt a curtain of dewdrop lights strewn from ceiling to floor. "How'd you get in?" I ask.

"How'd *you* get in, asshole?"

"We were invited," I say evenly.

"We thought we were being pranked by a mate," Goose says, nicking a charged glass of champagne from a tray held by a passing waiter. I think I notice a shift in Jamie's expression just before Goose downs the contents of his glass. "This is *splendid*," Goose says.

Jamie, back to his usual self, says to Goose, "Well, in a sense, that's true. You were pranked by a mate, if you consider me a mate."

"So those Tory dicks—" Goose starts.

"Just two dudes I paid with a pint. Easy prey," Jamie says.

"Worth it," Goose agrees.

"I've always considered myself to have a flair for the dramatic."

"One might think you actually go here, starting sentences with, 'I've always considered myself,'" I say, narrowly avoiding two women in high-necked dresses, their hair whipped up behind them.

"When in Rome," Jamie says, following my gaze. Then, "Is it just you guys?"

"What, here?" Goose asks. Jamie nods. "Indeed it is," Goose replies brightly.

"Why?" I ask.

"No reason," Jamie says, shrugging. "Thought maybe you might've met up with old chums here in Merrie England."

I search Jamie's face. "Old *chums*? No," I say cautiously. "What about our old chums from Brooklyn?" When he doesn't answer immediately, I specify, "Leo? Sophie?"

Can't ask about Mara or Daniel. Not yet. Shouldn't ask at all, if I want to keep my dignity.

Jamie shakes his head. "Haven't heard a peep. And wouldn't exactly call them *chums*." He looks around us. "This place is wild, right?"

It is, that. Everyone, Jamie included, is in formal dress—so good on Goose there, for that—and we seem to be underground, in an impressively large Gothic arcade. There are tables scattered about, set with china and navy linens, and every available sconce is lit with dripping candles, making the light flicker.

I reflexively scan the crowd looking for the face I want but am terrified to see. "Are *you* alone?" I ask Jamie, ever so casually.

"You mean, is Mara here?" Jamie arches an eyebrow.

There it is.

"She's in her childhood bedroom, waiting by the phone for you to call as she listens to R.E.M. on repeat," he says, and when he sees my expression he pats me on the shoulder. "Just kidding, she's totally over you."

This isn't what I expected when I allowed myself to be led here by Goose; it's worse. Far, far worse.

When I saw Jamie I considered, for the briefest of seconds, asking questions I now realise I've been desperate for answers to—where is she? What is she doing? Who's she with? But I refuse to give Jamie the satisfaction. Shan't.

"Lovely," is all I say.

Jamie flashes a phony smile. "What are friends for?"

"Is that what we are?" I ask him.

Goose throws his arms around both of us. "Gentlemen, gentlemen. On a night such as this, how could any man bicker?"

"I bring out the best in him," Jamie says to Goose, who starts edging us toward one of the tables. With food, I notice.

"So how *did* you find out about this?" I ask Jamie, still uncomfortable about all of it. The seeming randomness of it all. The invitations with our names on them, I could accept, especially if Jamie had them made—if he'd found out about the party, somehow, and Kate told him we'd be in Cambridge.

But how did *he* know about it? I can't hear his heartbeat or pulse, and so I can't know for certain whether he's lying. I wish for the first time that I could.

Jamie picks at one of the pomegranate seeds spilling out from a platter laden with paper-thin sashimi. "I know a guy who knows a guy," he says, pulling a plate nearer to us. "You gotta try the hamachi," he says to Goose. "It's marinated in yuzu."

"What's the name?" I ask. "Of the guy you know?"

"Is it so shocking that I'd have friends here?"

Fuck it, I decide. Might as well come right out and ask. "Was it the professor?" I'm not sure if Jamie flinches or if the candles have just flickered.

Goose shoots me an embarrassed look and mutters under his breath, "Mate, really?" Then, turning to Jamie, "Oh! Do you know Ceridwen?"

Jamie looks momentarily flustered—I think?—but recovers quickly. "No," he says, picking up another piece of sashimi. "Is she one of Noah's exes?"

"No, we just met her, and she's got this friend—"

"*Goose*," I say, and shake my head once. Jamie looks back and forth between us.

"What?" Jamie asks, picking another pomegranate seed from the platter, rolling it between his fingers.

Goose rolls his eyes. "Forgive him. He's having an off night. Feeling rather paranoid."

"You're not paranoid if they really are out to get you," Jamie deadpans.

I watch him, saying nothing. He seems off, somehow, and different, but Goose doesn't pick up on it, and it's fucking tiresome, not being believed.

"Here," Goose says, taking two glasses from the next passing tray. "This'll help." He offers the other to Jamie, who refuses.

"Since when do you not drink?" I ask Jamie.

"I'm not thirsty," he says, shrugging. I put down my glass as well.

"Come *on*," Goose says to me, rather exasperated. "It's *medicinal*."

I ignore him. "When did you get to England?" I ask Jamie. "What have you been doing here?"

"A couple of days ago," he says easily. "Sightseeing. You?"

"Sightseeing where?"

"Oxford first, but don't tell anyone here," Jamie whispers to Goose. "They call it the Other Place."

Goose smirks. "They do, that."

"Massive Tolkien fan, though. Couldn't not check it out."

"So you came to visit colleges," I say, affecting a bored tone. "And because Brooklyn was boring without us."

"I was being nice," Jamie says maddeningly. "I really meant that it was boring without Goose but didn't want you to feel excluded."

He's firing back with all the right answers. But they don't *feel* right.

I finally realise why. "You just *left* Mara?"

"No, *you* left Mara," he fires back. "Or don't you remember."

Of course I fucking remember. If only I could forget, because Jamie's right and I hate that he's right, and myself, of course, as always, which is possibly why I can't stop myself from asking, "Where is she?"

"You don't have the right to ask me that," he says.

"You're lying," I say, to provoke him. "I don't believe you just left her on her own."

He's growing angry, now. "I didn't. She's not a kid. She's not a thing. She wanted some time to herself and after what you did I don't blame her."

"What *I* did? Do you know what *she* did?"

A few heads turn in our direction at my raised voice. I notice and don't give a shit. Jamie notices, and does. "Nothing to see here, folks," he says to them, flashing a too-wide smile. "Keep drinking that champers."

"God, that's what my mother calls it," Goose says, disgusted. Jamie's hovering between focusing on Goose and dealing with the problem of me. He decides on Goose.

"I didn't know any better," Jamie says solemnly to him. "It'll never happen again."

"See that it doesn't," Goose says.

I'm of a mind to leave this rapidly congealing conversation; the part of me that has been hoping, naïvely, for a distraction, is dying an agonisingly slow death. But I'm not quite ready to trust whatever this is, yet, that Jamie's pulling.

Though maybe I can extract myself, somehow, and manage to watch him for a bit instead?

I start backing away from both of them. "I think I'm done for the night, chaps," I say. "Enjoy the party," I add to Goose.

Jamie leans his head back, looking up at the ceiling. "*Fuck*," he mumbles. Then, "Goosey, can you give us a sec?" He tugs playfully on his lapel.

"Of course," Goose says. Then Jamie steers me away from the table, not meeting my eyes.

"I'm sorry, okay? She's my best friend, and it doesn't feel right talking to you about her, now." He glances over his shoulder—at Goose? Someone else?—before looking back at me. Or, more precisely, my feet.

I can't know for certain whether he's lying. He might be, or I might be losing my mind—might've *been* losing it for a while now, and seeing him here's shoving me off the edge.

If I hadn't spent the earlier part of the evening with someone as suspicious of the world as Isaac, would I be acting like this? Jamie's the closest I've been to Mara since—

Since.

I'd whore myself for a cigarette right now, something to do with my hands, my mouth. I'm jumpy, anxious. Maybe I'll start in on the champagne, after this.

"Look," Jamie says, voice low. "All I'll say is this. She'll always choose the people she cares about over the people she doesn't, and she cares about you the most. She thought you knew her. She thought you got that."

"I do, but—"

"There's no 'but.' That's how she is. It's *who* she is."

"It doesn't *have* to be," I say, and immediately regret it. The last thing I want or need is to be drawn into this conversation right now, about her, with *him*.

Jamie's shaking his head. "You don't get to choose the version of her you want," he says quietly. "As long as she loves you, she'll choose you."

Kill for you, he means. Which I couldn't—still can't—accept.

"Does she?" I ask miserably. I couldn't despise myself more. "Still?"

Jamie looks impossibly more uncomfortable, shifting his weight.

Turns out I can.

"Forget I asked," I say, choking the rest of my questions about Mara down. I give Jamie a single nod. Then, trying to reclaim some pride, I apologise. "Sorry, for all that, before. It's been . . . an odd night."

Jamie smiles, but it doesn't reach his eyes. "It's cool." His hands are in his pockets, and he's facing away from me. He doesn't ask about my night, which is un-Jamie-like. Or maybe it's perfectly Jamie-like and I'm reading too much into it, or the wrong thing into it, or everything.

I'm still trying to scrape away thoughts of Mara from my skull when Goose interrupts us breathlessly. "Guys, I just saw graffiti from *1731*. One W. Kymer felt himself important enough to carve his name in stone. Do you know where we are? I think we're under the chapel," he answers himself. "There's loads of people buried here. Like, where we're walking."

"Actually, they're buried below the chapel floors," a familiar voice says from behind Goose. When he shifts, I see Victoria Gao standing beside him in a gown that looks like molten silver. "There was a project in the late eighteenth century to lower the steps leading to the sanctuary, but human remains were found inside intact lead coffins, which were disinterred. Noah," she says to me, holding out her hand. "Lovely to see you again."

Isaac's words come to mind unbidden.

Don't touch anyone you don't trust.

Isaac hasn't even fucked with my head, yet, and still he's fucking with my head.

Victoria's hand is still extended, so I'm faced with the choice of having to be publicly rude whilst privately acknowledging that Isaac's paranoia is warranted, or acting like a normal person.

Fuck it. I shake her hand.

40

YOU WILL REGRET BOTH

"FANCY MEETING YOU HERE," I SAY TO VICTORIA.
She looks perplexed. "You didn't get the invitation?"

I look to Goose, and Jamie. "What?" I ask.

"I asked them to leave it with your mobile. You didn't see? Odd," she says, as if that's what's strange, here.

"What invitation?" I ask her.

"Your father's company—*your* company, I should say— funds a foundation, which is hosting this benefit tonight," she explains patiently. "The planning committee thought it would be meaningful to have it here, at the university where he attended."

Suggest you go to Cambridge. Loads of family history there as well.

"I'm glad you're here, regardless. And that you brought your friends." She flashes a smile at Goose, Jamie. "Victoria Gao," she says, holding her hand out to them. "General counsel for EIC. And you are?"

"Goose Greaves," he says, shaking her hand.

"Jamie Roth."

"Lovely to meet you, Goose. James."

The hair rises on the back of my neck for some reason.

"It's Jamal, actually," he corrects her, politely.

She sighs, embarrassed. "I'm terribly sorry, forgive me, I shouldn't have assumed—"

"Victoria?"

"Kate!" Victoria says, as my sister appears behind her wearing a blush-pink structured gown. "How was the trip up? Was the driver all right?"

"Lovely, thank you so much," my sister says, teeth gleaming, smile bright. "Jamie, glad you could make it." She kisses him on each cheek before turning to chat with Victoria.

So, that's it then. Jamie must've found out about the party from Kate, decided to fuck with me. Victoria's appearance here is to be expected, given that she helped organise the event. Jamie's seemed off all night because we've always *been* off, he and I, before Mara, and neither of us knows how to act now that it's done.

I've been imagining a conspiracy where there is none. Goose was right again.

I run my hand through my hair, and notice it's shaking, slightly. I should be drinking, in this state, listening to Goose on that point as well. I nick his half-full champagne glass and bring it to my lips.

Before I can drink it, though, Jamie stumbles into me. The sound of glass shattering on stone draws heads in our direction.

"Sorry," Jamie says, but he meets my stare directly, now.

He isn't sorry.

"Had a bit too much to drink, I think," he says to Kate and Victoria.

He hasn't had a drop.

"Can I get you anything?" Victoria asks him.

"Thanks, but I'll be good once I get some food in me." He tips his head at one of the tables. "Boys?" He looks at me and Goose.

"Right," I say, grabbing a new glass of champagne, watching Jamie's eyes follow it. Something *is* happening—but he won't talk about it here, clearly. "We pregamed before we got here, but I've got loads of catching up to do, yet." Kate rolls her eyes. "Don't let any freshers spot you in that dress, for God's sake," I add before turning back to Goose and Jamie. I follow them to a table.

"Could do with a smoke," I say, aware I haven't got any.

Goose must have, though. And it's a perfect excuse to leave. "Goose? Got any?"

"Course," he says, feeling his pockets. He withdraws a few hand-rolled ones and I withdraw my lighter. That, I've kept.

"Think I can I smoke in here?" I ask Goose, then Jamie.

"Probably not," Goose says.

I sigh. "Everything's always so *complicated*," I say. Then, to Jamie, "Join us?"

His eyes dart around the room. "I think I'm good here, actually," he says.

Jamie is many things: Stupid is not one of them. Careless isn't, either. Whatever it is that's going on, he can't or won't talk about it—not here, at least, and he doesn't seem to want to leave, either. Which means he *has* to be here, for some reason.

What bloody reason, though? If I want answers, and I really fucking do, I'll have to force him out of here, and then force the words out of him.

"Well, I'm in need of the loo," I say to Jamie. "Can't even remember where we came in from, can you?" I ask Goose. Jamie points to a large, arched wooden door. I flag a waiter down with one hand, leaning exaggeratedly on the other elbow.

"Loo?" I pretend to slur.

"Outside the chapel, by the porter's lounge."

"Really?" Goose asks. "That far?"

"It's fine," I say, thanking the waiter. Then I stand, making a show of it, pretending to sway, before I jostle my way through clumps of people on my way out the door. I'm looking for a confrontation, something I'll need to be rescued from, preferably by Goose and Jamie both, when an excuse finds me, first.

A man in a pale blue plaid suit and a yellow tie grabs my hand, pumping it forcefully.

"Mr. Shaw," he says. "Jay Dee. Pleasure to meet you. Such tremendous work you're doing, with the foundation."

"Of course," I say, looking over his shoulder at the door. "Thank you."

"Caught a glimpse of you at the funeral, of course, didn't want to disturb you. Your father was a great man, a very great man. Such vision, he had! No one was doing what he was doing! Truly a great man, your father was."

The words come so easily. "My father was a cunt."

It's as though the entire room had conspired to stop talking at that exact moment. My voice seems to echo along the vaulted ceiling.

All in, why not. "What!" I shout, remembering Jamie's discomfort at my earlier volume. "He was!" I make out Jamie and Goose heading toward me, and catch Jamie whispering to Goose. Perfect.

"Apologies," Goose says to the man, and everyone in our general vicinity. "Terribly, terribly sorry—my usually charming friend's had quite a lot to drink." Once they're at my side, they each take an elbow. "Once again, my deepest apologies; we'll get him sorted. Please, go on and enjoy your evening."

They steer me toward the massive wooden door; the guests make way for us. I see Victoria standing on the opposite side of the arcade, without Kate, but she doesn't stop us. No one does.

I free myself from their grip and say, loudly enough, "Don't *touch* me. Fuck's sake, I can still *walk*." They escort me to the stairs, and up.

We carry on until we're in the chapel itself, which is entirely empty and utterly breathtaking. The dark wooden screen stretches at least midway through the chapel, acting, in our case, as a sort of shelter from the altar steps and Rubens's *Adoration of the Magi*. Dozens of candles are lit in the entryway, and the fan vault is dramatically lit to highlight every detail.

"Okay," Jamie says to me. "I appreciate this moment, I do, but I really want to get back to the party."

"*Why?*" I narrow my eyes at him. He narrows his in return. "Fine," I say. "Just—help me find the loo, first, all right?"

Jamie glares, but says, "Sure."

We walk in silence along the college building, but I stop before we get to the porter's lodge. The Front Court is empty, the passages are empty, so I finally, finally ask Jamie, "What the fuck is going on?"

"What?"

"Come on," I say to him, who, to my surprise, sits down right where he is, on the ground.

"What—"

He starts picking blades of grass.

"They *really* frown upon that, here," Goose says. Jamie doesn't answer; he's arranging the blades into letters.

LISTENING

I meet his eyes. Tip my head back at the chapel, and mouth, "Them?"

YES

My father's company? Something to do with Horizons, perhaps? We don't have much time, I realise, and I need to choose my questions carefully, but there's one I need to answer before the rest.

MARA? I spell out.

Jamie shrugs and mouths, "I don't know."

SAFE?

He mouths again: "I don't know."

I immediately want to ask when he last saw her, ask about Daniel and whether he's been in touch, but—

SPY, Jamie arranges on the ground. Points to himself. Then forms new letters: SHITTY

"You're a shitty spy?" I mouth, and he nods.

"Least we agree on that," I say aloud, and he kicks my shin with his foot as he starts to get up, but I force him back down.

"Who?" I mouth.

Jamie hesitates for a minute. Then tugs at his pendant.

I run my hands through my hair, nearly tearing it out in frustration.

"Why?" I mouth.

He looks at me for a moment, and I'm not sure if he's wondering what to say, or wondering what I meant by the question. Finally, he spells out the word:

HISTORY

I clearly don't get it, nor does Goose, because Jamie then spells: MINE, and points to his chest.

"Mates," Goose says aloud. "I think we've got to bail out."

Jamie is still arranging blades of grass on the ground, though. The next word is FAMILY.

I think immediately of Isaac, then, wandering Cambridge in search of a place to sleep for the night, or perhaps having gone back to Ceridwen's room after all. Does Jamie know about him?

"Mates, seriously." Goose is tugging on Jamie's shoulder with one hand, and at my jacket with the other. I look up.

Several porters are lumbering toward us with torches in their hands. One's got a radio on his belt.

"Chapel roof," a fuzzy voice says, coming from one of their radios.

"Bloody idiot freshers," one of them mumbles as he heaves past us. Another scolds Jamie on his way along.

"You're lucky you picked tonight, young man, or I'd have you suspended," the porter says to Jamie.

"What's going on?" Goose asks them. He is roundly ignored.

"Did you hear that? On the radio?" I ask Goose and Jamie. They shake their heads. I nearly repeat what it said, but remember Jamie's word:

LISTENING

So I point to the roof instead, where the porters' torches are now aimed in a dizzying frenzy, finally coming to rest on the distant outline of the person climbing it.

NO STAKES

"F UCK," GOOSE SAYS.

"My thoughts exactly."

Jamie mouths, "Let's go," and jerks his thumb back to the chapel, our entrance to the party. We follow him quickly. As we walk, we're joined by a smattering of students coming out of their rooms, approaching from different directions.

"Someone's night-climbing?"

"Total fucking legend."

"How can you be a legend if you're sent down before term even starts?"

"Who said it's a fresher?"

"I know one of them."

"One of the freshers?"

"No, idiot, a climber."

"*What?* Who?"

"Can't say."

"Pardon," Goose says politely to one of them. "Do you know what's going on?"

"Not really," she says. "Heard at first it was an initiation, now everyone's saying it's a night climber."

"Which is . . . ?"

"Seriously?" one of the guys says. "God, you lot are loathsome."

"We don't go here," I say, irritated.

"So a tourist, then," he says. "Even worse."

"It's an old soc," the girl Goose flagged says to me. "There's no record of who the first one to climb any of the buildings was, but over the years they've been responsible for the most classic pranks in uni history."

"They got an Aston Martin on the roof of the Senate House, once."

"And Christmas hats on the pinnacles of chapel, another time."

"*Vita aedificium est istam scande*," the student who claimed to know the climber says. "Life is to climb that building over there," he says, shooting us a superior look.

"So this is a thing people do," I say, making eye contact with Jamie.

"Not on the reg or anything," the girl says. "But it's been done, yeah."

"How high is it?" Goose asks, indicating the chapel ahead of us.

"A hundred and sixty feet."

"How does anyone even get up there?"

"Used to be the chimney, I think, but they blocked that. Now you need gear. Not as pure," says the smug climbing admirer.

The girl rolls her eyes.

The court is starting to get crowded, and a couple of the porters have turned their attention to herding students instead of the climber.

Jamie looks longingly at the chapel, tugging my arm.

"Think we can get back in?" I ask. He looks doubtful. Still won't speak. Who does he think is listening? And listening to *what*? From where?

"We can try, before it's surrounded," I say, then, to the girl, "Thank you."

"What, you're leaving?"

"We've got a party to get back to." Goose smiles.

We don't get far. A human chain of soft-looking guards is blocking the entrance to the chapel, which is our only way back into the party. Jamie swears.

I look to him, then the guards. "I'm guessing you can't . . ."

He's shaking his head so strenuously it's faintly alarming.

"Right." If he could've talked our way in or out of anything at the moment, he probably wouldn't be here right now.

"There's another way in, through the Backs," says a voice from behind us.

M glides over a corner of lawn to meet us, the colour of her gown blending with the grass.

"It's something, isn't it?" she says, glancing up at the chapel. "You never quite get used to it."

I should be used to *her* by now, turning up at random to nip at my heels when I've strayed too far from her quest.

She's standing in profile, her face obscured by shadow. She's always seemed familiar, but there's something especially so about her tonight.

Jamie must see it too, because his eyes swing from M, to me, to Goose, and back to M again.

"Hi," she says to him, extending her hand. "I'm Mara."

Jamie's mouth is slightly parted, his head cocked to one side.

"Long story," I say.

He looks like he's about to speak, but no words come out. His eyes never leave Mara's grandmother's face.

M beams charmingly. "Come, we'll chat over drinks."

Goose looks up again. "But what about . . . that?"

"You heard the Tabs," I say. "It's a prank." I don't believe it. I want to believe it.

I edge closer to M. "Why are you here?" I ask her.

"I was invited."

"Bollocks." Jamie's spying, for or on the professor. We've just left Isaac, who warned us about him. We're being listened to, supernaturally or otherwise, and now M is here, wanting a chat?

"I agreed to give a speech about your mum," she says.

"What are you on about?"

She shrugs. "The foundation asked me. Came across my name somewhere in her things. We *were* friends, you know."

"They didn't find your name in her things. *I* have my mother's—" Diaries. Journals. Packed up in boxes for me and sent to New York, and then packed up again and sent back to Yorkshire, courtesy of—

"You know Victoria," I say to M, as something clicks into place.

"Yes," she says. "I know Victoria. And the foundation *did* happen upon my name in your mother's belongings. The two aren't mutually exclusive." She looks infuriatingly amused before turning around. "Follow me," she says, leading the way through the Fellows' Garden, which is as quiet as we are.

We each follow her for our own reasons; Jamie is, quite obviously, on some sort of mission; Goose is game and curious, along for the ride as always; and I—I don't know what I am anymore, what I believe. Every instinct I have feels wrong. My compass is broken. I've never been more lost.

We reenter the chapel through a door near the altar. M leads the way with Jamie right behind her, and when she moves into a shaft of light, I see it.

The green silk of her dress dives into a V in the back, as it does in the front. The emerald fabric eddies with every footstep, and my own footsteps slow to a stop.

I know that dress. It belongs on someone else.

The chapel fills with the outlines of people, translucent and writhing in fancy dress. The stained-glass windows darken and the roof lowers and my skull is filled with what passes for music in Miami. Katie, in fairy wings, is beside me, regaling her friends with a tale I'd been valiantly attempting to listen to until I saw that dress.

Mara stands at the far end of the room, doe eyes wide. "Coming?" she asks.

It's the voice that drags me from the memory—M's voice, not Mara's. But the memory, the intrusion, feels ominous. A harbinger.

And then Goose's voice, beside me, as the bodies fade and the chapel ceiling stretches up, fans out: "This feels . . . sacrilegious."

"He'll forgive you," says Jamie. The acoustics reflect Jamie's voice so that the words *forgive you* follow our steps.

Goose puts one foot cautiously onto the red carpet. Then another, before he finally starts walking normally.

I, however, do not. It's been one thing to open my eyes and

find myself looking out through someone else's, to feel what they felt, to hear a thunder of heartbeats wherever I went. It wasn't good. I didn't *like* it. But I understood it. It was *my* normal.

Which is precisely what my thoughts aren't, not anymore. I feel trespassed upon, watched, like there are eyes on my skin, in my head, swarming like insects. I reach for my collar, what's beneath it, without thinking, only noticing I've done it when my fingers feel silk instead of silver. It feels wrong, all of us following in Mara's—no, M's—shadow. I'm suddenly vertiginous with panic, with paranoia.

"Stop," I call out, as M walks through the Gothic arch of the staircase. She listens.

We all do, as the air outside fills with screams. I catch a swift, dark silhouette moving past one of the massive stained-glass windows as the climber falls.

KNOW HIMSELF

FOR THE FIRST TIME, I FIND MYSELF GENUINELY shocked by someone's death.

I wasn't yanked into someone else's reality. I didn't feel anyone else's fear or sadness or shame. I watched someone die with my own eyes, from my own limited, blind perspective—just a falling shadow through stained glass.

It might be a stranger. Someone who isn't Gifted, someone I don't know.

It might be an accident. A prank gone wrong. A simple fall.

Or it might not be either of those things. I don't know because I *can't* know, not for sure, not without my Gifts. I'm still broken.

And glad of it.

Goose is ashen, ill-looking. "I can't—how did that—"

Jamie's eyes linger on the staircase, beyond M's feet.

M is looking at me. Waiting.

"Well?" she says finally.

"Well what?"

"Are you coming or not?"

She doesn't wait for my answer, though, before she begins the descent.

Perhaps I don't know what happened for certain. But I've seen enough, experienced enough, to begin to guess that it wasn't an accident. That none of this is.

I'm in it, though. As is Jamie, whatever his reasons. But Goose—

I pull him aside. "Listen, you can't chunder in the chapel. Go out the front way, we'll find you after, all right?"

He looks stricken. "Did he fall?" His voice sounds young, unsteady.

Goose is shocked and not thinking, not remembering, that I have no way of truly knowing, but now's not the time to remind him. Or to describe the shape that my suspicions are forming.

"Yes," I lie. "Go."

I'm tempted to get down on my knees and thank Jesus when he listens, but Jamie and M are almost out of sight. I hurry down the steps as quickly as I can.

We finally come to the enormous door. When M knocks, I'm afraid, for a moment, that when it opens, we'll be walking in on some sort of ritual, with everyone chanting in robes.

The door opens. It's just the same party.

Or what's left of it; there are soiled linens and empty glasses on the tables, along with half-eaten plates and discarded trays of picked-over food, along with a handful of tuxedoed waiters clearing up.

"Where'd everyone go?" Jamie asks.

"The news has probably spread—it would be easier for everyone to exit through other colleges."

"You can get to others from here?"

M nods as she walks. "Caius and Trinity are the closest. You don't have to come along, but I'd like to find out what happened to that poor boy."

I wonder, for a second, what might happen if I call her bluff; if I turn to leave, collect Goose, and get out of here.

But we've been followed every step. No reason to think it'll stop now.

So instead I ask, "How do you know it was a boy?"

"Antiquated gender conventions and past experience," she says, not turning around. "But feel free to assume otherwise."

I shut up the rest of the way.

We emerge from the arcade through another staircase, which leads to a corridor, which leads to yet another staircase, and then, finally a library.

Victoria is scrolling on her mobile, leaning against one of the grey walls. She's framed by mullioned windows draped in red-and-white-striped fabric. A girl our age, possibly older, crosses the wide planked wood floors in a chartreuse dress and whispers in her ear as we approach. Victoria looks up.

"Hi," Victoria says to M.

I don't know why, but that surprises me, too. I expected . . . something more formal. Significant.

"Quite an evening," M says, walking over to Victoria. They trade kisses on each cheek.

"Awful," Victoria replies. "But I see you've returned with the guest of honour, at least."

I bristle. "There's nothing honourable about me."

"On that we can agree," Victoria says. "But I wasn't referring to you." She looks at Jamie. "I am terribly sorry about tonight."

Jamie shrugs neutrally.

She can't mean—*Jamie?* I try to catch his eye without being obvious about it. He won't look at me. What's he got himself into?

"The police've fetched the body," a man's disembodied voice says. I try and locate the source of it, and notice a round-ish figure descending a rolling ladder, using both hands.

The fabric of his suit is so unusual I recognise him as the man who waylaid me earlier straightaway. What *was* his name?

"Do they know anything more, yet?" M asks.

"Not that they're sharing," the man says. He looks and sounds more familiar than he should, like I've known him long before tonight. "When they do, I'll let you know." I briefly notice the girl moving behind me out of the corner of my eye.

"Thanks," Victoria says to him.

The man withdraws a pale yellow silk handkerchief from his suit pocket and wipes his hands. "How do you do?"

"I've just watched someone kill himself," I say. "How do *you* do?"

"Very, very unfortunate," he mumbles. "Very unfortunate."

"Did the police determine it was a suicide?" Victoria asks the man. He shakes his head. "No."

Victoria turns to me. "How do you know he killed himself, then?"

"Can we cut the shit, please?" I say. Every nerve is frayed, on edge. They're taunting me. Playing with me. "I know that you know what I am. What we all are."

Victoria looks around the room awkwardly, then at me. "Are you sure you're feeling all right?"

"I swear to God—" I start, just as M puts her hand on my arm.

"Maybe you should have a lie-down," she says.

I shake her off. "Maybe you should tell me what Jamie's the fucking guest of honour of," I say, kicking myself for doubting myself earlier. "Why is he even here?"

"Dude," Jamie says. I shoot him a dangerous look and he backs away, arms raised.

"What, am I supposed to pretend this is normal? That there's some perfectly ordinary explanation for all of us being here?" I snap, having fucking had it. I round on M. "That it isn't dodgy for my father's solicitor to know you, given you're supposed to be dead?"

M pauses, studying me with concern. "Who exactly do you think I am?"

"Mara Dyer's grandmother," I say through clenched teeth.

M looks quizzically at me, then Victoria. "Who is Mara Dyer?" she asks.

I feel like screaming. "Your granddaughter. Daughter of Indira, who's *your* daughter with the professor. Both of them believed you killed yourself seventeen years ago. I thought that too until you showed up outside my flat in Brooklyn last week and told me I had to come back to England if I wanted to save Mara from the professor, whom you met in British India two centuries ago."

She looks at Victoria, then back at me. "Noah, my name is Em—"

"M," I repeat. "M for Mara, because she was named after you."

She's shaking her head as I'm nodding mine. "Em for Emma," she says. "Emma Sarin. Because my mother loved Jane Austen and Sarin is not an uncommon Southeast Asian name. I told you my name when we met at your family's manor. Your sister Kate was there." She looks concerned, well-meaning, and her expression's a copy of Indi's, I realise.

Victoria, the unnamed man, and Chartreuse look on as if to say, *See?*

Kate. *Kate.* I hope to God she's nowhere near here; there's nothing else I can do about it at the moment. I cross my arms, lifting my chin. "So, what then? You're here tonight because . . . ?"

"Because I was one of your mum's closest friends at college," she says. "I got to know your father a bit, after she died, and he put me in touch with Victoria, who helped me get involved with the foundation." Emma—no, *M*—looks to Jamie, now. "I started explaining that to your friend, when we saw each other at Front Court."

I look to Jamie, then, finally. He's sitting in a black leather wing chair opposite a globe. "Tell them. Tell them about Mara."

He looks uncomfortable. "She's your ex-girlfriend? What do you want me to say?"

"Tell them what you told me," I order him. "Tell them what you're really doing here." When Jamie shrugs helplessly, I say, "He told me he's a spy."

Victoria puts a finger on her lips. "A spy," she repeats.

"Goodness," the man says.

Em, or M, bites her lip before saying, "Just so we're all sure we understand you, you're saying you think I'm over a century old, and that your friend here is a teenage spy?"

"I'm *not* mad," I say. Insist, really. But then, that's what people who are mental always say, isn't it? The cracks are beginning to show through the paint.

"Why don't you sit," Em says to me. Chartreuse comes up, offers me a glass of water. I almost take it before remembering the champagne glass at the party—how Jamie knocked it aside before I could drink it.

"I'm not drinking your poison," I growl, withdrawing my hand so fast that Chartreuse stumbles, only just catching herself on my shoulder to avoid a fall.

"Heavens!" the man says, and again, that jolt of familiarity. His name—does it start with a D? "Dear girl, are you all right?"

"Just breathe," Em says to me, sounding like a twenty-five-year-old yoga instructor as she demonstrates how to do it. I've never felt more capable of murder.

"Please sit," Victoria pleads. "You look exhausted."

I *feel* exhausted. Wrung out. "Thanks, but no," I say, peeling Chartreuse's hand off my shoulder. I begin backing up toward the door. "I think it's time we leave."

No one responds. I'm almost to the door. It can't be this easy, can it?

"Jamie?" I ask him.

"Yeah?"

"You coming?"

"Okay," he says, standing up slowly. He turns to the bemused-looking adults. "It was nice meeting you all. Thanks for the food and stuff." He smiles at them, but it doesn't take.

"Make sure he gets some rest," Em says.

"And some tea," Dalrymple chimes in—Dalrymple! That's his name. "Tea always helps."

"Sure thing," Jamie says, adding a little salute before turning around.

I take another step backward. My legs collapse beneath me.

A wave pulls at my consciousness. I struggle against it, but the current's too strong. I hear Em's voice before the grey walls shade into charcoal, and deepen into black.

"It was Leo," she whispers in my ear. "It was Leo who died. Now sleep."

43

THAT IRONY IN LIFE

"THAT WAS MEAN."

"It was, a bit."

"A bit? I think you might've broken him."

"I feel slightly guilty."

"Only slightly?"

"One must find ways to amuse oneself."

"How true."

"He's coming round, ladies."

I blink stupidly, opening my eyes to the same odd library I passed out in, and the same people in it, with one addition.

Isaac is sitting opposite me. His body is draped casually in the leather wing chair Jamie had been occupying, but his expression is a mixture of anger and fear.

"James," Victoria says. She's out of my line of sight but I recognise her voice. Jamie appears in my field of vision, then, dressed not in a suit, but jeans.

"Hey," he says to me.

I try and sit up, but my muscles don't work. "What did you do to me?" I ask Victoria, over his shoulder.

"Charlie helped you sleep."

"You looked like you needed a rest," M says.

I clench my teeth to keep from screaming. "You drugged me?" I ask the girl, still wearing her gown.

"She doesn't need to use drugs," M says. "She's Gifted, like you."

"Like us," adds Victoria.

"Why? Why did you do this to me?"

They look at each other. "Do . . . what?"

"Lie to me," I say through gritted teeth. "Bring me here." A trickle of sweat rolls down my temple, onto my neck. I can't even lift my hand to wipe it. "Bring *us*," I add, glancing at Isaac.

Victoria glances at the floor. Mr. Dalrymple looks constipated. Charlie's eyes keep darting away, so it's M who says, "We needed a sacrifice."

Mr. Dalrymple makes a sound like he's choking, which turns into a high, keening laugh. After another moment, Victoria breaks into a grin. Charlie looks embarrassed.

"They're fucking with you," Jamie says. He turns to them. "Guys?"

"Sorry, sorry," says M. "It's just, you make it so *easy*."

Mr. Dalrymple starts laughing again, and then M joins in the giggle fit. M seems like a different person entirely; but she's never been anything she seemed to be, has she? She slid from one role to the next, changing her manner-isms, colloquialisms, speech patterns—sometimes in the span of a single sentence—gauging and reacting to whom-ever she speaks with, shepherding them in the direction of her choice.

"You said Leo's dead," I say, injecting as much venom into the words as possible. "Were you fucking with me then, too?"

That does sober them up. "Sadly, no," Victoria says, but she doesn't look particularly sad.

"You killed him," I say blankly.

"Your father killed him, actually," M says. "Or anyway, his science did." She sighs. "Never really was one of his strengths."

Victoria cuts in. "The researchers he hired used different versions of the protocol over the years. As far as we can tell, we think that whatever mechanism his geneticists modified to switch the artificial gene on and off had a kill switch, for lack of a better term."

Goose's theory. *Maybe it's just something that happens to the copies.*

"The stuff that's been happening," Jamie starts. "Everyone

you've seen who's killed themselves? They . . . self-destruct," he says sadly. "It isn't anyone's fault."

"Well, to be fair," M says, holding out her hands and looking at me, as if to say, "*Except yours.*"

"I'm responsible for my father's actions, now?"

"Who said that?" She looks around. "Did I say that?"

"*How* did Leo die?" I ask. "Explain it to me."

"You were there," M says. "You saw what we saw."

"More than that," Victoria says. "You've felt it, in the past, haven't you? Experienced what they experienced? A form of extreme empathy, yes?"

"I didn't feel it, when he died," I say.

"Because you don't want to feel it anymore," M says. "You don't want to *feel* anymore, full stop. That's why you tracked down our friend, here, isn't it?" She glances at Isaac, tsking.

She's wrong, obviously—at least the bit about tracking down Isaac is. Not that I'm about to correct her. "Spare me the psychoanalysis, please. It's boring and you're shit at it."

M breaks into a smile.

"Leo was going to die," Victoria says evenly. "There wasn't anything any of us could do to stop it."

In a twisted way, it's comforting to hear. Spares me the guilt from having ignored answering the suicide question the second they stopped violating my mind. The guilt from avoiding my ability; it didn't help Sam, or Felicity, so why bother trying to get it back? Easier to choke it down and keep it there, to believe they'd have died anyway. That there wasn't anything I could do to stop it, not then, not ever. I was never rebelling against what the professor and my mother and everyone insisted I should be; I was hiding from it. Like the coward my father always said I was.

I'm nearly sick just thinking it. I look at Isaac for anything, something, a hint, but he's expressionless and blank. If I hadn't seen him earlier, when he'd just woken up, I'd never know he was in there.

"Why can't he talk?" I ask.

"He can talk," M says quietly. "He chooses not to."

Something about those words flicks a switch in my mind, shining a dim light on a memory; of Mara, pale and dead-eyed and limp.

She could *move. She chooses not to.*

My jaw clenches. Have they done something to him? Originals with access to the fruit of my father's poisonous research—they could do whatever they wanted.

Or perhaps he's silent by choice—betraying nothing so they'll have less to use against him, by his reasoning?

Isaac's survived the longest of us, from my generation. I should follow his example.

But I can't seem to help my mouth.

"So why this little get-together?" I ask them. I'm tempted to ask more, but Isaac's presence reminds me that anything I say might play into their hands.

They're older than you and smarter than you and stronger than you.

Maybe. Probably. But we wouldn't be here if we didn't have something they want. That's leverage.

Mr. Dalrymple withdraws a tube of ChapStick from his pocket and lines his lips, popping them loudly. It's the only sound in the room.

"That's . . . not an answer," I say, when no one does anything else.

"When your father had his geneticists apply the Lenaurd protocol—it's a game of roulette, what ability a carrier ends up with," Victoria starts. Her voice is robotic, technical, an echo of Dr. Kells's. "Usually the abilities aren't replicated, or if they seem to be replicated, it ends up never quite being an exact copy, regardless."

"You're thieves," I say, the realisation dawning. They haven't been offing Carriers to stay hidden, like I thought, like I suggested to Goose. "You're *stealing* abilities—"

"When someone dies, as has happened naturally over time, of course, or unnaturally, due to your father's interference, we've seen others born with that same ability, eventually," Victoria says. I wait for her to explain further. She doesn't, leaving me to listen for what she doesn't say.

Eventually, she said. Eventually isn't now, though, is it. "You accelerate the process," I say. "By which I mean, you kill them."

Victoria hesitates. "The unique genetic imprint of a Carrier's ability seems to remain intact after they die."

"Allowing you to steal it."

"Recycle," M corrects.

I narrow my eyes, not sure who to aim my questions at. I settle on M, though she seems to be taking this less seriously than Victoria—*seems* being the operative word. Nothing they say can be trusted.

"How do you decide who gets which ability, once a Carrier's dead?" I ask, trying to sound neutral. "This can't be all of you. How many of you are there?"

"Normally, how it works is everyone gathers at a site of ancient importance, whilst wearing robes, and we draw lots and chant until the next person's chosen. That's why the party tonight, and the fresh local corpse." She *almost* keeps a straight face, but cracks at the end. "Fuck! Nearly had it."

She sounds like Mara, just then, and it's like a spike through my chest. She adapts, chameleonic, until all verbal traces of the past hundred and fifty years are stripped away. If I were blind, without my ability, I might not know the difference. I'm nearly speechless with horror.

Nearly.

"You're not funny," I force myself to say, flattening my voice so it hovers between contemptuous and bored. "Just really fucking sad."

"You're not exactly a barrel of laughs yourself," she replies. "I honestly can't puzzle out what my granddaughter saw in you."

"She was probably just using me for sex," I say, shrugging. Then, "You must be very weak, if you have to shepherd kids to their deaths, force them off ledges, platforms—"

"*No*," Charlie says. It's the first time I've heard her voice. "No one was ever forced before."

"Not by us, at least," M says lightly. But there's a spark in her eyes.

"Which one of you does it?" I press, looking at each in turn.

"None of us," says Victoria. M sucks in her lips, biting back a grin. A sprite, mischievous and teasing.

None of *them*. Which means . . . one of *us*?

The room shudders, and a film begins to form on my vision, like frosted glass. A crack spiders out from the centre top, splitting and branching until M, Victoria, Dalrymple, Jamie, Charlie, and Isaac are reduced to vague shapes and desaturated colours. Then it shatters. Everything's the same, every*one*'s the same except—

Sophie's wearing a chartreuse silk dress, standing in the spot Charlie occupied just seconds ago.

44

THE PASSION OF THE POSSIBLE

OLY SHIT," JAMIE MURMURS.

I went to school with Sophie Hall for *years.* Jamie, longer. She'd proven herself a liar already, having betrayed Daniel's trust, and that was shit, obviously, but normal, human shit. This—whatever this is, that I'm looking at, is . . . malevolence.

A wave of revulsion crests, breaks. Isaac's feeling it too— even his expert poker face can't disguise his horror at the betrayal.

She tucks her short blond hair behind one ear, an anxious expression on her face.

I can't fathom it. Don't know where to begin, what to say,

how to process the layers of deception and make sense out of whatever polluted motive is behind them. So instead I say, "Mara's going to kill you. And she's going to do it slowly."

Sophie's blue eyes are like water, translucent. "There are worse things than death," she says.

I nod calmly. "I hear psychological torture's pretty fucking brutal. Though you'd have to ask Felicity and Sam and Beth and Stella and Leo and whoever else you've manipulated about that. Or, I suppose not, since they're all either dead or brain-dead, in Stella's case."

Stella, who blamed Mara right up till the end. Everyone probably had, at one point—I'd even wondered myself. She was guilty of so much else, it was almost easy. M said it herself, didn't she?

If you spend your life in a house with no windows and no doors, if you've never seen a tree reaching for the sky, or felt grass under your feet, or heard a bird's wings beat the air, your eyes might be open, but how much can you see?

If someone controls what you see, that affects what you believe. And that affects what you do.

Sophie walked in our footsteps, painting over doors if we walked out of the room, hanging pictures over windows when we looked the other way. Manipulated the view.

But who designed the house?

"Daniel isn't dead," Sophie says, cutting into my thoughts. "Yet."

"Yet." I repeat the threat, or the promise, or whatever it is that invoking Daniel's name is supposed to do. I glance at Jamie, feigning scepticism to mask my anger. "I don't know, you think that'll save her once Mara finds out what she is?"

A rage, explosive and shocking in its suddenness, overcomes her. "I am what your father *made* me!" she screams, her short, slight frame trembling. "I had a *life* before him. He made it a living hell. I'm still living with it, every fucking day!" She's still shaking after she's gone quiet.

No one speaks, giving me time to consider what to say next. Jamie offers nothing, not a clue, no help at all, so I stay silent. Sort of.

I catch Sophie's eye, and rub my forefinger and thumb together.

She crosses the room and grabs my hand mid–tiny violin gesture, trying to crush my fingers in hers. She's much smaller than I am, but it *does* hurt when someone actively tries to rebreak one's fingers. I can't move due to whatever's been done to me by someone in this room—Charlie, I thought then. Could be Victoria, though—could be any of them. Anything I see, hear, think, might have some construction of theirs. Might not be real.

No wonder Isaac lives the way he does.

"You do understand that I rather enjoy pain, right?" I ask Sophie. The skin on her pale chest flushes, up to her neck and cheeks. A vein bisects her forehead.

I'm genuinely surprised when she drops my hand instead of hitting me.

"Like your father," she spits.

A beat. Then, to Sophie, "Please, *do* tell me your tale of woe," I say as flatly as I can, hoping to buy more time to work it out. "The origin story that made you betray and manipulate and murder your friends and lovers and everyone who trusted you."

"I didn't *murder* them—"

"Wrong," I say. "I heard their last thoughts, begging for help. They didn't want to die until you *made* them want it." I look to Jamie again. "So much for that self-destruct claim."

"We all wanted it," Sophie says, her face going pale again. "We all thought about it. That's how your father *engineered* us," she spits.

"Thinking's not doing, though, is it," I say. "You're still here, after all."

"That's not a reward, it's a punishment," Sophie says, her eyes filling with tears. Victoria interrupts us.

"You should go, Soph. Get some rest." A tear spills, rolls down Sophie's cheek as she nods. Victoria whispers something to her and strokes the crown of her head, once. Then Sophie wordlessly leaves the room.

"Well," I say to M, Victoria, and Dalrymple. "She's mad."

"Sophie wrestles with big emotions," Victoria says, and I nearly laugh out loud at the understatement. "She isn't delusional, but she struggles with reality sometimes, and—"

"And no doubt one of you *helped* her with that struggle," I say. "I don't care. Honestly, truly I don't. If she's sick or broken or Frankenstein's monster, it doesn't matter. We're all sick. We're all broken. We still have a choice."

M is nodding. It's deeply alarming, her agreeing with me. "You're right. We all have a choice. Sophie's daily existence is such misery she thinks it's merciful, to end it for others like her." Shades of the professor in her voice, now, the cadence and tone. "Especially once she knew she was helping some of us."

Dalrymple dabs at his forehead with his kerchief. "I was able to do what that young fellow Leo could, once upon," he says forlornly. "I helped find others like myself. I'd know everything about them. Names, histories, temperaments." His shoulders heave with a wistful sigh. "Even helped some of your family," he says, nudging me with his elbow.

Family. He was at my father's funeral, he said. And he was there when Sam died—Victoria, too.

It's M's face I watch, though, as Victoria speaks. M, who revealed herself in calculated fits and starts, unspooling just enough details each time to fit with what Mara might've told me, what I might've read in family letters and journals. Using them as a lure when baiting me with the promise of saving Mara didn't work, arranging them so they propped up a narrative casting the professor as the villain. And Simon, with him.

"You were right," she says. "Our Gifts age too. Like the rest of us. Not as fast, not the same, but they weaken, with time."

I look from her, to M, to Dalrymple, finally, beginning to understand. Leo's death returned his Gift. Made him stronger.

"The more of *us* there are, the weaker you get," I say. "Have I got it right?" I don't need to look at Dalrymple's reddening face to know that I am.

"Half right," M says. "You're one of us too. Born, not made."

I stare blankly for a moment, before turning to Victoria. "So, you've rounded us up, revealed the plot twist, fed me some answers wrapped in bullshit justifications. What now? The plea for assistance?" I turn to M. "Or wait, no—we're past that, aren't we. Is it time for the threats?"

"We don't need either of those things, thanks to your friend," M says. I glance at Isaac, then Jamie.

"James is here to encourage you to do the right thing," Mr. Dalrymple says.

"Which is what, exactly?"

"Your inheritance," M says plainly.

Congratulations on your inheritance, the professor wrote.

"Is that why he's here?" I say, tipping my head at Isaac, as much as I can move it at all. "To root around in my mind?" M has been chasing my memories from the start, haunting me until my resistance chipped away. And it worked.

"Your family started this madness," M says. "We want it to stop."

"All right, let's stop it," I say. "You needn't have wasted so much time and effort assembling this little tableau, though.

The drugs you gave me? They worked. I remembered Simon, the professor. All there, for the taking. Have at it," I say carelessly.

A slow grin spreads across M's mouth. "I didn't give you drugs. I gave you sugar and hinted that it was something else, to see how suggestible you are. And you are *quite* suggestible. Your mind filled in the rest."

"So why bother with them?" I say, tipping my head at Isaac, Jamie. "I'll tell you what you want, or you can take it, however the fuck that works, I honestly don't care."

"Because you're suggestible and stubborn. Anything I asked, you turned down out of contrariness, not caution. I tried a plea. It didn't work. I tried guilt. That didn't work on you, either. Neither did self-interest, or even threats." She looks at me appreciatively. "You're got a complex psychological profile. Hard to pin down." She looks at the others. "I'm not sure any of us would be here, if it weren't for Goose."

My muscles tense.

"The second I mentioned him, and you went to the hospital? We had it locked up." She smirks. "Knew we could use him to move you in the direction we preferred, and he did."

"His psychological profile is ... less complex," Victoria says.

"Where is he?" I ask. I don't mention Ceridwen, in case there's a chance, however fleeting, that they don't know about her. Information is currency.

"Around, I'm sure," M says with a shrug.

"He's close enough to be useful, and far enough that you needn't bother worrying about him, just now," Victoria says. "I must say, I didn't think you'd appear, tonight, for the benefit."

"Are you holding my sister hostage as well?"

M gives me an exasperated look. "Neither of them is a hostage. We didn't know you'd come—but we were certain Goose would. Vee was certain you wouldn't show because of the association with your father. Especially if you got wind that Kate might be there."

"I was sure you'd cancel it, honestly," Victoria says.

"But I've gotten to know you and Goose a bit, haven't I?" M asks.

"Why lie?" I ask Jamie, uselessly. He hasn't offered a single word of assistance yet. He's plainly out of sorts, but I've no idea what's happening, there.

"Jamie learned about tonight on his own," M says, eyeing Jamie with an amused expression. "He overheard us, planning. We wanted to see what he'd do."

"What he'd do?" I ask, looking at Jamie steadily.

"Whether he'd be in touch, beforehand. Warn you. He'd allied himself with the professor, which I believe you knew. But he's seen, now, that that was a mistake. When he overheard us, he volunteered to help himself. Thought it would play well to Goose."

Jamie's expression betrays nothing.

"All we want is to go back to before," Dalrymple adds

with a kindly smile. "When you feel . . . encouraged enough to make the right decisions, Isaac will help recover whatever memories you may have lost, over time. Dear old James will help encourage Isaac, and you, in sharing them."

"Really," I say tonelessly, my mind speeding off in a thousand directions as I try to work it all out. "And what are you getting in exchange for all this . . . encouragement?" I ask Jamie. *Or what are they threatening you with?*

No one speaks, until Jamie says, "Isaac's my brother."

Hardly surprising, given the resemblance, I suppose. I wait for more, but no one elaborates. "And?" I finish.

Jamie talks to Isaac directly. "No one knows if your Gift is original, like mine, or if it's been artificially induced, like Stella's." Then, turning to me, "If it's the second, you're going to heal him."

"Oh. Got it. Sure."

"I can hear your sarcasm font," Jamie says. "But you *can* do it. There is a cure for the protocol. The thing you've been looking for?" Jamie says to Isaac. "It's him." Jamie's pointing to me.

No sign from Isaac that Jamie's line has landed. Good. "Quite the little cheerleader, all of a sudden, aren't you," I say to him. Even if his abilities weren't gone—which they mustn't be, he was either lying, in New York, or they'd been restored for him—even if he *could* force Isaac to do what he wanted, we can't use them on each other, not without—

Goose.

I bite my tongue, knowing in the pit of my stomach that wherever he is, even if he's not a hostage, he can't possibly be far enough. "Fine," I say to Jamie. "Let's say you're right, and I can heal him. I'd do it anyway for you, without holding anyone you care about for ransom. You do know that, don't you?" I meet his gaze as steadily as I can, praying he *does know*.

When he doesn't answer, I ask, "How do you know they're telling you the truth? They've lied to all of us, just as the professor has. All of them—they've got every incentive to treat you like a condom."

"Goodness!" Dalrymple says.

"Condom?" M repeats.

"Used once and then discarded," I say. I study Jamie's face as I say it—he accused me of using Mara that way. If he breaks, cracks a smile, shows any sign at all that he's aware, I can use it, perhaps—

"We would never," Victoria says. "His ability is infinitely more valuable than yours."

"So he's more of an investment piece, then? A collector's item? Property?" I say to M, watching her eyes narrow at the word. I flick a glance at Jamie—does he tense a bit? I can't quite tell. "And where does Mara factor into all of these brilliant plans to hijack my mind and my life?" When no one answers, I say, "Whatever it is, you won't find her so amenable."

"She doesn't need to be," M says simply.

I can't work out if she's saying that because she knows something, or because she knows nothing.

It doesn't matter, I decide. "Mara will come for me. God help you when she does."

M stalks toward me, Mara's dress moving silkily with every step. She bends toward my ear and says, "I'm counting on it."

45

RESIGN EVERYTHING

S O I'M THE BAIT, THIS TIME. FITTING.

"Do you know what makes Mara so powerful?" M asks, her tone, her voice sliding back into something older. "She *chooses* to be. She's accepted herself, completely. Without judgement."

"I thought that made her a sociopath?"

She smiles. "It makes her dangerous. In your experience, when are people at their most destructive?"

When they have nothing to lose.

"Mara can be, and has been, exploited. Her love, her loyalty."

I know it. I've exploited them myself.

I've used Mara's loyalty as a weapon, her love as a key. I've held myself back so she would run toward me. Fled from her to see if she'd give chase.

I doubted her, mistrusted her, made her prove herself to me over and over again, and when she did, and trusted me enough with the truth of it, I said she'd proved it too much and walked away from her without looking back.

"So it's your turn to exploit her, is it? What do you think'll happen then?" I ask, my voice hoarse. They can't steal her ability—she's original, like me. They'd need something else—some*one* else?—if that's what they're after. M claimed she's a Shadow, Mara's precursor—and perhaps her ability weakened after all, with Mara's birth and manifestation. Or she could've been lying about all of it, lying even now. Victoria as well.

Dalrymple and Victoria exchange a glance, but it's M who speaks, again. "Mara will come for you, then he'll come for her. And I'll be here when he does."

"This is all about *him*?" I say. "You've let your life be dictated by a man you loathe—"

"I haven't let him do anything. I can't escape him." She says it matter-of-factly, but her expression is shuttered. Boarded up like an abandoned house.

I push her. "So, you'll bring the professor to you by getting the rest of us all together, finish him off, even though he knows the future, likely knows you're planning this. And then you'll, what, steal all our Gifts? That's quite a lot of power," I finish.

"It would be a lot of power," Victoria concedes, ignoring the first bit. "I expect we'll lose one of us before it's done."

Which one, though.

"So all that shite you fed me about saving Mara from herself, needing my memories or whatever—"

"Both are true," M cuts in. "Mara does need to be saved from herself. Your memories will help us do it, when she comes, and when he follows her. They'll help everyone—Mara, the teens who've been dying because of your father's legacy—"

"And you, most of all," I finish.

M doesn't reply, at first. Then she says, "I want what was taken from me. I want to know who I was before I gave myself this name. I told you the truth, about that."

"Why not have Isaac restore your memories, then?" I say.

Her eyes slit. "I would have been satisfied, once, knowing where I came from. But now I want to know why."

She could have my memories, if that were all she truly wanted. If that were all they'd be used for. But it isn't. There's something else she wants, and she needs me *and* Mara to get it.

I try to hide how sick I feel at the thought of whatever love Mara might still have for me being used against her, in any way. Because I've used her myself. Being with her was like walking with the shadow of death beside me, a door marked EXIT comfortingly within reach. Her power over it, and the power I unconsciously wished I had over her—it's intoxicating. Addictive. And every warning to stay away—from the professor, because she'd weaken me, or ruin me—only drew me in closer. Made me desperate to keep her in my orbit, whilst surrounding her with reminders of the worst moments of her life.

How much of who she's become is because of what he and Kells made her believe she should be? If she'd never been led to believe she was a murderer from the start? Who would Mara be if she'd never met my father . . . or me?

I ruined her. Not the other way around.

You were supposed to slay the dragon, but you fell in love with it instead.

My father's words.

Slay the dragon. Save your girl.

That's what M wrote before shepherding me here.

They were both wrong. I haven't saved my girl. I damned her.

To be used again by others, for their own ends, or to dangle her in front of me to make me serve them.

I don't have a full understanding of what Jamie's here for, not truly, not yet. And I've no idea who else they've rounded up—Goose and Ceridwen, likely, and God knows how they might use them.

I think back to what Isaac said before, about the originals appearing in my memories. A wanted man, he called me.

Whatever the thing you want most is, that's what they'll use to get what they want from you.

I've wanted many things. Not to have to feel any more

deaths. To protect the people I care about. To save Mara, most of all, though she doesn't need or want me to. Even leaving her was a way to try and change her, to get her to be the version of her I wanted, instead of the version she chose to be. The version I wish I could forget.

Maybe I can do both. Forget her *and* save her from being used—by anyone, even or especially me.

I look at Isaac, sitting now with one ankle crossed over his other knee. I don't know what choices are left to me, but I decide to put them in the hands of a stranger I trust, and a friend I don't.

"Mara is what I want most," I say to Isaac, meeting his gaze, holding it for dear life. "She's what I want most in the world." Then, to M, I say, "If my remembering is what you want, I'll do it. Just don't hurt Mara. I won't need any encouragement." My glance shifts to Jamie, who seems to be chewing on the inside of his cheek.

"Isaac?" M asks him. "Do you?"

He shrugs. "I don't care," he says easily, without hesitation. "I'm not the one who'll be stuck with them."

Victoria nods at Jamie. "I'd still feel more comfortable if you'd . . . say something. I'm sure you can understand."

Jamie obediently takes a couple of steps toward Isaac's chair. When he speaks, his voice is resonant and commanding. "Make Noah remember. Make him remember everything."

The room is silent. The three originals are completely still, waiting, watchful. All eyes are on Isaac, as his face relaxes, as he unfolds himself from his chair, and moves easily to mine. He stands in front of me, forcing me to look up. With one hand, he glances his open palm softly against my face, then crouches down in front of me, his stare unclouded and clear.

My heartbeat thunders against my rib cage, not knowing what he'll say, not knowing who I'll be after he says it. Whether I was right to trust him, or not.

"Forget Mara," he says, as the room begins to darken. The next words I hear are the last ones I remember, before everything goes black.

"Both of them."

EPILOGUE
ACCURSED CHANCE

MARA

COULD YOU BE ANY SLOWER?" I CALL OUT OVER my shoulder.

Daniel glares at me through the revolving glass door. "I could be faster if I weren't carrying your stuff *and* mine."

I roll my eyes once he's inside. "Gimme."

He hands me a massive stripey duffel bag as I rise up on my toes to check out the lines. "Where'd you get this?"

"Mom's closet," I lie. It was Noah's closet. Noah's bag. "Which line do we need to be in?"

He glances at the board. "Uh, that one, I think," pointing to a series of numbers. Flight 1821, departing in fifty minutes. "But I don't know that we'll make it—"

"We'll make it," I say, scanning to see if there's an opening in any of the lines. "Special Services! That's us."

"Pretty sure that's not what that means," Daniel says.

"Very sure I don't care." I muscle my way through an adjacent line and by the time we reach the agent at the Special Services desk, we've Drawn Attention to Ourselves. Oh well.

The agent, a harried-looking, mostly bald gentleman, asks us, "How can I help you?"

I smile my most nonthreatening smile and place my ID and Daniel's on his desk.

"Two tickets on the next flight to London," I say. "Whatever it takes."

ACKNOWLEDGMENTS

NONE OF MY BOOKS WOULD EXIST WITHOUT THE ENDURING support of my family. I'm deeply grateful to my mother, Ellen, and to Jeffrey, for going above and beyond for me and for this book—so much love and thanks to you both. Infinite thanks to my incredible sister Yardana, and my almost-equally incredible brothers Martin, Jeremy, and Bret, for being exactly who you are. Most of all, as I write this, I am thankful to Grandpa Bob, and my grandmother, Janie, ז״ל. You have been my champions in life since I was born. I am so lucky, and I have never and will never forget it.

Kate, Stella, Stephanie—thank you so much, always, for it all. Stephanie, you know what you did.

Many, many thanks to my editor, Liz Kossnar, for helping to shape this book; to Lucy Ruth Cummins, for designing yet another stunning cover; and to the entire team at Simon & Schuster for all they do to help make these books happen and for shepherding them out into the world.

To Dana Spector and Paradigm, thank you for never stopping. And extraordinary thanks are owed to my extraordinary agent, Faye Bender, for more than I can say.

Last but never, ever least, thanks to you, my readers, for being here, still and always. I appreciate you more than you know.

MICHELLE HODKIN is the *New York Times* bestselling author of the Mara Dyer series and its companion trilogy The Shaw Confessions, and her books have been published in seventeen languages. Michelle grew up in South Florida, went to college in New York, and studied law in Michigan, before settling in Brooklyn. You can visit her online at michellehodkin.com.

RIVETED

BY *simon* teen ♥

BELIEVE IN YOUR SHELF

Visit RivetedLit.com & connect with us on social to:

DISCOVER NEW YA READS

READ BOOKS FOR FREE

DISCUSS YOUR FAVORITES

SHARE YOUR IDEAS

ENTER SWEEPSTAKES FOR THE CHANCE TO WIN BOOKS

Follow @SimonTeen on

to stay up to date with all things Riveted!